"YOU MUST BE
A VERY STRONG MAN,"

Sylvie said at last, "to be so calm when you are in great danger." She leaned forward, her gown billowing out as she moved and giving Longarm a glimpse of her full white breasts. "I must find out for myself how strong you truly are. May I?"

Without waiting for Longarm's reply, she grasped his biceps in both hands and squeezed hard. Longarm could see the nipples budding pink from the creamy globes her low-cut gown now revealed. He accepted the invitation.

Sylvie lifted her head, her bright lips parting. Longarm bent to kiss her and he felt the pressure of her hands on his biceps relax, and in a moment he felt her hands on his thigh...

TABOR EVANS

LONGARM

IN THE BADLANDS

A JOVE BOOK

LONGARM IN THE BADLANDS

A Jove Book / published by arrangement with
the author

PRINTING HISTORY
Jove edition / September 1982

ISBN: 0-515-05603-0

PRINTED IN THE UNITED STATES OF AMERICA

Chapter 1

Longarm moved slowly through the early evening dusk, turning away from the isolated scattered shacks along the banks of Jersey Creek to enter Rattlebone Hollow, where the shanties stood in crowded rows. He'd been counting the streets as he passed them, and now, as his informant had told him to do, he turned to his right, away from the creek, and entered the little settlement whose houses stood higgledy-piggledy in the saucerlike depression that bordered the creekbed.

He'd hoped that when he got away from the sluggish green-brown waters of the creek and the wide stretch of dead-looking greasy mud that stretched in a wide border along both its banks, he'd also be free from the gut-wrenching stench that rose from the scummy streambed. But the smell still surrounded him as he walked along the dirt trail past dozens of tumbledown shacks. There were few people about, and the occasional whiffs he got of frying saltback and onions told him why; it was suppertime in the Hollow.

Longarm was relieved that the winding narrow street he'd chosen to follow was almost deserted. He tried not to be conspicuous as he made his way into the little settlement, but he knew that his efforts weren't very successful. His tall sinewy frame and the firm set of his jaw would have drawn attention

1

anywhere. So would his gunmetal-blue eyes and the sweeping curve of his full mustache that swept up on the sides of his tanned, clean-shaven cheeks like the curved horns of a range-tough Texas steer.

In Rattlebone Hollow, Longarm stood out like a starched white shirt spread on a coal heap. Here most skins ranged from pale brown to ebony-black, and mustaches were rare except on the wearily downturned faces of the few older men he'd encountered.

And nobody in the Hollow wore the kind of clothing that covered Longarm's tall, sinewy frame. The ragged hand-me-downs that hung from the stooped frames of the men he'd seen were a far cry from the well-fitting thigh-length coat and skin-tight snuff-brown whipcord pants tucked into polished cordovan stovepipe cavalry boots. The shapeless battered hats on the heads of the few he'd passed were a sharp contrast to his flat-creased snuff-brown Stetson.

Daylight was fading fast as Longarm walked frowning along the narrow meandering street, going deeper and deeper into the Hollow. The passageway barely earned the name "street"—it was more of an alley than a thoroughfare—and Longarm began to wonder if he'd counted the number of such passages correctly after reaching the first line of shacks.

Scraps of light were beginning to show now through the tattered curtains of the shanty windows and the cracks in their walls. But the scanty illumination that crept through the openings was so dim that Longarm had to walk more slowly as he strained his eyes, looking for the doorway streaked with white paint that was the object of his search. He turned to look back, and now it was dark enough for him to see the lights of Kansas City casting a pinkish glow on the early night sky.

Behind him, a ghostly white veil of night fog was creeping up the street from Jersey Creek. The odor that Longarm had first noticed as he approached Rattlebone Hollow grew even stronger as the mist crept closer. He stopped and fished a long cheroot out of his pocket, flicked a match across a horn-hard thumbnail, and lighted the slim cigar.

Old son, he told himself, *for all you know that yarn Toad Morton spun could've been just so much hogwash. Toad wouldn't be the first outlaw to spill a pack of lies when he lay dying. His kind's just mean enough to send somebody off on a wild-goose chase, away from where he knows his crooked*

2

partners are likely to be. But this sure is a likely place to look for a pair like July and Snag. So you better push on a little bit further, prowl a little bit longer, before you give up looking.

Puffing his cheroot, Longarm moved on slowly, peering carefully through the gloom at each door he passed. He'd almost reached the edge of the settlement when the whimpering cry of a woman led him to the white-streaked door he was seeking. He stopped outside the door, listening.

A man's menacing voice reached his ears. "You better tell me what I wants know, girl! You ain't got much longer to make up your mind to talk!"

"I've told you all I can!" the woman's voice replied, fear in her strained tones.

Judging that he had a moment or two before it would be time for him to take a hand, Longarm stepped aside from the door. Inches away, a wide crack in the plank wall spilled yellow lamplight from the interior of the shack. Longarm peered through the crack.

A hulking black man, sleeves rolled high to show arms that bulged with muscle, was standing in front of a young woman seated in a wooden chair. There was something strained about her posture, and when he looked closer Longarm saw that her hands had been pulled behind the back of the chair and tied tightly.

He had no time to look closely at the girl, but got the impression of a cascade of shining black hair falling over smooth shoulders, of full red lips, a thin delicate nose, and large, lustrous dark eyes in a creamy face. The eyes were pleading now as she looked at the big man who had made her his captive.

She'd been stripped to the waist, and the strained position in which she was bound caused her full firm breasts to thrust out boldly. At one side of the pair stood a small square table on which a kerosene lamp burned. A few inches to one side of the lamp there was a cast-iron brazier in which charcoal glowed redly. A length of strap-iron an inch wide lay across the lip of the brazier, one end buried in the coals.

Longarm took in the interior of the one-room shanty with a single glance to make sure there was nobody else inside. He did not need to waste time studying its details. It was almost bare of furnishings; a bed stood in one corner, a stove in another, and a chair at the end of the bed. A double-barrelled twelve-gauge shotgun was leaning in the corner between the bed and stove. Longarm judged the distance from the shotgun to the man just as the man spoke.

Bending toward the girl, the black man cupped one of her exposed breasts in his huge hand. "It's gonna be a long tahm afore that piece a'iron gets hot," he said. "Plenty of tahm for me to find out how a stuck-up octoroon acts when I push my big hard hunk of black meat into 'er. It's been a while since I had me a woman, 'specially a light-skin gal like you."

"I guess I can't stop you doing what you want to," the girl snapped at her tormentor. "But every time you get close enough for me to smell you, I want to puke!"

"Shet up!" he said, slapping the girl with a heavy backhand blow. He stood gazing at her for a moment, then continued, "July's gonna be the last man to put it to you, girl. Because by the tahm I get through fuckin' you, that hunk a 'strap-iron'll be red hot. And I'm gonna stripe them big soft titties and them pretty cheeks with it till no man ever looks at you again!"

"No, July!" the woman cried. "Don't do that to me! I can't tell you anything more about Judge Claypool! Please, you've got to believe me!"

Hearing the name of the Federal district judge was all that Longarm needed. Raising a booted foot, he kicked the door with a solid thud that splintered the casing inside and tore the bolt out of the half-rotten wood of the jamb as the door swung open wide.

"Hold it right there, July!" Longarm snapped. "I'm a deputy U.S. marshal, and you're under arrest!"

Even before Longarm started speaking, July was diving for the shotgun. The distance between the big black and the weapon was a bit more than an arm's length, which would give Longarm all the time he needed.

July's hand hadn't yet touched the shotgun when the slug from Longarm's .44 Colt caught the moving man in mid-stride. The big hunk of hot lead spun July around and shoved him into the back wall of the shanty. He stood spread-eagled against the rough bare boards for a moment, his face contorted with surprise and hatred, making ineffectual efforts to grasp the shotgun's barrel. Then he slid slowly down the wall and lay still.

After the reverberations of the shot died away, there was silence for a moment, then the woman spoke. "You—you're truly a lawman?" she asked, her eyes wide in fear.

"I sure am," Longarm assured her.

"Oh, thank God!" she sighed. "I've been tied up her since this morning. You must've heard what he was threatening if you were listening outside."

"I heard him all right."

Longarm couldn't keep his eyes from the young woman's bare torso. She noticed his glance and tried to cover her breasts. Longarm holstered his Colt and stepped behind the girl, took out his pocketknife, and cut the rope that held her to the chair. She stood up and pulled her clothing up around her shoulders.

Longarm told her, "I've been tracing this man and another one ever since their gang staged a break-out at the Federal prison a couple of weeks ago."

"Snag Collier?" she asked. "Is that the other man you're after?"

"That's right." Longarm indicated the dead man on the floor. "This one called July was all that was left of the gang besides Snag after they grabbed a couple of guards and took their rifles to shoot their way out. I've found out enough about the gang he used to boss to know that Snag won't be too far away from July. I don't guess you've seen him, have you?"

She shook her head. "No. But, from what July said, he'll be here sooner or later. The two of them were planning to kill Judge Claypool and the Federal attorney for sending them to prison."

"From what little I heard before I busted in, I guess you must work for the judge," Longarm said.

"I work at his house. I'm Mrs. Claypool's maid." She paused, then added, "My name's Fern."

"Mine's Long," he told her. "Custis Long, out of the Denver marshal's office."

Since the report of his pistol-shot had died away, something about his surroundings had been bothering Longarm. He finally put his finger on it. Nobody from the shanties around them had come to find out what had happened. The narrow, twisted street outside was silent. He stepped to the door to look out and as far as he could see along the street, the lights in the other shacks had been extingushied.

He turned back to face Fern. "What kind of people live around here? A lot of 'em must've heard my shot. How come nobody's showed up to see what happened?"

Fern's face twisted into a sad little half-smile. "This is

Rattlebone Hollow, Marshal. They call it that because anybody who lives here for a while gets the shivering ague. And folks who live here in the Hollow know better than to stick their noses outside when there's shooting. Rattlebone Hollow folks stay away from any place where something bad's happening, even if it's right next door to them."

"You know a lot about Rattlebone Hollow, don't you?"

"I ought to," Fern replied, a trace of bitterness in her voice. "I was brought up here. I'd still be here, I guess, if it hadn't been for Mrs. Claypool. My mother worked for her, before the judge got his Federal appointment. And there wasn't any place for my mother to leave me when I was little, so Mrs. Claypool let her take me with her to work."

"I see," Longarm nodded. Then he added thoughtfully, "Well, if there's not going to be anybody noseying around here and asking questions, maybe you and me better go back inside and do a little more talking."

"Do we have to? With July lying there dead—"

"Just don't pay attention to him. He won't be bothering you any more," Longarm told her. "And we got to have a talk right here and now so I'll know what to look for. My job won't be finished until I snap my handcuffs on Snag Collier. He's the most dangerous one of the bunch, from what I hear."

"Yes," Fern agreed as they went inside and Longarm closed the door of the shanty behind them. "I know a little bit about the gang, Marshal. I was working at the judge's house when he was presiding over the trial of Snag Collier's gang. I couldn't help hearing about the threats Snag and his bunch made then. But I didn't know they'd managed to break out of the pen." She frowned. "You'd think the judge would've said something to Mrs. Claypool about them escaping. He did know about the break-out, didn't he?"

"Oh, he knew about it, all right. I imagine he didn't want his wife to get scared."

"That'd be like him." Fern nodded.

"If he'd said something, he might've saved you from getting caught by July," Longarm went on. "How'd that happen, Fern?"

"I went to do the marketing for Mrs. Claypool. July must have been watching the house. He grabbed me when I went past an alley down at the market square. He held a hand over my mouth while he showed me a knife and told me he'd cut

6

my throat if I didn't go along with him quietly. I could tell he meant it, so I went with him, and he brought me here. He tied me up and gagged me and told me he was going to look for Snag Collier. Then he went away. He just got back a few minutes ago."

"But he didn't find Snag, or they'd've both been here now." Longarm frowned.

"July said he'd left word around town where he was," Fern told Longarm. "He started asking me things about Judge Claypool—what time he goes out, when he gets back home, how the rooms of his house are arranged. I answered his questions because I was afraid not to, but he wasn't satisfied that I was telling him everything. That's when he put that piece of iron there to get hot."

Longarm had been studying Fern's face while she spoke. She showed no traces of mixed bloodlines. Her skin was a delicately rich creamy hue and her brows were coal-black over dark expressive eyes. Her rich black hair shone above a smooth high brow puckered into a worried frown. She was in fact a beautiful young woman.

Longarm asked her, "Did July say anything about what he and Snag were planning to do as far as Judge Claypool's concerned?"

"Only that when Snag Collier got here they intended to kill the judge and his family."

"They didn't say how or when?"

"No. But from the questions July asked me, I got the idea they intended to try to kill the judge at home."

Longarm nodded slowly. "That'd follow, I guess. It'd be easier for them to get at him. In his courtroom they'd have had trouble getting to him, with bailiffs and such around. What's the judge's house like?"

"Well—" Fern's brow puckered. She seemed at a loss where to begin describing the house. Longarm waited patiently; he knew people sometimes had trouble putting into words the most familiar things of their everyday lives, the places they lived in and the objects that surrounded them.

Finally she said, "Well, it's a big house. Yellow brick, two floors and a big attic. That's where the cook and I have our rooms—in the attic. Cook's not there right now—she's gone to visit her mother in St. Louis—so I'm in the attic by myself. The judge and Mrs. Claypool have a bedroom with separate sitting rooms on the second floor. There are other bedrooms and two bathrooms on that floor. Then there's a parlor and sunroom and a dining room and library on the main floor. The kitchen's in the basement."

"Is there a lot of land around the place?"

"Oh, yes, a big yard. Mostly lawn, with some trees and a flowerbed along one side and shrubs in front of the veranda. In the back there's the stable and carriage-house, and in the loft there's a room for the stableman."

Longarm grinned wryly. "A man could get lost in a place like that, I imagine. And a man who's trying to sneak up on the house would find plenty of cover." He took a fresh cheroot from his pocket and lighted it over the lamp chimney, puffed thoughtfully for a moment, and went on. "All right, Fern. You've been a lot of help. I've got a pretty good idea what to do, now. We'll go into town and find the Federal marshal. I'm going to need some help to get things fixed up so as to fool Snag Collier when he comes looking for the judge."

"What about—" Fern gestured toward July's body, crumpled against the wall.

"I'll leave him for Snag to find. I want Collier mad enough so he'll take right out after the judge, and that's what I have a pretty good idea he'll do, soon as he gets here. Now, where's the nearest place we can find a hack around here?"

She thought for a moment. "We'll have to go into town, Marshal. There's a saloon not too far from the creek where the hackmen go for a late supper. I guess we can find a hack there."

"Let's head for it, then." Longarm leaned over the lamp and blew it out. He and Fern stood for a moment letting their eyes grow accustomed to the blackness. He said, "You don't seem to me like the kind that scares easy, Fern. You didn't let July get you a bit rattled when he had you tied up a while ago."

"If you want to know the truth, I was scared to death, Marshal, but I wasn't going to give him the satisfaction of knowing it." Then, uncertainly, she asked, "Why did you say that?"

"Because I got an idea how to handle Snag Collier. I'll need some information and some help from you to make it work, and we'll have to do some fast moving. But I figure you can do what's necessary. Question is, how do you feel about it?"

"Mrs. Claypool and the judge have been really good to me,

8

Marshal. If you need my help, I'll do whatever you want me to."

"I thought you'd say that. I'll tell you what I've got in mind on the way into town. Now, let's go find that hack and get away from here before Snag shows up."

Chapter 2

Fern stopped after taking the first few steps up the stairway leading to the second floor of Judge Claypool's house. "Are you sure there's not something else you want me to do, Marshal Long?"

Longarm shook his head. "Nothing I can think of, Fern, except one thing."

"Oh? What's that?"

"Well, we're partners in this deal we've set up, and it ain't right for you to be so formal. Will you just quit calling me Marshal Long?"

"Why—if you want me to, of course. Even if it does seem a little bit funny for a servant girl—"

"Stop thinking about being a servant, Fern. Like I just said, we're partners."

"I don't know your first name," she reminded him.

"No, I guess not. We haven't had time for a lot of chitchat. Most folks that know me call me by a sort of nickname I've picked up—Longarm."

"If that's what you want," she nodded, then after a moment of hesitation, added, "Longarm."

"That sounds better."

They had just come up from the basement to the main floor

of Judge Claypool's residence. In the parlor a clock chimed nine. Longarm realized with some surprise that only three hours had gone by since he and Fern had left the Hollow. During the hackney ride to the center of Kansas City, Longarm had explained his plan to Fern. They'd wasted the better part of an hour while Longarm had tried without success to locate the Federal marshal.

By the time they'd gotten into downtown Kansas City, the Federal building was closed. Not even a custodian had answered Longarm's repeated pounding on the ornate doors. The desk sergeant at police headquarters had given Longarm the chief marshal's home address, but the house was locked as tightly as the Federal office building, and looked as deserted.

"We could go back to the police station and see if they'd give you a man or two," Fern had suggested.

Longarm shook his head. "No, the best thing to do is to go straight out to Judge Claypool's house. We'll explain things to him and see if he'll go along with the scheme."

After hearing Fern's story of her abduction by July, then listening to Longarm's explanation of the scheme he'd worked out, the judge had tried to get Longarm to include him in the watch for Snag Collier.

"I remember the Collier gang quite well," Claypool had told Longarm. "He and his men had to be removed forcibly from the courtroom after I'd sentenced them, and the last thing that Collier shouted as they took him away was that he was going to make me and my family pay for my sending him to prison."

"Then I don't expect you'd mind staying downtown in one of the big hotels for tonight, while I try to nab him here at your house?" Longarm had suggested.

"Of course not! But surely you're not going to try to do what you've described single-handed. Suppose Collier's not alone?"

"I don't figure that's too likely," Longarm had said thoughtfully. "Sure, Snag and July have been out long enough to find some men. But the way I figure, they've got a personal grudge against you. They'd want to pay it off themselves."

"I just don't like the idea of you playing a lone hand, Marshal."

"It's the best way, Judge," Longarm had replied. "I can't seem to raise anybody from the marshal's office at this hour, and I don't feel like I can trust the local police."

11

"Well, I can agree with you there," Claypool had said. "The local force is both corrupt and inefficient. But if you'll give me two or three hours, I can have my bailiff round up some of the district marshal's men."

"Thing is, we ain't *got* two or three hours," Longarm had replied. "If I'm going to trap Snag Collier when he comes here looking for you tonight, you and Mrs. Claypool have got to leave in the next ten or fifteen minutes. Collier's going to start watching the house quite a while before he makes his move.

"That's why I didn't waste any more time trying to find the district marshal. Every minute we lose in getting you and your wife to where you'll be safe means there's more danger he'll see you two leave."

"I can take Mrs. Claypool to the hotel and come back to stand watch with you," the judge had suggested.

Longarm had shaken his head. "I appreciate you wanting to help, Judge Claypool, but I work better by myself."

"I'm not exactly helpless, you know, Marshal Long," the jurist had said tartly. "I served in the War. I'm no stranger to weapons and fighting."

"This ain't quite the same as a war, Judge," Longarm had replied. "Snag Collier don't play by any rules, the way army officers do. Besides, you'll want to be with Mrs. Claypool, to make sure she's all right."

After a moment's thought, Claypool had nodded. "You're right, of course, Marshal Long. I certainly wouldn't want to leave her by herself, worrying about me. We'll do things according to your plan. My wife and I will be out of here in ten minutes."

After Judge and Mrs. Claypool had left, Longarm had asked Fern to take him around the big yellow brick house so that he'd be familiar with its layout. He'd closed the shutters on all the windows, to make a forced entry unavoidably noisy, and had latched the windows, checked the locks, and made sure the bolts were thrown on all the outside doors.

"I guess that's about as tight as we can make things," he'd told Fern as they got ready to return to the main floor. "The door and window locks ain't going to stop him from coming in, but it's too late to do anything about 'em. Besides, Snag'd get spooked off for sure if he got the idea there'd been anything special done to the house."

"Before we leave the kitchen, can we please stop and eat?"

Fern asked Longarm at that point. "I haven't had a bite all day, and I'm starved."

"Come to think of it, I could use some supper myself. And a drink of whiskey, if the judge happens to have a bottle of good Maryland rye on the place."

"I don't know about Maryland rye, but if he's got any it'll be in the liquor closet over there." Fern pointed to a door on the other side of the kitchen. "And I'm sure Judge Claypool would want you to help yourself. You go look while I see what there is I can fix real quick."

Longarm found a bottle of Daugherty's instead of his favorite Tom Moore, but he was willing to settle for it. Fern was carving thick slabs of beef from a roast she'd taken out of the larder, and a loaf of crusty bread was on the table as well as butter, pickles, and mustard.

"I hope roast beef sandwiches will be all right," she said.

"Right now I'd be glad to eat pickled horsemeat."

They made a quick meal, with little conversation, and as soon as Fern had cleared the table they went back to the main floor of the big house.

"Now, you're sure you know what to do?" Longarm asked, as Fern started up the stairs to the second floor.

"I'm sure," she replied. "I'll light the lamp in Judge Claypool's sitting room, and then in his bedroom. They're the rooms you'll be using. Then I light the lamp in Mrs. Claypool's sitting room. After that, I'll go up to the attic to my room and light the lamp there. The light in Cook's room is already on, but I'll put it out a little while before I blow out the one in my room. Have I got it all straight?"

"Couldn't be straighter. You know, I got a pretty good hunch Sang Collier's been watching this house for the past two or three nights. Him and July could've been in Kansas City for the last week or so, if my figuring's right."

"If they've been watching the house, nobody's noticed them," Fern said, frowning.

"Snag'd be careful not to do anything you'd notice. He wouldn't stand around out in the open. He'd've have found some hideyhole to watch from. That's how his kind does."

"It makes me a little bit nervous, knowing somebody might have been watching the house here without any of us knowing it."

"Well, if I've got things worked out right, you won't have

13

to be nervous much longer, Fern. Snag's had time to figure out just how the judge and his wife move around every night when they're getting ready to go to bed. He had July grab you at the market today just so he could make sure his figuring was right. They'd likely have broken in tonight or tomorrow, if I hadn't spoiled his plans by shooting July."

"And getting me out of a bad situation," Fern said.

"That was just luck. After I'd asked around town a while, I got things pretty much narrowed down to where Snag and July'd be most likely to head. But all I had to go by was a tip about two men fitting their description renting that shack in the Hollow."

"Luck or not, I'm glad you got there when you did."

"Me, too. But let's get back to what we've got going here now, Fern. This house has got to look just like it does on any night when the judge and his wife are doing what they usually do. All Snag's got to go by, if he's watching, is the way the lights go off at bedtime. We can't tip our hand by having anything break that pattern he'll be looking for."

"Well, they do things pretty much the same way, night after night, just the way you've got our moves planned."

"Fine. Now, after you get to your own room, you leave the lights on this floor to me. I'll blow out the lamp in Mrs. Claypool's sitting room in about half an hour, and the one in the judge's sitting room a little bit after that. Then, a few minutes after I put out the lamp in the judge's room, I'll blow out the lamp in their bedroom. Then we'll just settle down and see if Snag shows up."

"How long do you think we'll have to wait?"

"Not much way of telling. If it was me doing what Snag's likely getting ready to do, I wouldn't make a move until about two or three o'clock in the morning. That's when most folks are sleeping the soundest."

"And I guess the only way I'll know whether your plan's working is if I hear somebody prowling around?"

"Chances are you won't hear a thing. And even if you do, you stay right in your room, where you'll be safe."

"Suppose you need help?"

"I can handle Snag by myself. If you're around trying to help, you might get hurt."

"You're sure you don't—"

"I'm sure," Longarm told her firmly.

14

Fern hesitated for a moment, then said somewhat reluctantly, "I guess I'll say good night, then."

"Don't worry," Longarm told her. "It'll all work out fine."

He watched Fern walking up the stairs until she reached the landing and was lost to sight. Then he went into the judge's sitting room, took off his coat and hat, and settled down in an easy chair. He took a swallow of whiskey and set the bottle of Daugherty's on a side table within easy reach. Lighting a cheroot, Longarm leaned back and watched the blue smoke from his cigar swirling in the updraft from the lamp chimney while he want over his plan.

Well, it don't look like there's anything you've overlooked, old son, he told himself when he'd finished his review. *Only thing you can't handle is whether Snag Collier's going to behave the say you figure he will. Because if Snag don't show up, what you're going to come up with is a whole lot of nothing.*

Standing up, Longarm stretched and blew out the lamp. He went into the adjoining bedroom, leaving the connecting door ajar. He walked over to the bed and pushed down on the mattress. To a man whose day had started before sun-up and had been filled with action, the bed felt too inviting to pass up.

Sliding his feet out of his stovepipe boots, Longarm took off his coat and vest and hung them on a chair beside the bed. He placed the vest over the coat, and arranged it to keep the pocket containing the derringer within easy reach.

After thinking about it for a moment, he unbuckled his gunbelt and hung it on the bedpost, arranging the holster to put the butt of the Colt where a single sweep of his right hand could bring the weapon into action. Then he blew out the lamp and stretched out on the soft mattress. Setting his mind to keep himself from sleeping, he lay gazing up into the darkness.

After several minutes, his eyes adjusted to the almost total gloom, and he could see the windows of the big bedchamber outlined against the gaslights that flickered along the street outside. The room's furnishings became visible as vague shapes in the darkness and the plastered pattern of interlocked circles in low relief on the ceiling above the bed slowly registered on his vision.

He was reaching into his coat pocket for a cheroot when the soft metallic grating of the door-latch in Judge Claypool's sitting room broke the silence. In one swift fluid blur of motion,

Longarm swept his hand around to grasp the butt of his ready Colt, rolled off the bed, and padded on silent feet into the adjoining room.

In the judge's sitting room, the curtains were thicker than those in the bedroom, the darkness was more intense. Longarm stopped just inside the door, pistol poised and ready, while he tried to pierce the blackness. A soft sound, the rustling of cloth on cloth, reached his ears. He turned to face the sound and brought up the Colt's muzzle. Then a soft whisper reached him from the darkness.

"Longarm?"

"I'm right here, Fern."

"I thought I heard you moving, but I wasn't sure."

Fern moved to Longarm's side. There was not enough light to let him see her clearly. Her features were a pale blur broken by the dark line of her full lips and the darker outline of her eyes. She had on a long light-colored nightgown that dropped in a straight line from her shoulders to her ankles.

"What's the matter?" Longarm asked. "Did you see something? Or hear something that bothered you?"

"No. I looked out my window after I'd blown my lamp out. There wasn't anybody on the street, so I went to bed. But I couldn't go to sleep." Fern was silent for a moment, then she asked, "Do you mind if I stay with you a while, Longarm?"

"Not a bit. I was just lying in the other room in the dark, listening. I guess two can do that as good as one."

"Your ears must be terribly good. I could've sworn I didn't make a bit of noise when I came in here."

"You didn't. The door did, though."

Longarm started back to the bedroom. Fern followed him. They stood for a moment in the center of the dark room, an arm's length apart, neither of them speaking.

At last, Fern said, "I'm not fooling you a bit, am I, Longarm?"

"That depends on what you mean."

"What I mean is that I'm sure you know a lot more about women than you've let on. You know perfectly well why I came down here. It's true that I couldn't go to sleep, but not because I was afraid. Because I kept thinking about you."

"I take that as a compliment, Fern. It does a man good to know that a woman thinks about him."

Fern stepped up closer to Longarm. He could feel the

warmth of her body and smell the musky fragrance of her perfume.

"It doesn't bother you if a woman makes the first move, does it, Longarm?" she asked.

"Not a bit." She was not the first woman to come to him without waiting for an invitation. And he was remembering Fern's full breasts and the silken texture of her creamy skin. He went on, "But if you came down here because you think you owe me something for getting you away from July—"

Fern broke in quickly, "No. That's not the reason. I'm here because I could tell from the first time I saw you that you're a man who knows how to please a woman."

"You're sure?"

"If you don't believe me, just tell me so, and I'll go back upstairs to my own bed and leave you alone."

"As long as you know what you're doing."

"I know, all right. Don't worry about that."

"Oh, I believe you, Fern. The only thing is, I wouldn't want us to get so busy we'd miss hearing Snag Collier, if he tries to bust in here tonight."

"You heard the clock strike nine just as we came up from the basement," Fern reminded him. "You said he probably wouldn't get here until two or three in the morning."

"That's about when I'd look for him, if he shows up at all."

"We've got half the night to wait, then. Can you think of a better way to spend it?"

When Longarm did not reply, Fern pressed her body against him, her upturned face a white blur in the darkness. Longarm bent to kiss her. Her tongue darted into his mouth. Longarm passed his free hand down Fern's back, pulling her closer. Their lips still glued together, tongues entwined, Fern swayed her body toward the bed, which was only a step or two away.

Longarm stopped when they reached the side of the bed. He slid his Colt back into its holster and started to unbotton his shirt. Fern's fingers moved to the buttons of his fly, and when she'd loosened them, pulled Longarm's trousers down over his slim hips. While Longarm unbuttoned his balbriggans from the neck, she was freeing the buttons up from his crotch. Their hands met and together they peeled down his underwear and trousers to pull the two garments off together.

With a shrug and a twist, Fern let her nightgown slip off her shoulders to fall in a heap on the floor. She stepped out

17

of the ring of cloth and pressed against Longarm. "Sit on the bed," she whispered.

Longarm sat and Fern dropped to her knees in front of him. She cradled his beginning erection in the palms of her hands and bent to run her tongue along its stiffening length. Her lips closed softly around his tip and she drew Longarm into her mouth.

For a moment Fern held him engulfed. Then she released him and Longarm felt the soft rasping of her tongue darting along his burgeoning shaft. He bent forward and cupped a breast in each hand as her head moved back and forth.

Fern drew her head back, releasing him. Looking up, she asked, "Do you like to come this way, Longarm?"

"Why, sure I do, if that's what you enjoy."

"Oh, I enjoy it, but that can wait till later. Right now, I need to get you into me."

Fern straddled Longarm's thighs and guided his erection to the apex of the black bush that formed a vee between her own thighs. He sank back on the bed while she positioned him and shoved down on his shaft. She leaned forward, bracing her arms on the mattress above his shoulders.

Her breasts were dangling over Longarm's face. He lifted his head to take the pebbled tip of one soft globe into his mouth and ran his tongue over it. Fern sighed with a deep inhalation of satisfaction. She began to buck her hips, working them in quick short strokes, her torso twisting from side to side. In a few moments, her breasts were heaving and tossing so wildly that Longarm could no longer catch their tips with his mouth. He lay back and let Fern set her own pace.

She slowed the quick gyrations and moved more deliberately. Her body sank down, her soft full breasts pressing hard on Longarm's face, allowing him to return to caressing them with lips and tongue while she raised her hips high and then slowly lowered them until her pubic arch was pressed firmly against his.

Long moments passed while Fern kept up her slow deliberate movements that sent Longarm's rigid shaft deeply into her. Then, almost without warning, a soft cry burst from her throat and in a moment Fern was bucking wildly again, her breasts heaving, her hips gyrating from side to side in the sudden, frenzied bouncing that came to an abrupt halt only after a scream of joy burst form her throat and she fell forward, her body limp and quivering.

Seconds ticked into minutes before Fern grew quiet, her trembling stopped, and Longarm felt her muscles grow taut as she lifted her shoulders and looked down into his face.

"You're still hard as a rock. You didn't come, did you?" she asked.

"Not yet. It takes me a while, Fern."

"Can you stay hard? Or do you want me to finish you off?"

"Oh, I'll stay up, all right. But you do whatever pleases you the most."

Fern was silent for a moment, then she said, "If you're sure you can stay hard, I like the feel of you inside me. God, you're big! You make me feel so good, I'd hate to let you go right now."

"There ain't no need for you to. I feel pretty good myself, only I'd feel better if we got a little bit more comfortable."

"I'd like that, too."

Putting his hands under Fern's armpits, Longarm levered them both up onto the bed until the mattress supported their legs. Then he turned Fern with him until they lay facing one another, one of her thighs under his side, her other leg draped across his hips. Fern cradled his cheeks between her palms and kissed him lingeringly but gently.

"I think I could stay this way all night, if you could keep hard that long."

"Well, I'll keep up for a while yet, but we ain't got all night ahead of us, regardless of how much we like it."

"That's what I was thinking. I'm ready to start again, Longarm, whenever you are."

Longarm responded by pushing into Fern a bit deeper. She raised her thigh to let him complete his penetration, and for a few moments he stroked gently and slowly while their lips clung in a tongue-twisting kiss.

When Fern began responding to his long slow strokes, Longarm speeded up. In a few moments she started to writhe her hips each time he went into her, and Longarm braced himself on his elbow while Fern moved to let him get above her. She raised her legs until her knees were just above his shoulders.

"Now," she whispered. "Now, Longarm! Fuck me deep and fast and hard!"

Longarm drove into her, Fern lifting her hips to meet his long fast thrusts. He was still minutes away from his climax when she began to cry out, animal yelps rising from deep in her chest. Then she began trembling and sprawled with her thighs spread wide, her entire body tossing out of control as Longarm pounded to his orgasm.

Fern lay limp by the time he'd jetted and thrust into her with a final deep penetration, holding himself against her until he was totally drained. Then he let himself slowly down on her still-quivering body and lay quietly, relaxed and spent.

Chapter 3

Fern was the first to stir. When Longarm felt her moving he lifted himself to let her roll to one side of the bed.

"You are one hell of a man, Longarm," she said.

"And you're one of the prettiest young girls I've ever run into," Longarm told her.

He groped in the pocket of his coat for a cheroot and match. When he flicked the match into flame by dragging it across his thumbnail, he saw that she'd propped herself up on an elbow and was gazing at him. He blew out the match. In the darkened room, the glowing tip of the cigar shed enough light for him to see Fern's face.

"I don't know why it makes me feel so good to hear you say that, Longarm, but it does," Fern told him.

Faintly from downstairs they heard the chiming clock strike one. For a moment, neither Fern nor Longarm spoke.

Fern said at last, "We've still got a little time left, haven't we?"

"No, Fern. If we get started again, we'll just keep on going. And if we were having so much pleasure we didn't hear the clock strike twelve, we sure as hell won't hear it strike two. Now, you go on back upstairs. If Snag Collier's going to show up, it'll be in the next two hours."

"What if he doesn't show up?"

"If he hasn't tried his luck by three o'clock, he won't be here tonight, and I'll wait for him again tomorrow night."

"Can I come back downstairs at three, then, if he hasn't arrived by then?"

"Sure you can. And I'll be ready and waiting. But you go on now, and let me put my mind on what I've got to do."

After Fern had gone, Longarm dressed in the dark, groping to get his clothing straightened out, fumbling on the floor for his boots, and finally strapping on his gunbelt. He went into the judge's sitting room, and by the light of a match he touched to a cheroot, made his way to the easy chair where the bottle of Daugherty's stood. He took a healthy swallow and leaned back against the soft leather upholstery, his ears tuned to catch the slightest sound.

A veteran of many such vigils, Longarm was too experienced to be deceived by the structural creakings a house makes during the night hours. He paid no attention to these noises, but when a soft grating against one of the outside shutters' slats sounded from the floor below, he became instantly alert. Standing up, moving slowly through the darkness of the unfamiliar room, he started for the door.

If anything, the hallway leading to the stairs was darker than the room Longarm had just left. He felt his way down the hall, keeping the fingertips of one hand brushing along the wall, until the arm outstretched in front of him bumped softly into the newel post of the stairway.

Planting his feet as close as possible to the wall to avoid the the slightest creaking, and lowering each booted foot with the utmost care, Longarm started down the stairs. He was halfway to the first floor when he heard the ticking of wire on metal, followed by the snapping of the catch and the creaking of the hinge as the shutter was pulled slowly open.

None of the noises Longarm had heard thus far would have been audible during daylight hours, and in the early evening they would have been lost in the casual sounds of normal household activities. Nor would they have been heard even in the silence of the early morning stillness by those with ears less keen than Longarm's, ears which were not straining to catch them.

By the time the next noise sounded, the tick-tick-tick of metal on metal, Longarm was standing in the hallway trying to determine which of the three rooms opening off the hall was the one from which the sounds were coming. He recognized the sound at once as being the blade of a knife inserted between the sashes of a double-hung window, tapping against the curved latch that kept the window locked. Before Longarm had decided which room it came from, the tiny noise had stopped.

Then he heard the whisper of wood sliding on wood as a window was raised. It was louder than the ticking, and he located its source at once. The sound came from the room immediately in front of him, the parlor. His footsteps noiseless on the rug, Longarm moved toward the center door. As he crossed the few feet of space between the stairway and the door, he drew his Colt.

Shielding his body behind the doorjamb, Longarm peered into the room. The window formed a rectangle of dim light in the dark wall across the room. Centered in the lighted rectangle was the silhouette of a man's torso.

In a casual conversational tone, Longarm said quietly, "I got you covered, Snag."

A shot replied to Longarm's words. His Colt spoke back, as the bullet from the intruder's gun tore into the doorjamb in front of Longarm's chest.

He heard a sharp cry of pain followed by the muffled thud of a body hitting the floor. By the light of the muzzle flash, Longarm had seen his adversary crouched in the window frame, one leg inside the room. He was about to enter the room when a second shot from the intruder ripped through the darkness and another slug thunked into the wall.

Longarm swore silently at himself for being careless. He hadn't anticipated the second shot and hadn't been prepared to use its muzzle flash to locate his target's new position.

You should've shot the first time to kill the son of a bitch, old son, Longarm told himself angrily. *Murderers like Snag Collier don't deserve mercy.*

Frowning into the darkness, Longarm called back from his memory the layout of the three adjoining rooms facing him: entry, parlor, and dining room. He chose the entry, for he could reach its doorway without exposing himself to Snag Collier's fire and would have the door's opening on the side of his own gunhand. He moved quickly but quietly down the hall to the entry door.

From the parlor, he could hear the soft scraping of Snag

23

Collier dragging himself across the carpeted floor. Longarm knew that he'd hit Snag, but the darkness hid the extent of Snag's wound. Before shooting again, Longarm decided to try persuasion. He didn't have much hope of talking Snag into surrendering but he thought he might be able to get an idea of how badly the outlaw had been wounded.

"Snag!" he called. There was no reply, but Longarm hadn't expected one. He repeated, "Snag! There's no way you're going to walk out of here alive, unless you throw in your hand! I know you're hurt, and that's an edge I got that you can't get past!"

Another shot from the darkness was Snag's only answer. Longarm had anticipated the shot, knew that Snag would be shooting blind, and this time he was ready. He blinked with the muzzle flash, then kept his eyes closed to preserve for as long as possible the image that had been imposed on them in that split-second when the outlaw's revolver had spat flame.

Now Longarm knew roughly where Snag was located in the dining room. He knew, too, that his enemy couldn't be aware of the door that opened into the dining room from the hall.

Even as the slug from Snag's revolver was tearing into the wall, a foot or more from the door from which Longarm had been speaking, Longarm was moving back toward the hallway. He bumped into the newel post of the stairway in his haste, but that gave him the orientation he needed to lead him quickly to the door between the hall and the dining room.

This time, Longarm didn't bother to take cover behind the doorjamb. Standing squarely in the center of the open door, he called loudly, "Snag! Give up!"

In the silence Longarm heard the rustle and scrape of movement the outlaw made when he turned around. Aiming at the sound, Longarm triggered the Colt, then let off a second shot just to make sure.

No shot was fired in reply and, though he strained his ears, Longarm could hear no sound of movement from the other side of the dining room.

After he'd stood quietly for a full minute, listening for the sound of breathing from across the room, Longarm struck a match. A quick glance convinced him that the corpse he looked at was that of Snag Collier. The dead man lay with his head and shoulders propped up against the wall, his revolver fallen from his lifeless hand. His mouth, opened wide in the grim grin of death, held the worst set of crooked, snaggled teeth Longarm had ever seen.

When the match burned down until he could no longer hold it without scorching his fingers, Longarm blew it out and struck another. He lighted a cheroot with this one, gazing over the end of the long slim cigar at Snag's body. Then he used the match to light his way up the stairs to the attic floor, where Fern was waiting.

It was a typical late-summer morning in Denver when Longarm stepped out of George Masters' barbershop, carrying with him the aroma of the bay rum that was still making his cheeks tingle. He started down Grant Avenue, heading for the Federal building.

Longarm's contentment evaporated instantly when he stepped into the office. He needed nobody to tell him that there was a stormy session ahead.

Without saying a word, Henry, the pink-cheeked clerk in the outer room telegraphed the message by pretending not to see Longarm. Instead, the spectacled youth bent close to the keys of the newfangled writing machine of which he was so proud and let Longarm go past him with protesting. The door of Chief Marshal Billy Vail's private office was ajar, and Longarm pushed it open further.

Vail looked up from his paper-piled desk. When he saw Longarm his lips tightened and his jaw thrust out so far that it almost hid the double chin he was growing. The chief marshal didn't speak either. Longarm recognized that as another bad sign.

He stood in the doorway while Vail stared at him as though he was looking at a stranger, and entered only after his boss jerked a thumb at the red morocco chair that stood against the wall near his desk. Longarm sat down and waited for the storm he knew was about to break.

"It's nice of you to favor us with a visit when you find the time," Vail said mildly. His face was growing redder by the minute, and only someone who knew the chief marshal as well as Longarm did would understand how much effort Vail was exerting to keep himself from shouting.

Vail went on, "I don't suppose you've read the book of rules the Justice Department issued two or three years ago? Rule Eleven is the one I'm referring to. It states that deputy marshals are expected to keep in close touch with the office to which they're assigned and that only in extreme emergencies shall they allow more than three days to pass without reporting in person or by telegraph to that office."

By this time, Longarm was ready to touch off the storm he knew was coming in order to save his chief from bursting a blood vessel. He said, "Now, Billy, you know nobody pays any mind to those damn fool rules. The bunch of pencil-pushers back in Washington that wrote 'em up don't know from a gnat's ass what goes on when we're out in the field."

"Goddammit, Long, you've made me look like a fool!" Vail exploded. "I sent you to take a prisoner from here to the penitentiary, and you just dropped out of sight!"

"Well, I knew where I was, Billy," Longarm pointed out.

"I sure as hell didn't!" Vail retorted. "I had to get a long telegram from the chief marshal in Kansas City before I even knew where the hell you were! I still don't know why you were in Kansas City, Missouri, or what you did there! But I do know that I had to send off a wire of apology to the district chief!"

"Now, wait a minute, Billy!" Longarm protested. "I done that man a favor! I cleaned up Snag Collier and his gang before they could murder a Federal district judge!"

"You also got the chief marshal into a dispute with the Kansas City police for jumping in on what should've been handled by the local authorities. Damn it, you killed two men there and had the police force going crazy trying to find out what happened!"

"It was me kill those bastards or let them kill me, Billy," Longarm replied. "I don't imagine you'd've done any different if it'd been you."

"What I might or might not have done isn't the point!" Vail snapped. "It's what you did! You made the chief marshal there in Kansas City look like the same sort of fool you made me look like, because he didn't know you'd come into his territory any more than I did!"

"Billy, I tried to find that chief marshal to tell him I was in his district and ask him for some help handling Snag. I could've taken Snag alive if I'd had another man or two along. The way it turned out, when I finally got him cornered I was all by myself, and the only choice I had was to kill him."

Vail had worked off much of his anger in his first outburst and was calmer now. He kept his eyes narrow, though, as he watched Longarm light a cheroot. Then he said, "If you've got a good reason for what you did, I guess I can keep this mess between me and the marshal in Kansas City. If I give him all the facts, it might keep him from making an adverse report to Washington. Maybe you'd better tell me the whole story."

Longarm spent the next quarter of an hour giving Vail an only slightly censored version of his activities. He started from the day of his arrival at the Federal penitentiary with the prisoner being transferred from Denver. He'd gotten there, Longarm reminded Vail, late in the afternoon of the day Snag Collier and his gang had staged a dawn break-out. The prison had been in confusion after Snag and July had gotten away, leaving two guards and two members of Snag's gang dead.

"Now, I was right there—the closest Federal officer the warden had to turn to," Longarm told Vail. "He needed all the guards he had to keep the prison under control. So he asked me to take on the job of tracking down Snag and the other man."

"Why the devil didn't you go to the chief marshal right off when you'd tracked your men to Kansas City?" Vail asked.

"Billy, there just plain wasn't time. Snag and July had covered their trail pretty good after the fracas at the pen. It took me three or four days to catch up to 'em, and for all I knew they might've been planning to keep right on moving. Then, after I found out they were planning to murder Judge Claypool, things just happened too fast."

Vail shook his head. He tried hard to hide his smile, but Longarm got a glimpse of it and knew that he was in good standing again.

"Well, after hearing your story, I guess you made all the effort you could reasonably be expected to under Rule Eleven," the chief marshal said. "I'll write to the marshal in Kansas City and refer him to Judge Claypool. I suppose the judge will stand up for you?"

"I'd be mighty surprised if he didn't, Billy."

"As far as I'm concerned, then, you're in the clear," Vail went on. "And I'm just as glad you are, because there's a case up in Dakota Territory that I want to put you on."

"Well, that'll be a real change from Kansas City. What kind of case are you talking about, Billy?"

"I'm not quite sure. In fact, I'm not sure it's a case for us at all."

Longarm frowned across the desk at Vail. "Wait a minute, now. If you ain't certain about it being our case, why're you sending me out on it?"

"Because the Interior Department in Washington couldn't seem to handle it themselves, so they passed it on to the Justice Department. Our bosses back East decided that they wanted it looked into by this office instead of the one up there in Dakota Territory."

Longarm said thoughtfully, "That smells like there might be some inside skullduggery going on that they figure somebody either in our department or the Interior Department's got a hand in."

"Something like that." Vail nodded.

"All right, Billy. Go ahead and let me have the bad news in one dose instead of throwing it to me a little bit at a time."

Vail began shuffling through the papers on his desk, moving them from one pile to another, until he finally found what he was after. Longarm saw the fat envelope his chief was opening and sighed inwardly. He lighted a fresh cheroot and leaned back in his chair ready to listen.

"There's no use in me reading all this to you," the chief marshal said, pulling a thick sheaf of folded papers from the envelope. "I'll boil it down and you can go over the file later on. What it amounts to is that two Land Office clerks are missing, with nobody knows how much government fee money."

"That'd be a straight case of embezzlement, then," Longarm observed. "And nobody that's been stealing from the government's going to stay around the place where he done the stealing. Now, you know good and well, Billy, it ain't going to help things a damn bit for me to traipse clear up to Dakota Territory looking for a couple of Land Office clerks when they're most likely living high right now in Chicago or San Francisco or New York."

"This is more than a simple case of embezzlement," Vail replied. "Those two clerks didn't drop out of sight at the same time, Longarm. The first one, a fellow named Smothers, just stopped sending reports about eight months ago. Two months ago, the Western Division of the Land Office in Chicago sent another clerk named Alberts to find out what was wrong, and—"

"You don't have to tell me," Longarm broke in. "He disappeared, too."

"He may never have gotten there," Vail said. "He hasn't been heard from since he got on the train going West."

"Is that all there is to it?"

"Not by a long shot. There was a big boom in land—claims and leases and purchases—going on up in Dakota Territory for a long time before the first clerk disappeared. Right now, the Interior Department doesn't know whether it has stopped or is still going on. They don't know in Washington how much public land up in the Territory has been leased or sold or claimed."

"Don't seem to me like they pay much attention to business."

"You still haven't heard all of it. The main office over in the western part of the Territory seems to have been shut down without Washington having been told about it, and everything connected with the Interior Department in that part of Dakota is in one hell of a mess."

"Well, I guess this won't be the first time we've had to go in and clean up a mess somebody else has made," Longarm said. "When do you want me to go up there?"

"Right away. The clerk's already got your travel vouchers and other papers ready. Get out of here on the first train that'll get you there, and read that file I gave you on the way up," Vail said. "This isn't just a Land Office mess, Longarm. It's a mess that's got a lot of high political muck-a-mucks interested."

"That's the way it always seems to be," Longarm said as he stood up. "Nobody seems to get excited over a mess unless there's politics in it somewhere. All right, Billy. I'm on my way."

Chapter 4

With a snort of disgust, Longarm began gathering up the sheets of paper that made up the case file Billy Vail had given him. There were letters to Smothers from his superiors in the Land Office, replies from the agent, correspondence between the Chicago Land Office headquarters and officials of the Department of the Interior in Washington, and dozens of notes and memoranda between individuals in both of the offices.

Assembling the papers was a job that took several minutes, for the foolscap pages lay two and three deep on the bed in Longarm's sparsely furnished room. He folded the documents as neatly as possible and stuffed them back into the dog-eared envelope in which they'd travelled from Washington to Denver.

He dug his watch out of the pocket of his vest and found there was still plenty of time left before he'd have to leave for Union Depot to catch the eastbound train. Glancing around the room, he made sure he wasn't overlooking anything vital, for the trip might well turn out to be an extended one.

He looked at the little heap of necessaries that stood by the door—his McClellan saddle neatly cinched up with all its gear, his rifle leaning across the saddle, and his bedroll and saddle-bags standing beside it.

Longarm had crammed into the twin leather pouches of the saddlebags the essentials that always went with him on a long journey: a box of fresh ammunition for each of his guns; extra shirt, balbriggans, and socks, the clothing carefully wrapped around an unopened bottle of Tom Moore; his field telegraph key; a supply of long slim cigars with a new box of wooden matches; oilskin pouches full of parched corn and venison jerky.

He'd checked his Colt, derringer, and Model '76 Winchester before cleaning and oiling them. They'd been the first items to receive his attention. In the inner pocket of his coat, his travel vouchers and expense warrants were folded inside the sealskin wallet that also held his badge. Getting ready for what might be an extended field trip was something Longarm had done so many times that his preparations had become almost automatic.

Lighting a fresh cigar, Longarm took a healthy swallow from the almost empty bottle of Tom Moore that stood on the floor beside the bed. As he returned the bottle to the floor, the bulging envelope on the counterpane caught his eye.

Damned if a man couldn't write down just about everything there on the back of a penny postcard, Longarm told himself. *It'd read something like this: More land's changed hands in Dakota Territory this last year than since they found gold in the Black Hills in '76. The Land Office in Washington don't know how much because the agent, fellow named Claude Smothers, got lost eight months ago. Another Land Office man, Arthur Alberts, went to find Smothers but he never did send in a report. Nobody knows where Smothers or Alberts is now or how much money in government fees is missing. Matter of fact, nobody in the Land Office seems to know anything.*

The bureaucratic fumbling that had led to his present assignment irritated Longarm greatly. He formed in his mind a picture of vast offices filled with rows of desks occupied by faceless men, their shirt-cuffs kept neat by black muslin sleeve protectors that covered their arms from wrists to elbows, all scribbling away eight hours a day. For a moment he looked at the battered envelope as though it was a personal enemy who'd just insulted him.

Then his good humor returned as he told himself, *Don't get too upset at them pencil-pushers back in Washington, old son.*

If it wasn't for their damn fool rules and mistakes, you wouldn't have enough work to fill up your time on the job.

Noon of the following day found Longarm swinging off a creaking daycoach of the Chicago, Milwaukee, St. Paul & Pacific Railroad at Fargo, on the eastern border of Dakota Territory. He was hungry, bleary-eyed, and bone-shaken after twenty-four hours of continuous travel, east from Denver to the junction of the UP and the CMStP&P, then north to Fargo, where a Northern Pacific train would carry him part of the long way he still had to travel before he'd reach his destination.

Tucking his Winchester into the crook of his elbow, Longarm trudged up the splintered planks of the station platform to claim the rest of his gear from the baggage car. He was still standing with his saddle, bedroll, and saddlebags at his feet when the train chugged out of the depot. The dry ham sandwich he'd bought from the butcher boy on the train a short time before it reached Fargo had done little to relieve Longarm's hunger. With food on his mind, he studied his surroundings.

Far to the north a ragged line of bluffs rose above the flat prairie; in all other directions the rolling plains stretched in a seemingly endless expanse. The Red River of the North rolled in low banks down from the bluffs across the prairie, defining the eastern border of Dakota Territory. Fargo stood on the west bank of the Red, the town itself cut into two sections by a small tributary stream that flowed east into the larger Red River.

Fargo was just emerging from the log cabin era. Along the north bank of the tributary low-roofed cabins were scattered. Beyond them the raw stumps of what had until a few years ago been timberland showed where the lumber had come from to erect the large frame houses and business buildings that were crowding out the few log cabins which still stood among the more recent structures south of the stream.

A baggageman pulling a flatbed cart came out of the depot and stopped beside a pile of luggage a few yards away. "Has the railroad got a lunch counter here in the depot?" Longarm asked him.

"What passes for one. What you'll get there in the depot is the same stuff the butcher boys sell on the trains."

"You know where there's a place to eat close by?"

"Friend, you're on the wrong side of the river to get a good meal. This here's Fargo-in-the-Timber. You'll have to go across the river to Fargo-on-the-Prairie to get decent grub."

"That'd be the new part of town, there to the south?"

"Yep." The man finished loading his flatbed and started back to the baggage room. Over his shoulder, he said, "You might do better at the NP depot than you will at this one here, but neither one of 'em puts out a meal worth bragging about."

From where he stood, Longarm could see the Northern Pacific depot, a short distance away. West of the depot, there were a few small buildings scattered along the right of way past a series of stockpens that hugged the tracks; in the pens the horns and rumps of restless steers provided the only movement the vista afforded in that direction.

Looking the other way, he gazed at the converging lines of the CMStP&P tracks, which angled northeast to the railroad bridge across the Red River, into Minnesota. The Northern Pacific rails branched off the bridge and made a beeline to the west along the banks of the little tributary. He studied the small shabby station where he was standing, comparing it with the more imposing two-story depot of the other line.

Even as hungry as he was, Longarm decided that the effort involved in crossing to Fargo-on-the-Prairie wasn't worthwhile. He threw his saddlebags over his shoulder and tucked his bedroll under his arm. Carrying his saddle in one hand and his rifle in the other he started trudging toward the NP depot.

As he got closer to the depot, it looked less impressive than it had from a distance. Like the station he'd just left, the NP's building showed signs of neglect. Its paint was peeling, the heavy timbers of its steps and loading platform were splintered and cracking, and half the rails on the sidings in the yards that stretched beyond the depot were rusted from lack of having been used.

Recurring financial panics had played havoc with the new roads like the Chicago, Milwaukee, St. Paul & Pacific that were just beginning to provide connections between the lines of the main east-west transcontinental roads. Even the established lines such as the Union Pacific and the Santa Fe had been hurt, and roads that had started construction late, as had the Northern Pacific, had been set back even more severely.

East of Denver, the CMStP&P was the only railroad spanning the five-hundred-mile gap between the Union Pacific main line and the uncompleted Northern Pacific. The NP train to which Longarm was changing would take him west only to the Missouri River. Panics had twice stopped the NP's rail-laying at the river.

Mounting the short flight of steps to the station platform, Longarm looked around for the baggage room. He saw the sign at last, over a pair of wide sliding doors at one end of the building, and carried his load down to them, but also saw as he drew closer that they were padlocked.

Turning around, he walked back along the platform to the depot doors and went inside. Only one ticket window was open. The benches that ran around two of the walls and extended into the room itself were unoccupied except for a man sprawled out and snoring loudly on one of the wall benches. The lunch counter that stretched across one end of the waiting room was without customers or attendants. The clatter of an open telegraph key sounded through the grille of the open ticket window. Longarm dropped his gear on the nearest bench and went to the window.

He glanced through the window and saw no one at the chattering telegraph key. "Anybody back there?" he called.

After a long silence, a sleepy voice called, "Westbound's due at seven. Eastbound at eight tomorrow morning."

"I know the schedule. What I want is something to eat."

"Lunch counter opens at six," the unseen man replied.

"It just happens that I'm hungry right now," Longarm said.

"Sorry. There ain't nobody around now to fix you nothing."

"Is there anyplace else to eat around here?"

"Not unless you wanna go over to Fargo-on-the-Prairie. It's a right long hike, down to the river and across the bridge, but there's a café or two there."

"And you're sure there's not anyplace where I can get a meal on this side of the river?"

"Well—now that you reminded me, the Union Saloon over by the stockpens puts out a free lunch most days. They'll likely have a pretty good spread out today. The ranch hands that come in with some cattle on the eastbound this morning ain't got nothing to do but drink till the westbound gets here."

"Now, that sounds good to me. This Union Saloon's not far off, then?"

"Just walk west a little ways along the tracks till you run

into it. There's a couple of whorehouses down there, too."

"Thanks, but all I'm looking for is food. How about the baggage room? Can you open it up so I can check my gear till train time?"

"You taking the westbound?"

"That's what I got in mind."

"Hell, mister, just leave your truck in the waiting room. Won't nobody come in here till a little while before train time. Stuff it under one of the benches. I'll keep an eye on it for you."

Longarm doubted that the unseen speaker would be vigilant in watching any items left in the waiting room, but on the other hand there seemed little likelihood that there'd be any passenger traffic to watch until just before the westbound train arrived. Hunger made up his mind for him. He stowed his saddle, bedroll, and saddlebags under one of the benches and with his Winchester tucked into the crook of his arm started down the dirt road that ran parallel to the tracks toward the stockpens.

Before he got within a hundred yards of the saloon, Longarm could hear the boisterous whooping and shouting of its cowhand customers. The noise grew louder as he drew closer and when he pushed through the batwings the din of drunken shouts and raucous laughter battered at his ears.

For a moment, Longarm stood just inside the swinging doors looking at the barroom. It was small and narrow and crowded. Wherever he looked, there were men dressed in the scuffed working boots, faded Levi's, and gingham shirts favored by working ranch hands.

Longarm's arrival went unnoticed. He lowered the angle at which he carried his rifle, bringing the barrel as close to his body as possible, with the weapon's muzzle pointing almost straight down to the floor, and started working his way toward the bar. The cowhands were letting off steam by leapfrogging, hand-wrestling, or free-style clog-dancing in the small amount of open space the floor provided, and they paid no attention to Longarm as he dodged around them.

Men were standing shoulder to shoulder at the bar, and others stood two and three deep at the small round table that was heaped high with cheese, sliced sausage, and thick slabs of ham between dishes holding pickles, onions, and hard-cooked eggs. As politely as he could, Longarm shouldered between

35

two of the men standing at the bar. He tossed a cartwheel on its scarred wet surface and the barkeep looked questioningly at him.

"Maryland rye, if you got any," Longarm said.

"There's a bottle of rye whiskey around someplace," the barkeep replied, turning and searching until he found a dusty, unlabelled bottle with only a quarter of its contents remaining. He set the bottle and a glass in front of Longarm and shoved a pitcherful of water along the bar to rest beside the bottle and glass.

"Now, I didn't ask this redeye what part of the country it come from," he told Longarm. "But if it ain't to your taste, you can drink the same kind everybody else does."

"I imagine it'll suit me," Longarm said. He pulled the cork and sniffed. He nodded, looked at the amount of liquor left in the bottle, and went on, "It don't look to me like there's a dollar's worth left here, but if you figure that cartwheel's enough, toss it in your till and I'll take the bottle. Then I'll pick up a bite to eat at your lunch table and find me a quiet corner where I won't get in nobody's way."

"It's damn near worth a dollar to me to get rid of that orphan liquor," the barkeep replied. "It's a deal."

Settling the butt of his Winchester a bit more firmly over his left forearm, Longarm turned the glass over and put it on the bottle's uncorked neck. He picked up the bottle in his left hand and began pushing his way up to the table where the free lunch was spread. He had worked his way through the outer row of the men crowding up to the table and was trying to reach between two of the cowhands in the front row when one of them grabbed his wrist and twisted his body around to glare into Longarm's face.

"Wait your turn," he began. Then he saw Longarm's neat black coat, gray flannel shirt, and string tie and added, "City dude."

Longarm could tell that the man had downed a few drinks too many and ignored the remark. He twisted his wrist free and met the cowhand's eyes with his own steely gaze.

In the irrational fashion of drunks, the man became offended. He said angrily, "Look here, dude, you better step back and take your turn after us working men has got our share."

Longarm had no intention of getting involved in a saloon

brawl with a man who was obviously drunk. He said levelly, "You go on and take what you want. When you're done, you can step aside and I'll get myself something."

"Now, don't go telling me what to do, slicker!" the drunk snarled. He drew his head back to get a better look as Longarm and for the first time saw the rifle nestled in his armpit. He grinned and said, "Well, look here! The dude's got him a long gun! What's the matter, city man? You afraid to go outside without a gun to protect you?"

One of the cowhands across the table from the drunk said, "Peebles, you better lay off that fellow. He ain't the dude you've tagged him for. Be careful or you'll get in trouble."

"Mind your own business, Stitch!" the drunken hand retorted. "I guess I know a city dude when I see one! Look at that buttoned-up collar and necktie!" Turning back to Longarm, he went on, "You know how to handle that gun?"

"I manage," Longarm replied, his voice still low and level.

"Maybe you better let me take care of it for you," the cowhand went on. "Hell, you prob'ly don't even know whether or not you got the safety on. You might shoot somebody accidental."

With as much of a lurch as he could manage in the crowd, the drunk reached for the Winchester. Longarm's right hand was free; he brought up his palm and planted it on the drunk's chest to push him away.

By the time Longarm moved, though, the cowhand had grasped the rifle's action. Somehow he managed to push the safety off and get a finger inside the trigger guard. The Winchester cracked as the slug from its muzzle ripped into the board floor under the lunch table. The rifle's recoil jarred the bottle of whiskey from Longarm's hand. The bottle thudded to the floor and the glass flew off the neck. Glass and bottle shattered with a tinkle that sounded loud in the dead silence that had gripped the crowd after the shot.

Longarm wasted neither time nor motion. His right hand, which had been pushed against the drunk's chest, clamped on the cowhand's wrist and twisted the man's hand away from the rifle. Without stopping, Longarm jerked the cowhand's wrist forward and down, used the impetus he'd given the man's body to pull him a step forward and at the same time twirl him around and bring his imprisoned wrist up his back between his shoulderblades.

"Let go, damn it!" the drunk yowled. "That hurts!"

"Not any more'n it ought to!" Longarm snapped. "Anybody drunk enough to put a hand on another man's gun needs to learn better!"

By this time the shock of the shot had worn off. The other ranch hands began moving toward Longarm and their friend.

"You men keep back!" a man standing at the bar commanded loudly. "Don't mix into this! Whatever Peebles gets, he's got coming to him!"

Evidently the speaker's authority was recognized by the cowhands, for they stopped in their tracks, the more sober ones restraining those drunk enough to try to interfere.

Longarm frog-marched the drunk to the bar, laid his rifle on the mahogany, and, when his hand was free, flicked off the drunk's hat. Picking up the pitcher of water the barkeep had placed in front of him earlier, Longarm poured the water over the drunk's head in a slow, steady stream until the pitcher was empty. The cowhand sputtered and tried to pull his wrist free, but his strength was not enough to break Longarm's iron-hard grasp.

From the end of the bar, the man who'd commanded the others to stay clear of the fracas walked up to Longarm. "You can let go of him now," he said. "I'll answer for his behavior." When Longram looked at him, the man added, "Pebbles is one of my hands. He'll do what I tell him to."

With a nod, Longarm released Pebbles' wrist. The cowhand spun around angrily, his fists coming up. He saw his boss standing beside Longarm and let his hands drop, a sheepish look on his face.

"I didn't know the gun was going off, Brad," he said. "I was just funning the dude. Honest."

"You'd better go outside and walk around in the fresh air," Brad replied. "Get yourself sober enough to tell a dude from a man when you see one."

When Pebbles had started toward the batwings and the other cowhands had begun to turn away from the scene, Brad said to Longarm, "I'm sorry that happened, but I'll square accounts as best I can." He called to the barkeep, "Slim, give this gentleman back whatever he paid you, and put it on my bill. And set him out a fresh bottle."

"Now, you don't have to do that," Longarm protested.

"I'll feel better if I do. My name's Easley, by the way." He extended his hand. "I don't guess I need to tell you that Pebbles didn't mean to get out of line, Mr.—"

"Long." Longarm shook his hand. "No hard feelings on my part, Mr. Easley. Your man just had a few too many."

"I'm glad you see it that way. We've just finished rounding up that bunch of steers you saw out in the pens, and the men needed to let off steam."

"Sure."

The barkeep set an unopened bottle on the bar and laid a silver dollar beside it. "I got no more rye whiskey," he said, "but that's good bourbon Brad's buying for you."

Longarm nodded and turned back to Easley. "I ain't going to take your bottle, Mr. Easley, much as I appreciate it. But I'll have a drink with you just to show there's no hard feelings."

"Whatever you say, Long. But I still owe you. My spread's the Lazy G. It's about a hundred miles west of here, between Jamestown and Bismark. If you're ever around there, stop in and visit for a while."

"Thanks, I'll remember that. Now let's have that drink, then I'll get me a bite of that free lunch, which is what I came in here for in the first place, and we'll call it all square."

Chapter 5

Longarm found the Northern Pacific depot still deserted when he got back to it. The same sleeper occupied the bench against the wall, no one had as yet showed up to start cooking at the lunch counter, and the telegraph key still chattered away unattended behind the window of the apparently deserted ticket office. Checking his gear, Longarm found it undisturbed. He laid his rifle along the backrest of the bench above the spot where his equipment rested and stretched out to catch forty winks himself.

A rattling of cooking utensils from the lunch counter roused Longarm from a deep sleep. Instantly alert, he sat up and looked around. A man was behind the lunch counter pulling pots and pans from the oven of the stove and piling them on top. There was something familiar about the man. Longarm studied him for a moment before recognition dawned. Unless he was badly mistaken, the man now getting ready to begin cooking was the sleeper who'd been occupying the corner of the bench along the back wall.

Longarm took a cheroot from his pocket and lighted it. He puffed at the long slim cigar until it was drawing evenly, then stood up and walked across to the lunch counter. The man had taken the lids off the pots he'd just removed from the oven.

One held beans and the other stew. There were two pans of biscuits as well.

As he stood looking at the food, Longarm grew angrier by the minute, remembering how hungry he'd been when he first entered the station earlier in the day. The cook was now putting kindling into the firebox of the range that stood behind the counter. Glancing at Longarm, he said over his shoulder, without interrupting his work, "Too early to get anything to eat. Can't you see I'm just getting the stove heated up?"

"I didn't come over to eat. I just wanted to ask you a question."

"What?"

"Wasn't that you, sleeping over there on the other side of the depot till a few minutes ago?"

"Sure. What about it?"

"I came in here a little while after noon, hungry as a bitch wolf with nine cubs. The fellow back of the ticket window said there wasn't anybody around to cook me up something."

"Well?"

"Well, if you were here all the time, why in hell didn't you do what the railroad pays you to do, and dish me up a bowl of beans or stew and some of those biscuits? Damn it, I was hungry enough to've eaten 'em cold."

"Mister, I'm paid to have grub ready when there's a train due in. That's when the eastbound's due in the morning and when the westbound's due in the evening. In between times, what I do is my own affair."

"It wouldn't've hurt you a bit to fix me something."

"Listen, friend, if I'd've heard you saying you was hungry, I might've come over and fixed you up. But when I sleep, I sleep all over, and I didn't hear you nor nobody else say nothing about being hungry. That answer your question?"

"I guess it does," Longarm replied, shaking his head. "But it's one hell of a way to run a lunch counter."

Turning away, Longarm walked out and began pacing the station platform to work off his temper. The sun was dropping to the flat western horizon now. Longarm paced back and forth on the platform until he'd cooled down, then went back into the depot.

He sat on one of the benches until the thought of a hot meal won out over his irritation. He decided he was ready to swallow his pride, as long as he could swallow along with it a plate of

41

stew and biscuits. He went over to the counter and ate. The stew wasn't as bad as he'd expected, and when he'd finished his meal and drunk a second cup of hot coffee, the delapidated depot didn't look quite so dreary any more. The stationmaster appeared behind the ticket window and Longarm went over to have his travel voucher stamped.

"Federal marshal, eh?" the stationmaster said when he saw the voucher. He looked at the travel authorization closely. "I need to fill in where you're going before I can stamp this for you, Marshal Long. It doesn't say here where you're headed."

"The office clerk couldn't find out how far west the NP tracks go these days," Longarm replied. "He says you still don't have rails west of the Missouri, but I went past the river a good while back, to a little town called Interior."

Well, you and the clerk in your office are both right and you're both wrong. We've got trackage west of the Missouri, but it's not in shape yet for regular traffic, so our orders are not to issue any tickets beyond Bismark."

"As I recall, Interior's a good hundred miles west of that."

"It is. We had service to Interior for a while. Then when we laid off track crews during the panic, some of the men got mad and ripped up a lot of roadbed that we still haven't finished rebuilding."

"How far west of the river will the NP get me, then?"

"If you don't object to riding a work train past Bismark, I can fix it for you to cover another fifty miles. That'll take you to the section camp, and if you've got saddle gear, I'll wire the foreman to lend you a horse you can ride to Interior."

"I'd be obliged if you'll do that, then. I figured I'd need a horse when I got here, so I've brought my gear. Used to get a cavalry remount, but since the army's wiped up the Indians, there's not as many forts around here as there used to be."

"That's the truth, Marshal. But the way settlers are pouring in, it won't be long till there'll be towns with livery stables any place you look, so I guess you'll still be able to get around. Well, you make yourself comfortable, and I'll fix up your voucher and arrange for that horse."

Longarm was still waiting for the voucher when Brad Easley and his cowhands arrived. The men were not in the best of shape. Several were still so drunk that they had to be supported by their companions. A few others were sober enough to stay erect and walk in a staggering sort of way, and the balance had reached the glum stage of sobering up. In the depot's big waiting room there didn't seem to be as many of them as there had in the crowded bar, and Longarm counted them quickly as they straggled in. There were fourteen, not counting Easley, who'd come in last. When the rancher saw Longarm, he waved and came over to where he was sitting.

"You didn't tell me you were waiting over at the depot, Long," he said. "Which way are you heading, east or west?"

"West."

"I'm going east, to market my steers. I was hoping you might be heading that way, too. I figured that since the east-bound won't pass through until morning, we could go into town and have supper together."

"I'd've liked that," Longarm said. He looked at the ranch hands, who were settling down on the benches, and asked, "Your men going along with you?"

"Oh, no. They're going back to the ranch on the westbound. They've got to cut another bunch of steers out of my main herd to ship out two weeks from now."

"Well, they ain't quite as rambunctious as back there in the saloon. I reckon they'll make it."

"They're a tired bunch right now," Easley said. "But they've had their blowout, and they're sobering up. I don't think they'll give you any trouble on the train."

"If they do, I can handle it."

"I'm sure you can, after seeing the way you handled Pebbles this afternoon. But if they—" Easley broke off as the station-master called Longarm's name.

Longarm excused himself and went over to the ticket window.

"You're all fixed up, Marshal Long," the stationmaster said, handing Longarm's travel vouchers through the window. "I just made your vouchers out to Bismark. After you cross the river you'll be riding NP accommodation to the section camp. There'll be a horse waiting for you at the camp. Anything else you need, just tell the section foreman, and he'll see that you get it."

"I'm obliged to you. You've been real helpful." Longarm turned to find that Easley had followed him to the window and had overheard the stationmaster.

"You're a lawman?" Easley frowned. "Marshal? Federal, I'd guess, since you're certainly covering a lot of territory."

"You guessed right. I'm going on a case over near the Montana border."

"No wonder you didn't have any trouble handling Pebbles. He really did misjudge the kind of man he was tangling with."

"Oh, I saw right off he wasn't going to be no trouble. And I sure wasn't about to arrest a man just because he'd had too much to drink and made a fool of himself."

"Why the devil didn't you tell my boys who you are? They'd have respected your badge and left you alone."

"Why, I look at it this way, Mr. Easley. If I can't handle a man without waving my badge in his face, I ain't fit to be carrying that badge in the first place."

Easley was silent for a moment, then he nodded thoughtfully. "Yes, I see what you mean. Well, I'm glad things turned out the way they did, with no harm done. Don't forget, you've got a standing invitation to stop in at the Lazy G whenever you find yourself up this way."

"I'll remember that," Longarm promised. "A man in my job don't ever know where he's going to be, or when, but I'll likely be passing this way again."

"When you do, don't pass by the Lazy G without stopping," Easley said. A locomotive whistle sounded in the distance, and Easley said, "That's the westbound. I'd better see about getting tickets for my men and rounding them up."

Easley stepped up to the ticket window, and Longarm began gathering up his gear. He got it assembled and carried it out to the platform. He looked down the track to the west; the locomotive of the westbound was already in sight, crossing the Red River bridge. Behind it the sky was deepening from the pale blue of daylight into the deeper blue of evening. The train was close enough now for Longarm to hear the metallic whine of steel on steel, brakeshoes being clamped on wheels, as the engineer began slowing for the station stop.

Longarm waited until the locomotive crawled past him. He watched as the first four cars rolled by; they were all crowded. Then he began walking along the platform, keeping abreast of the baggage car. The sun was in his eyes now, a thin arc of flashing yellow above the flat rim of the prairie to the west. The train stopped just before the baggage car reached the end of the platform. The baggage car door rolled open. Longarm tossed his saddle, bedroll, and saddlebags inside, but kept his rifle tucked into the crook of his elbow.

"Hold on there!" the baggageman called as he appeared in the open door. "I can't take on baggage until I've unloaded!"

"Take mine as a special favor," Longarm told him. "Name's Long, Deputy U.S. Marshal. I'll pick up my gear at Bismark."

Without waiting for the baggageman to reply, Longarm turned away from the car and began retracing his steps to the rear of the train. His walk was a short one, as there were only two passenger coaches and a parlor car behind the baggage car. The door in the vestibule of the center coach was the only one open, and the conductor stood beside it, helping detraining passengers alight. The cowhands from the Laxy G had gathered in a little knot outside the station door and were listening to Brad Easley.

"Board!" the conductor called. "All aboard!"

Longarm stepped aside to let the Laxy G hands get on the train first. They filed past him, one or two nodding to him. Peebles passed by, but did not look at Longarm. Easley had not followed his men to the train; he was standing in the depot door, watching them. He flicked a quick wave at Longarm, who nodded in reply.

"If you're going on this train, mister, you'd better get on," the conductor told Longarm. "We're ready to pull out."

Longarm stepped up into the vestibule and turned back to the conductor. He said, "Soon as we get rolling and you've got a minute to spare, I'd like to have a little talk."

"About what?"

"About some of the passengers you might've noticed on this run. My name's Long, I'm a Deputy U.S. Marshal, and I'm looking for two men who more'n likely rode this train."

"I'll be glad to help you all I can, Marshal. I don't guess you're in a real big hurry for us to talk, are you?"

"No. Whenever you get a few minutes free."

"Just as soon as I take up the tickets and get my trip book in order, I'll stop by wherever you're sitting."

"Fine. I'll be in the parlor car."

As Longarm walked through the center coach, habit led him automatically to give each passenger a quick look. The Lazy G hands had disappeared into the front coach, and only about half the seats in the one Longarm entered were occupied. Most of the passengers were men in business suits; mentally, Longarm divided these into two groups, drummers on regular selling trips and merchants or storekeepers from Bismark. A few of

45

the latter were accompanied by women, but of the twenty or so passengers on the coach only five were female.

There were even fewer passengers occupying the wicker lounge chairs and sofas in the parlor car. A game of whist was being played by four drummers in the corner just inside the door. A young couple occupied one of the sofas in the center of the coach; they had their heads close together and were talking in low tones.

Far in the back of the coach a young man, his head bent down toward the book he was reading, sat in one of the chairs across the car from the miniature bar that occupied one corner of the car's end. No one was sitting in any of the half-dozen other chairs in the front of the car or on the other sofas which stretched along the sides of the parlor car with small tables between them.

Longarm liked to sit as far back in a railroad car as he could manage, facing forward. He made his way to the rear of the car, and, after placing his rifle on the floor beside the wall, sat down in a chair across the aisle from the man who was reading.

Only after he'd settled comfortably in the chair did Longarm notice that the reader was more youth than man. In spite of— or perhaps because of—the thin puffed-out sideburns that extended almost to the young passenger's jawbones, and the small gold-framed spectacles he wore, Longarm judged the young man to be no older than twenty-two or twenty-three.

A leather case stood open on the table next to him and a small bottle of red wine and a wineglass rested beside it. Looking more closely, Longarm saw that the case was filled with sandwiches and that the youth held one in his hand. He was engrossed in his book, and did not notice Longarm.

Two quick blasts sounded from the locomotive's whistle, and the train began to creep ahead. Longarm looked out the window until the stockpens and the cluster of houses around them had been left behind, but tired quickly of watching the forest of tree stumps that were the only feature of an otherwise empty landscape.

Turning away from the window, he took a cheroot from his pocket and lighted it. The first heavy plumes of smoke that rose from the long slim cigar swirled across the coach and wreathed the head of the passenger across the aisle. The young man waved a hand to clear away the smoke, raised his head from his book, and looked at Longarm.

"Now, I didn't intend to blow that puff in your direction," Longarm said at once. "Maybe I'd best move someplace else, if cigar smoke bothers you."

"It doesn't bother me at all," the young man replied. His voice was high-pitched but not unpleasant to hear. He went on, "In fact, I'll light up myself and keep you company." He placed the half-eaten sandwich in the leather case and took a fat Corona from one pocket of his vest, a cigar-knife from another.

Methodically, he clipped the end from the cigar, ran the stiletto blade of the knife up the clipped end, and returned the knife to his pocket before taking out a match and puffing the cigar alight.

"Aha," he said. "Now that's just bully." Exhaling, he picked up the wineglass and took a sip of the red wine it contained. Then, suddenly aware that Longarm had been watching him, he said, "Nothing like a good sturdy Bordeaux to go with a cigar. In fact, I really prefer it to brandy. I say, would you care to join me in a sip? I have a spare wineglass here in my case."

Longarm shook his head. "Thank you kindly, but I ain't much of a wine drinker."

"Do you wear the white ribbon, then?" Before Longarm could reply, the young man went on, speaking very rapidly. "If you do, I'd enjoy discussing with you the dichotomy of those who are advocating abstinence in the guise of temperance. My father was fond of pointing out how selective they are in their citing of Biblical authority for their views. They quote the passage from the book of Ezekiel, 'Strong drink is a mocker,' but ignore St. Paul, who said, 'Take a little wine for thy stomach's sake.'"

Concealing his surprise at the spate of words that gushed from the young man, Longarm answered, "Oh, I ain't temperance by any manner of means. But about the only kind of liquor that suits my taste is good Maryland rye, so I pretty much stick to a swallow or two of Tom Moore when I take a drink."

"Now, that's very interesting, to find someone here in the West whose palate is sensitive enough to distinguish between brands of rye. I must confess, I haven't yet acquired the ability to identify brandy, much less whiskey."

"Well, it ain't all that hard to tell what kind of whiskey you're drinking," Longarm said. "Leastways, not for me."

Their discussion was interrupted by the train's butcher boy, who leaned over Longarm's chair and said in a secretive whisper, "Marshal Long, the conductor said to tell you he's got time to have that talk you wanted, if you'll go up to the baggage car."

"I'll be right there," Longarm said. He stood up and said to the young man across the aisle, "You'll excuse me, but I got a little bit of business to tend to right now."

"Certainly, certainly. We'll continue our discussion later."

Swaying with the motion of the train, Longarm started for the baggage car. As he passed through the second day coach, he noticed that the Lazy G cowhands were sitting in a group at the back of the coach.

They paid no attention to him as he walked down the aisle. They'd brought several bottles of liquor with them from the saloon, and were passing them from hand to hand. Longarm made a mental note to caution the conductor about their tendency to get boisterous, then decided that the trainmen on this portion of the run must be used to handling a few drunken ranch hands, and went on into the baggage car.

"Sorry I had to keep you waiting, Marshal," the conductor apologized as Longarm came into the car.

"I wasn't in a hurry," Longarm replied. "It just occurred to me that there aren't likely to be too many regular passengers on this stretch of road, and that you'd know most of 'em."

"Well, that's right, Marshal. I've been on this run since the NP began trying to restore service west of Fargo, and if the men you're after do much travelling, I probably know them."

"They're both government men, so they'd be travelling on vouchers, like I do. Except these fellows work for the Land Office. One of 'em ran the office at Interior for quite a while. Claude Smothers is his name. That ring a bell with you?"

"Oh, I know Smothers, of course. Or did. He was a regular between Bismark and Fargo for quite a while, but I haven't seen him lately." Frowning, the conductor added, "It's been six months or longer, I guess."

"Would you happen to remember which way he was travelling on the last trip he made with you?"

Frowning, the conductor shook his head. "It's been a while, Marshal, and I can't say offhand. But give me a little while to think. It might come back to me."

"I'd be obliged. Now, the other man's name is Arthur Alberts. He'd have showed up maybe two or three months ago. Do you recall seeing him?"

Again the conductor shook his head. "As you said, Marshal, there aren't many passengers on this run who use government vouchers, and you'd think I'd remember the ones who do, but it's not all that easy. Give me a little while to think back. Maybe I can remember something." He paused and asked, "I don't guess you can tell me why you're after Claude?"

"Well, I ain't exactly after him. His boss in Chicago got worried because all of a sudden he just stopped sending in reports. They sent the other man, Alberts, to find out why they didn't hear from Smothers, and now he's dropped out of sight, too."

"You think something's happened to both of them?"

"That's what I aim to find out. Now, I'd appreciate it if you don't say anything about our talk, and I'd sure be interested in hearing anything you can think of that might help me when I get to Interior."

"Interior's not on the NP line, you know, Marshal Long. If something's happened there, I might not have heard about it."

"Sure. I understand. But you do some hard thinking, and if anything occurs to you that might give me a lead, it'd be right helpful."

"I'll do my best, Marshal."

Satisfied that he'd done all he could for the moment to get his investigation going, Longarm started back to the parlor car.

Chapter 6

Walking through the first coach on his way back to the parlor car, Longarm noticed that the seats which had been occupied by the Lazy G hands were now vacant. The empty whiskey bottles on the floor around the seats told him why, and he moved a bit faster as he went through the next day coach. The minute he opened the vestibule door and entered the parlor car, he heard loud talking. At the back of the car, the Laxy G men were drawn together in a tight knot in front of the miniature bar, haranguing the butcher boy. The young couple who had been sitting on the sofa had retreated to chairs across the aisle from the four drummers, who'd stopped their card game and were looking toward the crowded rear of the car.

Longarm leaned over the table and asked the nearest of the drummers, "What the hell's all the fuss about back there?"

"Damned if I know. We were involved in our game, and when those cowboys came in, we didn't pay much attention to them until the shouting started."

"They're angry at the price the barkeep's asking for his whiskey," the young man across the aisle volunteered. "Nellie and I heard what was said before all the shouting started. When it looked like they might get into a fight, we moved up here."

"If that's all it's about, there's no call for me to mix into it," Longarm said. "Best let 'em talk themselves out. If they don't settle it after a minute or two, the cowhands'll get tired and go back to the front coach."

"I hope you're right," Nellie said.

"I'll move on down to where I was sitting," Longarm told the couple. "Then, if things get out of hand, I can calm 'em down real fast."

He walked slowly down to the end of the car and sat down in his chair. The Lazy G hands were so engrossed in their angry argument that they didn't notice Longarm's return. Across the aisle, the young man had put his book aside and was watching the dispute with open interest.

"Looka here," one of the Lazy G men was saying when Longarm sat down, "we don't wanna buy out your whole stock. All we want is a coupla bottles to keep our whistles wet for the rest of the trip."

"I told you what the company says I got to charge for a bottle of liquor," the barkeep said.

"Oh, hell, tell 'em you busted a bottle!" one of the men called out.

"I can't. I'm responsible for breakage. If I say a bottle got busted, I have to pay for it."

One of the cowhands in the back of the group had noticed the bottle of wine on the young passenger's table. He turned to call to the others, and Longarm saw that it was Peebles, the ranch hand he'd had trouble with in the saloon in Fargo.

"Hey, you fellows!" Peebles called. "This little four-eyed kid's got some liquor here. Maybe he'll sell us some that won't cost as much as the barkeep's!"

Three or four of the men nearest Peebles turned around to look. One of them said to the youth, "How about it, stranger? Got any more of that stuff with you?"

"As a matter of fact, I have," the young man replied. "But I don't think you'd like it. I gather you men are after whiskey, and what I have is wine."

"Whiskey, wine—don't make that much difference," Peebles said. "How about selling us some?"

"I'm afraid I can't accommodate you gentlemen. I brought along just enough for my own needs, and I'm not interested in selling any of it."

"Now, look here, little fellow, don't be stubborn!" the man

51

standing beside Peebles said menacingly. "Where we're going, all we'll get to drink for the next month is water or coffee. We're going to get ourselves tanked up before we get off this train or we'll know why not!"

"I'm sorry," the young man replied. "I'd like to help you, but aside from the fact that the wine I have isn't something you men would appreciate, I don't have any to spare."

"What d'you mean, we wouldn't appreciate it?" the cowhand bristled. "You saying we ain't good enough to drink your fancy wine?"

"That's not it at all. It's simply a fact that a taste for wine has to be cultivated. And confirmed whiskey drinkers seldom enjoy fine wines."

"Well, toot-de-ooh!" Peebles snorted. "Listen to the little dude will you?" He turned to his companions and winked, a grin spreading over his face. Then he turned back to the seated youth and went on, "I guess I'll just have a swig or two out of that bottle of yours and see if I like the taste of it."

"I don't believe that would prove anything. Now, I suggest that unless you men can strike a bargain with the barkeep for whiskey, which is what you really want, you forget the entire matter and go back to your seats."

"If we don't, I guess you'll make us?" Peebles asked.

"That isn't what I said, sir. The conductor is in charge of the train. It's his job to keep rowdies from bothering the passengers, not mine. I'm only concerned with having you stop annoying me with ridiculous suggestions."

"By God, I'll show you what annoying is!" Peebles snapped angrily. He took a step and reached for the bottle of wine. "I'll have a taste of this stuff whether you like it or not!"

Longarm was on his feet the instant the hulking cowhand stepped toward the table. He couldn't believe what he was seeing when the youth grasped Peebles' wrist before the man could grab the wine bottle and stopped the cowhand's movement.

Peebles tried to twist his arm free, but failed. Longarm had pushed aside the two or three men who'd been between him and the hulking Peebles and had almost reached the cowhand when Peebles took a roundhouse swing with his free left hand.

Still seated, and without seeming to move more than an inch or so, the youth ducked under the blow. He hadn't released his hold on Peebles' wrist when Longarm grabbed both of the cowhand's elbows and immobilized him. Peebles glanced over

52

his shoulder, saw who was holding him, and stopped struggling.

"All right, damn you," he told Longarm. "You can let go of me, Marshal. I'll leave the little pipsqueak alone."

"Let him go," the young man invited. "I can protect myself without assistance."

Peebles snorted in disgust. "I can wipe up the floor with any little four-eyed son of a bitch like you with one hand tied behind me!"

Longarm still had not released the big cowhand in spite of the young man's suggestion that he do so. His jaw dropped when the youth stood up and began unbuttoning his vest.

"I really regret this," the young man said as he slid his arms out of both vest and coat and laid the garments over the back of the chair, "but it's against my code to allow myself to be called a son of a bitch by a bully. And you, sir," he added, speaking directly to Peebles, "strike me as being a bully of the most obnoxious type."

"Now, wait a minute!" Longarm broke in. "Let's not have any fighting in here!"

"I'm afraid there'll have to be a fight," the young man said calmly. He took off his glasses, leaving his face looking strangely naked, then began undoing the gold links in the cuffs of his shirtsleeves. "In fact, I insist on it. A bully such as this man needs to be taught a lesson."

There was an assurance in the youth's tone that told Longarm he wasn't talking idly. He remembered the grip the young man had maintained on Peebles' wrist, and the unruffled manner in which he'd dodged the big man's roundhouse swing.

He asked, "You're sure you know what you're getting into, young fellow?"

"Certainly I do." The youth had removed the gold links from his starched white cuffs and put them in the lid of the case beside his glasses. As he spoke, he was rolling up the sleeves of his shirt. He patted the folds of the sleeves into place and stepped aside from the table. He said, "I'm quite ready now. You can release the man whenever you wish."

With a mental reservation that he could always step in and stop the fight before the young man was hurt too badly, Longarm let go of Peebles' elbows.

With a roar like that of a just-roped bull, Peebles launched a wide sweeping swing with his right fist. The young man lifted his chin just before the blow connected and Peebles' fist swung past his opponent's face with a force that pulled the big man a quarter-turn toward the smaller one. The youth buried his fist in Peebles' unguarded belly and stepped back as the big man grunted and counter-punched with a left jab.

A fist thrown up at the last moment deflected Peebles' blow and the young man stepped into a straight right, his fist again finding a target in Peebles' midsection. Peebles grunted as the blow landed, pushing him back almost a foot.

He advanced quickly, though, this time working his fists like battering rams in a series of short jabs. The youth ducked under the high-swinging attack and got both his right and left fists home in rapid succession in Peebles' breadbasket.

Peebles' mouth was open now. The series of blows he'd taken had driven the wind out of him, and he was gasping for breath. He ducked his head and bored in, his fists low to protect his face. Somehow, the youth got a left jab through Peebles' guard and landed a hard blow on the big man's nose, which started to bleed copiously.

The sight of his own blood flowing drove caution out of Peebles' mind. He raised his head, gulping air, blood streaming across his open mouth and dripping off his chin, his fists cutting through empty air inches away from his opponent's face. The young man ducked below Peebles' pumping arms and brought his right fist up with an uppercut that slammed the big man's mouth shut with a clash of cracking teeth.

Peebles tottered. The young man stepped back and waited calmly. Looking at him with open curiosity, Longarm saw that he was not even breathing hard.

For a moment, it looked as though Peebles was going to recover, in spite of the stunned, vacant look on his face and in his glazed eyes. Then, after he'd stood shakily for a few seconds, his knees gave way and he crumpled to the floor.

For a moment the ranch hands stood unbelieving. Then two of them started for the young man. Before they reached him, Longarm had stepped across Peebles' unconscious form to take a position in front of the winner of the short, savage fight.

"Now, that's enough!" Longarm said sternly. "This young fellow knocked your man out fair and square, and you other men ain't going to gang up on him to get even! It wasn't him that started the argument, remember, it was Peebles!"

"He's right, boys," one of the men at the rear of the group called. "Peebles started it, the young rooster finished him, and that's that. Now, we better get back to that other car where we

54

belong before the conductor hears about this ruckus and gets us all in trouble with Brad."

"Are you the man Mr. Easley left in charge?" Longarm called to the speaker over the heads of the men between them.

"That's right, Marshal. Joe Fitch. I guess you'd call me a sorta strawboss, till we get back to the Lazy G and the real foreman takes over."

"You think you can make your men toe the line until you get where you're going?"

"Oh, they won't give you any more trouble. I'll answer for 'em if they do," Fitch replied.

"All right. Go on back where you belong, then, and take Peebles with you."

Peebles was stirring now, groaning feebly. Two of the men nearest him lifted him by the armpits and started toward the front of the parlor car. The others shifted around, getting ready to follow.

"Wait just a minute!" the winner of the fight called. The men stopped and looked around at him. The young man went on, "Barkeep, give these men two bottles of good whiskey. It's on me, just to show there are no hard feelings."

There was dead silence for a moment, then a chorus of laughs and "Hurrahs!" sounded as the barkeep handed Fitch the bottles of liquor.

Longarm spoke up quickly. "You sure you can handle your crowd if they get a few too many, Fitch?"

"Hell, Marshal, two bottles amounts to only about two drinks apiece. That's not enough to get any of these copper-gulched bastards drunk."

After the Lazy G men had disappeared through the vestibule door, the young man said to Longarm, "I think I owe you a drink, too, Mr. Marshal. You could've stopped me from teaching that cowboy not to bully somebody smaller than himself. I could see that you didn't believe I could handle him."

"For a minute, I didn't. Then I remembered how you'd held onto Peebles's wrist when he was trying to break loose, and how you'd ducked that first swing he'd taken at you. But I wasn't sure I hadn't made a mistake until after you dodged the first couple of punches he threw."

"You must be a pretty important man around here, to control that bunch of wild cowboys the way you did, Mr. Marshal. What's your first name, by the way?"

"You got things a little bit mixed up," Longarm replied.

"Marshal ain't my name. It's the job I hold."

"I have made a mistake, haven't I?" The young man grinned, showing a broad expanse of oversized teeth. "You know, it didn't occur to me that those men were addressing you by a title instead of your name. What's your name, then?"

"My name's Long, Custis Long. And I'm a deputy U. S. marshal, working out of the Denver office."

The young man put out his hand, and Longarm shook it. "I'm glad to meet you, Marshal Long. I certainly appreciate your backing me up the way you did. My name's Roosevelt, by the way. Theodore Roosevelt."

"I'm pleased to make your acquaintance, Mr. Roosevelt. You live in the East, I take it?"

"New York. And this is my first trip west. I think it's just bully to be meeting a genuine U. S. Marshal. I hope we can talk a while, now that the excitement's over. Why don't you sit down with me, and I'll finish my wine while you have a drink of—I think you said you preferred rye whiskey, if the barkeep can supply it. And perhaps I can persuade you to try one of my very excellent Corona cigars while we chat."

"I won't say no to a glass of whiskey, Mr. Roosevelt. I got a fresh bottle in my saddlebags, but they're up in the baggage car with the rest of my gear. If you don't mind, I'll stick to my own cigars, though."

Within a few minutes the two men were seated at the little table. Young Roosevelt had put his glasses on again, rolled down his sleeves, and donned his coat and vest. He refilled his wineglass and motioned to Longarm to pour himself a drink from the fresh bottle of Tom Moore the barkeep brought to the table.

Longarm said, "I'm real curious about something. Where did you learn to fight the way you do?"

"At Harvard University. I was a member of the college boxing team during my last two years there."

"Well, your teacher did a right good job."

"I'll be truthful with you, Marshal Long. I really didn't care for boxing when I began learning. I took up the sport only because I didn't weigh enough to make the football team."

"One thing I've noticed, Mr. Roosevelt. Size don't mean a whole lot when you measure a man's spunk. And you got plenty of that."

"It makes me feel bully to hear you say that, Marshal. By the way, I still feel a little uncomfortable when I'm called Mr.

Roosevelt. It seems to me that name belongs to my late father. My family and friends all call me Teddy."

"Well, I got a nickname, too, that my friends call me. It's Longarm."

"Of course," young Roosevelt smiled. "An obvious derivation."

Longarm looked at him blankly for a second before he nodded and said, "You sure have a way with words, too."

"That's something I've worked very hard to acquire, Longarm. If this trip west has the result I hope it will, a facility with language is going to be a necessary part of my equipment."

"You're out here on business, then?"

"Personal business. I'm hoping to find a place out here where I can live for a while and get rid of an affliction that's been my curse since childhood."

"You look pretty healthy to me," Longarm observed. "And you sure don't fight like a sick men."

"In one sense of the word, I'm not a sick man. I have a chronic asthmatic condition that lays me low from time to time. A spell or an attack comes over me without warning, and until it passes I'm virtually an invalid."

"How do you figure being out here's going to help?"

"I'm not sure it will. About all I have is hope. You see, doctors don't really know what causes the type of asthma I have. They're still treating it by trial and error."

"You mean they don't know any kind of medicine that'll cure it? Sort of like smallpox, only not as bad?"

"Something like that," Roosevelt replied. "The big difference is that asthma's not infectious. No matter how long I might be around someone else, I can't pass my asthma on to them."

"And you say there ain't no cure for it?"

"None's been discovered yet. When my father took our family to Europe a number of years ago, he had me examined by several specialists, and none of them knew what caused the disease or how to cure it. But when I'm in the clear, pure air of the mountains I feel as good as the next man most of the time."

"Well, if you're looking for mountains, you've come to the right place."

"That's what I'm hoping. Actually, I shouldn't be here now at all. You see, I'm going to be married in a short time to the dearest, sweetest girl in the world, and I should be with her right now, making our wedding plans. But I don't want her married to an invalid, Longarm."

"Well, that's a sentiment that does you credit. But I don't guess I understand all the ins and outs of what you've been explaining to me."

"That's my fault for not starting from the beginning. You see, I began reading for the law even before I graduated from Harvard last year. I overdid my studies, and my asthma recurred. My brother Elliott was planning a trip to Texas to look over some property he has there, so he suggested I go with him. Alice agreed it was vital for me to recover my health, so I came west with Elliott." Roosevelt paused to take a sip of his wine.

Frowning, Longarm observed, "Texas is a long way from Dakota Territory, Teddy. How'd you get up here?"

Roosevelt smiled. "As it turned out, Elliott knew very little about Texas and I knew even less. We found that there are no real mountains there, even though the air's clean. I felt so much better that when Elliott went back East, I came up here to the Rockies, where I'd find both clean air and mountains."

"You'll be staying here a while, then?"

"Until just before the wedding. After Alice and I are married, we'll probably come back and live here until I'm cured, or until I decide there's no hope for a cure. Of course, I'm hoping it'll be the former."

"If you find this part of the country's good for you, why don't you just stay out here and live?"

Roosevelt shook his head. "That's a long story, and this isn't the time to tell it." He paused and looked across the table at Longarm. "Since we've been talking, though, I've gotten an idea. I don't know that it's practical, but I'd like you to tell me whether it is or not."

"Now, how would I know that, Teddy?"

"Because my idea concerns you."

"How do I come into it?"

"We seem to get along pretty well together, Longarm. You know the country out here and I don't. If the case that's brought you up here doesn't make it impossible, I'd like to go along with you and see how you resolve it."

Chapter 7

For a moment Longarm stared at young Roosevelt as though he didn't quite believe what he'd heard. Then he said, "Now, that just ain't possible, Teddy. I don't know where in hell this case might take me, or what kind of trouble I'm likely to run into."

"I can't think of a better way to learn the country than from a man like you, who knows it."

Longarm shook his head. "What travelling I do ain't just for the fun of it, Teddy. Besides, I got a pretty good hunch that my chief down in Denver might not like it too much if I was to take an outsider along on a case."

"Suppose you give me some idea of the kind of case you're on," Teddy suggested. "Maybe I can help you decide."

"Now, wait a minute!" Longarm objected. "What makes you think I need anybody to help me make up my mind?"

"I didn't mean it that way at all. But if this case is more or less routine—one that's not likely to involve a lot of danger—I don't see any reason why I shouldn't go with you."

"Teddy, when I pull out of Denver on a case, I don't ever know what I might run into. Sometimes cases that don't look like they'll be much of anything turn into big ones, and some that look like they're going to be big just fizzle out."

59

"Is there anything secret about your present case? Anything I shouldn't know about?"

After a moment's thought, Longarm shook his head. "No, I can't think of anything offhand. A couple of Land Office agents dropped out of sight up here in Dakota Territory, and I'm supposed to find out what happened to 'em. There's a chance some government money might be missing, too."

"But you're not after a gang of outlaws on a case that would be likely to involve a lot of gunfighting?"

"Like I just said, you never can tell beforehand, but it don't seem likely I'll run into much of that."

"Then why can't I just travel along with you? I'd stay out of your way. All I'd be doing would be watching you work. And I'd also be learning a lot about the country while we travelled."

"I don't know—" Longarm began.

"Let me ask you a hypothetical question," Roosevelt broke in. "Suppose you were on a case out here and were riding along a trail and we happened to run into one another. Would you let me ride along with you to your next stop?"

"Why, sure, unless I was chasing somebody real hard. But if I was just travelling, I'd do what anybody else does—say, 'Ride along with me and welcome.'"

"And you wouldn't have to report to your chief that you ran into me and we rode together, would you?"

"No, of course not."

"Suppose we were more than a day's ride away from wherever you might be going, and we camped by the trail together overnight before going on. Would your chief object to that?"

"I don't see how he could." Longarm shook his head. "Oh, now, wait a minute, Teddy! I see what you're getting at, but it don't hang together. If we just ran into each other accidentally, that's one thing, but if I was to invite you to go along, I'd be responsible for you."

"Don't invite me, then," Roosevelt said. "But don't send me away if I just happen to run into you. Don't tell me anything that would harm your case. And I'll guarantee not to get in your way. How does that sound?"

Longarm refilled his glass and took a swig of rye before he replied. "The way you put it to me sounds all right, Teddy. But suppose there's trouble?"

Instead of giving Longarm a direct reply, young Roosevelt

said, "I didn't mention to you that Elliott and I did quite a bit of hunting while we were in Texas. Up in the baggage car, I have all the saddle gear and outdoor clothes I need. I also have a brand-new .41 Winchester repeater and a very fine *drilling*. In my suitcase I have a .41 Colt double-action revolver. I know how to use all of them. I'm a reasonably good shot, Longarm. And you've already seen that I won't turn and run from trouble."

Again Longarm sat silently thoughtful for several moments before he answered. "All right, Teddy, you're a pretty good shot and you say you've done a lot of hunting. Did you ever hunt anything that could shoot back."

Now it was Roosevelt's turn to think for a moment. At last he told Longarm, "No, I have never faced a man with a gun, which I'm sure is the point you're making. But I'm positive I wouldn't panic in a showdown."

Longarm nodded slowly, "I don't suppose you would, just judging from how I saw you act a little while ago."

"Do we have an agreement, then?"

Choosing his words carefully, Longarm replied, "If we just happened to run into each other on a trail, going the same way, I sure wouldn't say no if you asked if we could ride together for a spell. And if you happened to be around when I got into some kind of scrape, I'd like to have you on my side. But if something came along that ain't any of your affair and I asked you to get outa my way, I'd expect you to do it."

"That's all I ask for," Teddy grinned.

Longarm found the young man's smile so infectious that he had to grin back. He said, "You mentioned something about studying law, Teddy. You never did get to be a lawyer, did you?"

"No. I still have a bit more work to do before I'll be prepared for the bar."

"Well, you got a good start. I'd say you just won your first case."

Roosevelt laughed delightedly and said, "You know, Longarm, I think we're going to get along just bully together."

"It wouldn't surprise me none." Longarm drained his glass and lighted a cheroot. Then he looked across the table at young Roosevelt and said, "Now we got everything squared away, Teddy, let me ask you a question."

"Of course."

61

"What in hell is a *drilling?*"

Roosevelt looked surprised as he replied. "Why, that's the European name for an over-and-under gun—two shotgun barrels over a rifle barrel. It's a gun that hasn't become popular on this side of the Atlantic. Mine happens to be 16-gauge over a 40/70. It's not European, by the way; Thomas in Chicago made it up for me."

"Oh, hell, I've seen them. I just never did hear 'em called that before. I never paid much attention to 'em because they wouldn't be much good in my line of work."

"I took it to Texas because I'd heard there were places where big game and birds were close together. I didn't use it there, and I don't suppose I will here."

"Not likely. I don't look for this to be a case where there's going to be much need for guns. Mainly, the Interior Department's concerned over how much money they'll lose in filing fees and land sales."

"What do you know about the case?"

"Not much." As succinctly as possible, Longarm sketched the details he'd been given. After he'd concluded, he said, "Now, there are just two reasons I can think of for that Smothers fellow to disappear. One is that he'd been stealing out of the fee money he got, and the other one is that somebody made him disappear."

"You're talking about murder?" Roosevelt asked.

"Yep. Let's say this Smothers fellow was dipping into money he collected for the Land Office, filing fees and land lease payments and such. Maybe he'd be in cahoots with somebody, say he'd had to forge names to false collection statements, something like that. He might've had a fuss with his partner, and the partner killed him."

"You'd have to do quite a lot of digging into Smothers's affairs, and establish his partner's identity," Roosevelt said, frowning thoughtfully. "After that, you'd have to find the partner and prove he committed the crime."

"That's right. One thing leads to the next in this business."

"What about the other man—what was his name?"

"Arthur Alberts. I don't have any idea why he never got where he was going, but with a little bit of luck, I'll find out sooner or later."

"I hope I'll be with you when you do," Roosevelt said. "What about this little settlement you mentioned—Interior? It's an odd name for a town."

"Oh, it was named that after the Interior Department. All it was back then was a land office and a saloon or two. It was supposed to be on a railroad, but the little jackleg road that was going to run through it went under in the panic. The Northern Pacific bought up its stock at a penny on the dollar. I don't suppose there's much of a town left there now, but we'll find out in a day or two."

Longarm and Roosevelt reined in at the rim of a long gentle slope that stretched down into the small valley where Interior lay, and looked at the town. Longarm still wore the clothing he'd worn on the train, but Teddy Roosevelt had discarded his neat suit and starched white shirt.

He'd donned his outdoor togs, unpressed trousers of light tan duck and a loose-fitting hunting jacket. The hip-length jacket was fitted with cartridge loops in twin rows on the front breast and had huge side pockets that bulged with Roosevelt's personal necessities: spectacle case, cigars, a number of folded handkerchiefs, extra shells for the .41 Colt that hung from a holster low on his right hip and for the Winchester in his saddle scabbard. A fur cap sat jauntily on his head, and he wore heavy laced boots that were almost too large to fit into the stirrups. Longarm had not commented on the young man's outfit, but had made a mental note to try to steer him toward more practical clothing.

"Hell, this place ain't as dead as I figured it'd be," Longarm remarked after they'd both lighted cigars. "I guess there's still quite a good bunch of folks that didn't leave when the railroad line fell through."

Although the setting sun stretched the shadows of the two riders in long dark misshapen streaks along the rim of the small saucerlike depression, the town itself was in deep shadow. Lights were twinkling through the early dusk from the windows of the sixty or so houses and buildings that made up the little settlement.

Longarm and Roosevelt had been in the saddle for the better part of two days. At Bismark, Longarm had succeeded in persuading the conductor on the westbound NP train to include young Roosevelt in the deal the Fargo stationmaster had made of transportation to the section camp some fifty miles further west. He'd wangled a horse for Roosevelt out of the section foreman too. Then Longarm and Teddy had started on the trail to Interior.

Keeping to the trail hadn't been difficult. They'd needed only to stay with the crisscrossed ruts of the wagon wheels that had been scored deeply into the dry rock-studded soil. They'd camped for the night beside a small stream, low now toward summer's end, that tumbled merrily over a bed of rainbow-hued stones.

Starting again at daybreak, they'd ridden steadily up the gentle rising slopes, the first hint of the great upthrust Rocky Mountains, still almost five hundred miles west. At last they'd reached what was left of the abandoned right-of-way of the little jackleg railroad which had been intended to bring progress and prosperity into that part of Dakota Territory. Once they'd hit the wide swath cleared for the rails that were laid but never used, and had now been pulled up and hauled south for use by the NP, Longarm had been on familiar ground.

He'd studied the broad graveled expanse of the abandoned right-of-way; it was cut with the tracks of wheeled vehicles as well as horses. "All we got to do from here on is what everybody else that's going there does. We'll just stay on the right-of-way till we get to Interior."

Now, with the day dying, they'd reached their destination.

"I hope there's a decent place to stay down there," Teddy said as they nudged their horses to start them down into town.

Longarm pointed. "You see that big three-story building in the middle of the town? It was about half finished when I was here before. The Railroad Hotel, it was going to be. The way it looks, it's still in business."

Though dusk had settled down, there was still enough waning daylight for them to see details of the settlement when they rode into town. There were no pedestrians in sight, no wagons or carriages, no other horsemen. Lights glowed from a number of the small frame houses they passed as they approached the town's business section.

Longarm and young Roosevelt slowed their horses to a walk as they meandered toward the few lights that glowed in the area in front of them. Longarm recalled the town as it had been during his previous visit, bustling with zest and activity, looking toward a bright future. It had turned out to be the twin to a hundred other such frontier towns he'd seen. It was a place of brave beginnings that had not provided a happy ending. Bypassed by the railroad, the town had stood still.

"Where are all the people?" Teddy asked.

"In the houses eating supper, I'd guess. And if you go by the places that ain't got lights burning, there ain't a hell of a lot of people living here any more."

They rode on along the main street. On both sides, frame buildings stood close together but the growing darkness did not hide the fact that most of them had not been occupied recently. Peeling paint had almost obliterated the signs that once adorned the fronts of the unoccupied buildings, but some of them were still legible.

As they rode slowly down the street, Roosevelt pointed and said, "There's the Land Office building, Longarm. Or at least, it's where the Land Office used to be."

The building was dark. Dust and windblow debris were piled in its doorway.

Longarm said, "I'll have to take a closer look at it first thing tomorrow."

"From the looks of the building, that office must have been closed longer than six or eight months."

"I was thinking the same thing, Teddy. That's something else for me to look into."

As they neared the center of town, the number of occupied buildings increased. Longarm noted three saloons, a general store, a barbershop, a doctor's office, the post office, and the office of the town marshal. There was also a single-story brick building bearing on its doors the words "First Bank of Interior."

The bank stood on one corner of Interior's main intersection. Across from the bank stood a large saloon. A third corner was occupied by the Railroad Hotel. Lights were glowing in some of its upper windows. Catercorner from the bank, so modest that it could easily be overlooked, stood a small frame building with a large sign covering its front.

Longarm glanced at it briefly, turned to inspect the hotel again, then reined in and stared once more at the small building. More to himself than to Roosevelt, he said, "Now, just what in hell does that sign signify?"

Huge letters read LAND OFFICE and below, in smaller lettering, 1000s OF ACRES OF VIRGIN GOVERNMENT LAND. Bright lights shone through the glass pane in the building's door and the two curtained windows that faced the main street. Through the door panel they could see people moving about inside the structure.

"Maybe the Interior Department was mistaken in thinking

the Land Office here was closed," Roosevelt suggested. "It may just have moved."

"If it did, the officials in Chicago don't know about it," Longarm replied. "But before I go in there and start asking questions, I'll do a little noseying around town. Then if whoever's running that place starts lying to me, I'll know they're lying."

"What do we do in the meantime?"

"Go in and register at the hotel. But it strikes me that we better not go in together. There might be a time when it'd be a good idea if we didn't seem to know each other. I've been here before, remember. It ain't likely many folks who'd remember me are still here, but one's all it takes."

"I don't understand." Teddy frowned.

"Something smells bad to me," Longarm replied. "And when I get a bad smell in my nose that generally means there's something rotten someplace. Just call it a hunch and play it my way, Teddy."

"Somebody's certain to have seen us ride in together."

"Maybe. It was getting pretty dark by the time we hit town, though, and we ain't seen many people on the street."

"I'll do what you think is best, Longarm. How will we find a chance to talk and compare notes, though?"

"We'll both be at the hotel. From the looks of the place it'll have a café, maybe a saloon, too, and a gambling hall. If we can't talk there, we'll ride out from town a ways and meet."

"I suppose you'll find a way to get word to me?"

"Sure. Don't worry about that."

"What do you want me to do, then?"

"Just what I aim to do, for tonight at least. Walk around town. Have a drink or two at the saloons and listen a lot. You can ask a lot of questions. You said you might be looking for a place to live in these parts later on."

"Of course. Why, I might even look into some of that land the sign says that place across the street has for sale."

"You might at that."

"By Jove, Longarm! I think this is going to be bully!"

"Don't get so excited that you forget to look over your shoulder once in a while," Longarm cautioned his young friend. "Now, go on and sign in at the hotel. I'll go across to the saloon there and have a drink, and check in a little while later."

Longarm twisted the reins of his horse around the hitch rail in front of the saloon and pushed through the batwings. Two customers stood at the long bar and a drunk was asleep at a table by the wall. The men at the bar looked incuriously at Longarm and went back to their conversation.

Longarm looked around the saloon's cavernous interior. In the rear of the building, covered by oilcloths, were three gaming tables and half a dozen poker tables.

Tossing a cartwheel on the bar when the aproned barkeep came up to serve him, Longarm said, "Rye. Tom Moore, if you got any."

The barkeep turned to fill Longarm's order, reaching a bottle down from a high shelf and setting a glass in front of him. "I ain't seen you in here before. New in town?"

"Just passing through. But I'll be here a day or so, if there's a decent place to stay."

"There's the Railroad Hotel. They'll have plenty of rooms right now."

"I'd imagine so. The town's quiet tonight," Longarm commented, filling his glass and lighting a cheroot.

"It'll stay that way a few days. Then things'll liven up."

"Oh?" Longarm lifted his glass. "What happens in a few days? Circus coming to town?"

"As good as. There's a new bunch of immigrants due in."

"Immigrants from where?"

"It's a mixed bag. There's a few comes from back East, but mostly them that's coming now is from Europe. A lot of Germans and some Polacks and Bohemians."

"How in hell do they find their way to this place, way off the railroad like it is?"

"Oh, Delaney and his men make it easy for 'em. I guess you followed the old railroad right-of-way into town?"

"Is that how the road here came to be so wide?" Longarm asked innocently. "I just figured somebody'd put in more road than a place this size would need."

"Not likely anybody'd take that much trouble. There was a railroad supposed to run in here, but it failed when the panic hit. The NP bought what little of it there was, and took up the rails and ties, so we just started using it for a road."

"And that's how the immigrants come in, then?"

"It sure is. Delaney runs a regular haul up here from Bismark. Wagons, shays, buggies, all of 'em full of immigrants."

"I guess there's a lot of new farms and ranches around here, then," Longarm said casually. "It's funny, though. I didn't notice any."

"You wouldn't, coming on the old right-of-way. The land on both sides of it's railroad subsidy land. The immigrants are settling to the north and west."

"Ain't that part of the Territory folks call the Little Missouri bandlands?" Longarm asked. "I got the idea from someplace that the bandlands ain't good for much of anything—farming or mining or cattle."

"Oh, there's plenty of good rangeland out there. Some of it makes good farmland, too, if it's got water."

"I'd always thought it was real dry."

"There's enough water. Killdeer Creek, Greenheart Creek, the Little Knife River. It can be farmed."

"I guess you'd know about that better than I would." Longarm poured himself another drink and lighted a fresh cheroot.

"Well, farming ain't my line of work," the barkeep said, "but Delaney wouldn't sell nobody land for farming if he didn't think they could make it pay."

"You've mentioned that name before," Longarm said. "Mind telling me who Delaney is?"

"Why, he runs that land office across the street. You must've seen the sign over the door."

"I did, but I figured it was a government Land Office, and didn't pay much attention to it."

"Delaney's business hasn't got anything to do with the government. Matter of fact, the government Land Office that used to be here closed down quite a while back."

"Why, I thought the government was in charge of selling all the land in Dakota Territory that hadn't gone for railroad subsidies or Indian reservations."

"Maybe it did, but it don't any more. The government moves too slow. Why, this town was just dying away when the railroad went under. Of course, I wasn't here then, but that's what I've heard folks say. The government just sat back and waited for the farmers to come in and buy. It took a pusher like Delaney to get things moving."

"This Delaney sounds like he's quite a man."

"Oh, he is that! If you've got it in mind to buy land around here, you'd better get acquainted with him."

"I intend to do just that," Longarm said, finishing his drink.

Chapter 8

Longarm had already finished breakfast the next morning when Teddy Roosevelt came into the hotel dining room wearing the same field clothing he'd worn the day before. The hour was late, and only three or four tables of the twenty or so in the dining room were occupied.

Teddy chose the table next to the one where Longarm was sitting with a final cup of coffee in front of him. Neither of them spoke as the young Roosevelt took his place, his back toward Longarm, but within whispering distance. Longarm lighted a fresh cheroot and refilled his coffee cup from the silver pot on the table while he waited for Teddy to order.

"I didn't see you in any of the saloons last night," Teddy said as soon as the waiter had left. He did not look at Longarm, and spoke softly.

"I knocked off early and came on to the hotel," Longarm replied, his voice equally low. "I ran into a few things I had to study out."

"Did you hear the name Delaney as often as I did?"

"Enough to make me curious."

"Unless you object, I plan to drop in at that land office this morning," Roosevelt said.

"That jibes with what I need to do. I'll be checking on the

old Land Office and noseying around town a little more."

"How will we get together and compare notes?"

"Let's ride out west of town right after noon," Longarm suggested. "There's a trail runs off that cross street. We'd better go a mile or so over the ridge before we stop. Whoever gets there first can just wait by the trail."

"I'll look for you out there, then."

Longarm finished his coffee and strolled leisurely out of the dining room. He walked through the deserted lobby to the street and started down the main thoroughfare toward the abandoned Land Office building he and Teddy had noticed when they rode in.

There was very little more activity in town at this hour of the morning than there had been the evening before. The chief difference was that the businesses which had been closed and dark were now open, though few of them seemed to be attracting many customers. A man stood in front of the town marshal's office, his badge gleaming in the morning sun. He watched Longarm, but made no gesture of greeting.

Reaching the deserted Land Office building Longarm cupped his hands around his eyes and peered through the grimy window. A long counter ran the width of the single room inside. He could see a rolltop desk standing open against the wall behind the counter. Shelves covered the other side wall, but all of them were empty and covered with a thick coating of dust. Loose papers were strewn on the counter and on the floor between the counter and the door.

Longarm tried the door, but it was locked. He looked through the window again and saw that there was a back door in the rear wall. Squeezing through the narrow passageway between the side of the Land Office building and the equally deserted store next to it, he tried the back door. The lock was flimsy, and Longarm tried the key to his room in Denver in the keyhole. It turned the bolt halfway, and when he applied a bit of extra pressure to the key the bolt grated and then yielded fully. He pushed the door ajar and sidled inside.

Dust disturbed by his entrance roiled up from the floor but settled quickly. The floor behind the counter was as thickly covered with loose sheets of paper as the section that had been visible from the door. Longarm picked up several of the sheets and shook the grime off them. One was a five-year-old transfer of a homestead deed, the location meaningless to him, as it was given in surveyor's terms. Another of the papers was a receipt covering payment of a homestead filing, also five years old; a third was a transfer record similar to the first one. All of them were signed by Claude Smothers as Land Agent.

Moving to the desk, Longarm checked the papers that lay on it. They were much the same as those he'd picked up from the floor, outdated anywhere from three to six years. The pigeon-holes in the top of the desk were all empty, but a row of small drawers down the center of the top invited investigation. Longarm opened the first and found it empty except for dust. He was opening the second when a harsh voice grated from the door.

"Just stand real still, now," the speaker commanded. "I got a gun on you and my finger's real nervous on the trigger."

Longarm froze.

"Leave your hands just like they are," the voice went on. "And turn around slow, so I can get a look at your face."

Longarm obeyed. He found himself looking at a pudgy dough-faced man who wore tight trousers that caused his belly to slop over his belt in a fold. He wore no coat, and his vest lacked six inches of meeting in front. On the breast of the vest was pinned a badge in the form of a star with a wide rim circling it. On the rim were stamped the words "Deputy Marshal."

Longarm registered these details at a glance. He also took note that the long barrel of the big Remington revolver the man was holding on him was as steady as a rock and twice as ugly.

"Damned if you look to me like you're dumb enough to think a place like this would have anything in it worth busting in to steal," the pudgy man said after he'd inspected Longarm for a moment. "What'd you break in here for?"

Longarm knew that he was about to have his introduction to whoever enforced the law in Interior. He'd be forced to reveal his identity, and he'd been wondering just how much of his case he wanted to disclose to the locals. He decided now that a bit of stalling was in order.

"I broke in here to save time," he said. "I'm on the same side of the law you are, so you can put your gun away. My name's Long. I'm a deputy U. S. Marshal out of the Denver office. The reason I'm here is to find out what's happened to the Land Office agent who used to be in charge of this place."

"Well, now," the pudgy man said. The tone of his voice

gave away his indecision, but he did not lower his pistol. "Well, now, that's a real pretty story, but can you prove you are who you say you are?"

"My badge is in my inside coat pocket. I'll take it out if you say so, or you can come get it yourself."

After taking a step forward, the fat man stopped. "I don't guess you'd be lying about something as easy to prove as that," he said. "Just the same, I think I'll walk you down the street to the office and let my boss listen to what you've got to say. And, just to be on the safe side, I'd better take care of that gun you've got under your coat."

"You think you can trust me to take it out and hand it to you?" Longarm asked, trying to control a smile.

"If you're who you say you are, you'll hand your gun over. If you ain't, and you try to work a fancy draw on me, I oughta be able to pull my trigger first."

"That's very sensible, and I'm a sensible man. I'll hand over the gun without any tricks."

Moving slowly and carefully, Longarm drew his Colt, grasping it with two fingers clamped on the butt, and held the pistol out. The deputy marshal stepped up and grabbed it.

"I'm beginning to believe you," he said. "I'll take a look at your badge, now, before we leave."

Longarm took his wallet from the breast pocket of his coat and flipped it open to show the badge pinned inside.

The pudgy man inspected it carefully and nodded. "It looks real enough," He said. "All right, we'll go out that door you busted open and walk up the alley to the office and go in the back door there. I won't put the cuffs on you, but I won't holster my gun, either. Remember, if you're thinking of trying anything tricky, I'll be ready."

"I said I was a sensible man, so give me credit for being one," Longarm replied. "You've got my gun, and yours is in your hand. No man with any sense would try anything under those conditions."

They walked side by side up the alley until the local marshal jerked his head toward a door. "In there," he told Longarm. "You open the door. We don't keep it locked in the daytime."

Longarm pushed the door open and found himself in a short narrow corridor between two steel-barred cells. At the end of the passageway another door stood ajar. The pudgy deputy marshal motioned him to go ahead, and Longarm went into the room adjoining the cells.

He found himself in what was obviously the main office of the Interior town marshal. Desks stood on the two side walls and a table in the center of the floor. In the far wall, narrow windows flanked the open door that led to the street. A tall, thin man stood there, his back to the office, leaning against the doorjamb. He turned when he heard the two men enter.

"Well, I'll be damned!" he exclaimed. "Look at what the cat's dragged in!" A broad grin cracked his cadaverous face as he asked the deputy, "Is this the one that busted into the old Land Office, Pudge?"

"Yep. I caught him inside, Magruder. He says he's a deputy U. S. marshal out of the Denver office, and he's got a badge to back up his story, but I figured he'd better talk to you."

"You mean you don't know who he is?" the marshal asked.

"He said his name's Long, and that's the name on his badge."

"Goddammit, Pudge! Didn't you ever hear of Longarm?"

"Why, sure, but—Oh, gawdamighty!" the local deputy said. "You mean that's who he is? Why, hell's bells! He's famous!"

"Oh, this is Longarm, all right," Magruder assured his deputy. He faced the Federal marshal again and asked, "What're you in town for, Long? On somebody's trail?"

"More like trying to find out about somebody," Longarm said. He remembered Magruder from his earlier visit to Interior. At that time, the town marshal had been a deputy. There hadn't been any real enmity between them at that time, but they hadn't exactly seen eye to eye on much of anything, either. "Now that your man knows I am who I said I am," Longarm went on, "you'll ask him to give me back my gun."

Magruder nodded to Pudge, who took Longarm's Colt from his waistband and handed it over. "Sorry I didn't believe you," he said.

"No grudges, Pudge," Longarm said. "You done what you thought was the right thing, not knowing me."

"It'd've saved us all some trouble if you'd stopped in and told us you was in town," Magruder said, "and what you was planning to do. Just what did you have in mind, busting into the old Land Office building, anyhow?"

"I guess you knew that Land Office clerk that dropped out

73

of sight," Longarm said. "Claude Smothers."

"Oh, sure," Magruder replied without hesitation. "Everbody knew him, even if he was pretty much of a loner."

"I don't guess he had a wife, did he?"

"Smothers?" Magruder shook his head. "No. Like I said, he was a real loner. Didn't mix into anything in town. I don't suppose anybody missed him when he dropped out of sight."

"Did you look for him after he disappeared?"

"No. But I never did get a 'Wanted' on him, so I just figured he'd quit and left town without letting anybody know."

"He didn't let his boss in Chicago know, either," Longarm told Magruder.

"Look here, Long," the town marshal said, "Smothers has been gone for months, now. How come everybody's all of a sudden getting worked up about him?"

"Somebody else has been looking for Smothers?"

"No, no, I didn't mean that. But it looks like to me that it took his boss in Chicago a hell of a long time to start worrying about what happened to him."

"It looked that way to me, too. But I found out that the Chicago office sent a man out here to find out what was wrong, a fellow named Arthur Alberts. Now he's disappeared, too."

Magruder frowned. "You mean this other fellow got here and then disappeared? Or did he ever get here?"

"I haven't got an answer to that myself. All anybody seems to know is that he's gone." When Magruder made no comment, Longarm went on, "What about the Land Office records, Magruder? Do you happen to know when they were hauled away? Or who took 'em?"

"I didn't know they was missing."

"Seems to me there's a lot of things you don't know about in a town where you're supposed to be upholding the law."

"Well, who in hell would think anybody'd be interested in a closed-up Land Office in a town this size?" Magruder demanded.

"You mean to stand there and tell me you didn't pay any more attention to that place than to let somebody steal the record books that list every sale of land in this district?"

"Listen, Long, I've got enough to do to keep my own office records straight. I can't be worrying about Federal records. That's the Land Office's job."

"Well, you got a point there. But the office is cleaned out, just the same—books, maps, plats, all of it."

"Who in hell would want stuff like that?"

"All I can think of is that another land office might."

"Now, hold on, Long!" Magruder snapped. "You're as good as pointing a finger at that new office Creighton Delaney opened a while back."

"That'd be the one down on the corner, I guess?"

"Don't be funny. You've seen it, if you've been here more than an hour or so. It's the only land office left in town."

"This Delaney who runs it—is he a friend of yours?"

"Not especially. But I happen to think he's a fine man. He's done more for this town than anybody has, even the damn little railroad that started it!"

"I wasn't accusing him of anything," Longarm said mildly.

"Well, it rubs me the wrong way to hear an outsider like you come into town and start bad-mouthing a man you don't even know!"

"Don't get your back up, Magruder," Longarm advised.

"All right," Magruder said sullenly. "Now, I'll forget about that burglary you pulled off at the Land Office, but next time you wanna know about something in this town, you come to me and I'll tell you where to look for answers."

"If I run into anything I figure you should know about, I'll tell you, Magruder." Longarm felt free now to light a cheroot, and did so. Through the smoke, he asked, "Are you through with me now? Can I get on with my business?"

"Whenever you feel like it," the town marshal replied grudgingly. "But don't make any trouble for me and my men, you hear?"

Walking the short distance to the Railroad Hotel, Longarm tried to remember more about Magruder. The man had played a minor part in the case that had brought him to Dakota Territory earlier, but as far as Longarm could recollect, Magruder hadn't done anything outstanding. He remembered him only as a shadowy, sneering minor figure in the background of the previous case.

At the hotel, when he failed to see young Roosevelt in the lobby, Longarm glanced into the dining room and bar, but his unofficial assistant was not in either place. After getting his rifle from his room and stuffing a fresh supply of cheroots into his pockets, he went downstairs to the stable which the hotel maintained as a service to its patrons. Roosevelt's horse was gone, and as soon as the stableman had saddled his mount, Longarm started out from town.

There were no trees left in the saucer in which Interior was located, and the fairly dense growth of pines and junipers that Longarm remembered as having stood beyond the crest of the ridge that outlined the valley had been sharply thinned. Longarm remembered the area beyond the ridge quite well. He'd covered it thoroughly while looking for Boots McGinnis. He reined in just past the crest and looked for Teddy, but saw no sign of him, so continued to follow the trail.

After dipping down into a long shallow valley beyond the crest of the saucer, the ground began to rise again. Longarm had covered only a short distance when he saw Teddy ahead. Young Roosevelt was sitting on his horse on top of the ridge a mile or so away, staring toward the west. He was so engrossed in the scenery that unfolded beyond the ridge that he did not hear Longarm until his horse nickered and bobbed its head. Then he turned, his eyes wide and shining behind the ovals of his spectacles.

"You didn't tell me about this!" he said as Longarm reined in.

Turning back in the direction he'd been looking, young Roosevelt swept a hand at the vista that unfolded beyond the ridge. Longarm had seen it before, but he looked again at the seemingly unending vista of rugged cliffs and freestanding buttes that rose in rounded domes, steep conical pyramids, and huge hulking pillars—shapes no architect could imagine— above short level stretches and deep gorges.

There were more hues than the eye could encompass at once in the stripes that zigzagged across the faces of cliffs and the walls of the freestanding buttes. Reds predominated, ranging from deep copper to almost vermillion, and in places fading to delicate pinks. The reds appeared in swaths that varied from a hundred yards in width to tiny stripes that seemed no wider than a finger. Setting off the red hues were patches and stripes of coal-black, buff-gray, dark brown, and billiant yellow.

"Why, that's just worthless land, Teddy," Longarm said. "A lot of that black is coal, but not enough to mine, and I guess there's some copper in the red places, but there's even less of it than there is coal. And all the colors have something in 'em that sours the ground and poisons what little water is left standing when it rains, which is seldom. All that'll root in it is sagebrush and salt cedars. There ain't graze enough for it to be rangeland, and it won't grow crops. That's why folks hereabouts call it the bandlands."

"I don't care what they call it," Roosevelt said. "This is one of the bulliest places I've seen, and I've travelled over all of Europe and quite a bit of Africa and up and down the East Coast here at home."

"Well, I'm glad you like it," Longarm said, bewildered by his companion's enthusiasm. "Me, I never was one to admire scenery much."

"Like it? I think I've fallen in love with it!" The young man saw the surprise in Longarm's face and said quickly, "Oh, not the way I love Alice. But I'm coming back to this place, Longarm. I'm coming back here to stay for a while. As soon as Alice and I get married and have time to settle down, I'll bring her here, and we'll build some kind of a house, even if it's just a cabin we can stay in for a few weeks every year."

"That's a good idea," Longarm said. "I sure hope you get to do it. A man ought to be able to do the things he enjoys."

Young Roosevelt suddenly became businesslike. He turned his back on the scenery and said, "Let's ride down the slope to that grove of trees there. I know you want to talk about the case, and as long as we're up here, where I can see this view, my mind won't be on telling you what I've found out."

They reined around and started down the slope, Teddy turning from time to time to look back at the badlands until the crest of the ridge hid the scenery from view. He did not seem inclined to talk as they rode toward the grove of salt cedars, and Longarm did not try to make conversation. Reaching the grove, they dismounted and walked a few feet away to lean against the trees. Teddy produced one of his fat Coronas, Longarm pulled out a slender cheroot, and they both lighted up.

"Well?" Longarm asked. "How'd you do when you went in to talk to Delaney?"

"Not as well as I'd hoped. He was cordial and distant at the same time."

"Which I take to mean that he gave you a big welcome but didn't say anything that meant much."

"I couldn't have put it better myself, Longarm." Teddy grinned. "I did learn two things about him, though."

"Go ahead."

"He's a very smooth bunco artist and he hasn't been away from the East Coast very long."

"What makes you say that?"

"Every time I put a key question to him, Delaney avoided giving me a direct answer. Honest men selling an honest product don't act that way. That's a lesson I learned from my father." For a moment young Roosevelt hesitated, then he said, "I haven't said much about my family, Longarm, but we are quite well off."

"I figured that out myself. Does it make any difference?"

"I just mentioned it so you'd understand that my father was plagued by bunco men selling all kinds of odd stocks and trying to get him into their shady deals. As soon as I was old enough to understand, father insisted that I sit with him sometimes while these men made their pitches, so I became quite familiar with the breed. And Creighton Delaney belongs to it."

"All right, Teddy, I'm ready to take your word for that. Now, how'd you figure he ain't been away from the East long?"

"To start at the beginning, I recognized his accent as being what I call 'hokum cultured.' He tries to speak like a prep-school and college graduate, but he doesn't quite bring it off. And, as for his having been out here only a short time, his suit was tailored in Boston or Philadelphia not less than two years ago, but his haberdashery was bought west of Chicago, and more recently."

"Now, how do you know that?"

"I was brought up to notice such things."

"So far, you've done right good. I'll take your judgement about Delaney's clothes, too."

"Does what I've told you help any, Longarm?"

"Sure. Delaney's mixed up in some kind of land swindle, and I've got a pretty fair idea what it is. I got another hunch that he's got something to do with my real case, which is to find out what happened to Smothers and Alberts and if there's any Land Office money missing. Now all I have to do is tie everything together."

"And how do you go about doing that?" Roosevelt asked.

Before Longarm could answer, a burst of shots rang out from somewhere down the slope. Lead slugs whistled through the scanty branches of the trees over their heads. One of the bullets thudded into the tree against which Teddy was leaning and Longarm felt the hot wind of another brush past his cheek.

Longarm wasted no time. Grabbing Teddy by the arm, he dragged him to the ground, flattening himself down beside him.

"What— Those were shots fired at us, weren't they?" Teddy asked. There was no fear in his voice, just curiosity.

"They sure as hell were," Longarm told him. "Which means we got things stirred up down in Interior. And it means we're going to have to do some shooting back to get ourselves out of here!"

Chapter 9

An intense silence seemed to blanket the bright afternoon for an instant after the shots sounded, but the illusion was shattered by two more rifle-blasts in quick succession. One of the slugs plowed into the ground at the edge of the salt cedar clump in which Longarm and Teddy were sheltered. The other tore through the low-growing limbs just above their heads. Reacting instinctively, both men drew their revolvers, even though they both knew the snipers with their rifles had them out-ranged.

"Whoever is shooting at us, they're in a place where they could see us drop, but they don't know whether they hit us or not," Longarm said. "They're trying to sting us into doing some shooting of our own so they can tell what's what."

"You pulled me down so quickly I didn't get a chance to look around," Teddy told Longarm. "As far as I'm concerned, whoever it is could be almost anywhere."

Lying prone as they were, their faces pressed close to the hard, dry earth, neither of them could see more than a few yards in any direction.

"At least one of 'em is down the slope," Longarm said. "That slug that whizzed past me couldn't't've come from any other direction."

"Are there only two men out there?"

"From the way the first shots were spaced, I'd guess that's all."

"Well, you've been in situations like this before," Teddy said. "You know better than I do what our next move should be."

"What we need to do first is to get our rifles. If I'd figured anybody was skulking after us, I never would've left mine on my horse."

Teddy twisted around to look back at the edge of the copse, where their horses stood a few feet apart. The shots had not bothered the animals; they had not moved from the positions in which their riders had left them at the edge of the cedar clump, reins looped loosely over branches. The forefeet of the horses were almost in the copse, but their hindquarters were exposed.

Longarm's horse stood in front of Teddy's. The scabbard holding his Winchester was tied to the saddle straps horizontally, the muzzle behind the horse's foreleg, the butt just in front of its haunches. Teddy had secured his rifle vertically in front of the saddle; its butt protruded above the horse's shoulder.

"I think I can crawl back and get between the horses," he told Longarm. "I can reach my rifle without any trouble, but the way you carry yours is going to make it hard to reach."

"That's where you're wrong, Teddy. Mine's easier to get out of the scabbard because you hung your scabbard on your horse like a tenderfoot most always does."

"It's the way I've always carried a rifle in a saddle scabbard," the young man said, a bit miffed at Longarm's calling him a tenderfoot. "I don't see anything wrong with it."

"Nothing, except it's backwards. If you're not in your saddle you got to be standing straight up by the horse to draw it, and when you stand up, whoever's shooting at you is likely to take your head off."

"I can move fast enough to get it out of the scabbard before whoever's out there has time to aim."

"I wouldn't want to bet my life on it. But we can manage with one rifle right now. I'll go get mine."

Longarm belly-crawled through the copse, moving slowly and carefully to avoid touching any of the branches that spread close to the ground. He reached the edge of the trees and rose to his hands and knees to cover the short distance that remained between him and the horse. He sat down beside the animal's

81

hind leg and, without exposing himself at all to the snipers beyond the copse, reached an arm up, grasped the butt, and slid the rifle out of the scabbard. Within two minutes he was back beside young Roosevelt at the downslope side of the copse.

"Now let's see if we can persuade those fellows out there to show us where they're at," he told Teddy. "Take that pig-sticker of yours and cut off a limb about three feet long."

Teddy drew his hunting knife and hacked off the limb Long-arm asked for. He held the branch out. "Here you are."

"Keep it. You play sitting duck this time, and let me do the shooting. It ain't that I don't think you're a good enough shot, but I know how this rifle's sighted in, and you don't."

"What shall I do? Put my hat on the end of the stick and lift it up above the trees to draw their fire?"

"You catch on quick." Longarm grinned. "Don't raise it up till I get clear of this brush, though."

Flat on his belly, moving slowly and deliberately, Longarm inched his way to the edge of the trees. He levered a shell into the Winchester's chamber and held the rifle ready while he scanned the downslope area. Then he said, "Go on, lift your hat up now."

Teddy raised the stick with his hunting cap on it until the cap was an inch or two above the low tops of the brushy cedars. The cap had no sooner become visible than a rifle barked and a slug cut through the tops of the trees. It missed the hat but cut off the tip of a branch beside it.

Longarm had already chosen three or four spots on the long slope below them as the most likely hiding places of the snipers. There were two humps of ground that would give a man cover, and a couple of stands of mixed juniper and cedar that would conceal someone lying beneath their branches. He was concentrating his attention on these spots when he told Teddy to show the hat.

He glimpsed movement in one of the wooded patches and in the few seconds that were required for the downslope shooter to bring Teddy's hat into his sights, Longarm triggered the Winchester. His shot came so closely on the heels of the one fired by their enemy that the two reports sounded as one. Then Longarm quickly let off another shot that raised a puff of dust from the hump.

"Bully shooting, Longarm!" Teddy exclaimed. "Did you score any bullseyes?"

"Not likely. There's two of 'em out there, though. One's in that clump of brush about two hundred yards to the right and the other one's behind that little hump a hundred and fifty yards off to the left."

"I saw where your bullets kicked up the dust. You came close for such fast shooting."

"Well, I imagine you've done enough shooting to know how tricky it is when you're aiming up or down a slope and trying to draw a quick bead."

"I certainly do! Why, a few years ago, when I was hunting up in Maine, there was a deer—" Teddy stopped and shook his head. "That can wait until later, I guess."

"I guess," Longarm agreed. Then he said, "I'm real sorry I got you into this, Teddy. I didn't figure this case was going to turn out this way."

"Don't worry about me, Longarm. I won't say I'm enjoying being a target, but I'm not afraid. I've always wondered how I might feel in a situation like this, and now I'm finding out that it doesn't bother me."

"I give you credit for having plenty of spunk. And we'll get out of this all right. Just being shot back at with a rifle's giving those bushwhackers something to think about. Now they know they don't have the range on us any more, they ain't so likely to try to get any closer."

"What do we do now?" Teddy asked.

"Stay right where we are. The men out there might throw a few more shots at us, but I imagine they'll be satisfied just to hang around a little while longer and then sneak back to town."

"But we still won't know who they are, or whether they'll try again."

"Not for a while. But I don't figure it'll take me long to find out about 'em. Right now, I think I better make a quick sneak back to the horses and get your rifle. Then we'll be able to match 'em shot for shot."

"No. It's my rifle, Longarm," Teddy said stiffly. "I'll go after it."

"You will in a pig's ass! Damn it, Teddy, you're not even supposed to mix into what this case has turned out to be!"

"Well, I'm not going to leave you in the lurch!" Young Roosevelt's eyes were serious behind his oval spectacles. "It was my idea—I asked you to let me go with you!"

"So you did, but you said you'd step out if I asked you to.

83

And I'm not asking you to now. I'm telling you to step out of it right this minute."

"Maybe you'll tell me how I can get away from here right this minute, then," Teddy suggested, showing his big teeth in a broad grin.

A grin matching his companion's grew on Longarm's. "I guess I can't do that. Whether I like it or not, you're in it until we get out of this mess. But after we get back to town, we'll have to change our plans."

"In the meantime, I'd better go get my rifle."

"No." Longarm's voice was firm. "I know how to do that better'n you do. You take my Winchester and, when I tell you to, let off one round at that stand of brush where one of them damn bushwhackers is holed up."

Handing his rifle to Roosevelt, Longarm snaked back through the copse to the horses. He went on a short distance beyond the point where Teddy's horse was tethered and crawled to the left side of the animal, putting its body between himself and the snipers. Hunkering down, he got ready to spring, then called to his companion, "Now!"

When the shot fired by young Roosevelt rang out, Longarm was already in midair, reaching across the horse's withers to grasp the butt of Teddy's rifle. A shot from one of the snipers down the slope whistled harmlessly above his head as he was dropping to the ground, the weapon safely in his hands. For a moment, Longarm sat where he'd landed. Then he snaked back through the copse and handed the rifle to Teddy.

"I hope you got a full magazine in this thing," he said. "I didn't figure on running into any trouble like this, so I didn't bring any spare ammunition, and there's four shells used out of my magazine now."

"We'd better start counting our shots, then," Teddy said, then added cheerfully, "Don't worry, Longarm. I've got a full magazine."

"We'll just wait 'em out, then," Longarm said. "And I don't imagine they'll stick around much longer. We'll just make ourselves as comfortable as we can and sit tight for a while."

They settled down to wait, watching the downslope, saying little. After almost half an hour had gone by, Longarm's keen eyes spotted a small dust cloud far down the slope.

"It looks to me like our friends got tired quicker'n I expected," he remarked. "Nobody's gone by us, so I guess that's them heading for town."

"I don't suppose there's any chance of catching up with them?"

"Not a ghost of one. We're likely to run into 'em again sooner or later, though."

"Do you think it's safe for us to start back now?"

"I don't see why not. There damn sure wasn't but the two of 'em, so we might as well go in, too."

"They gave up pretty fast after we got our rifles into action," Teddy said as he and Longarm stood up and stretched before mounting their horses for the ride back to Interior. "I don't see why though."

"Well, they likely figured out they weren't being paid enough to risk getting killed. They'll tell whoever hired 'em that they couldn't get us, or something like that."

Longarm and Roosevelt mounted and started down the slope. As they rode slowly toward town, the young man asked, "How could those men have known we were going to be out here, Longarm?"

"I don't imagine they did. And I don't imagine they figured on you being here, either. What I figure to be most likely is that they was sent to follow me out from Interior and get rid of me the first chance they got."

"But why, Longarm? You've only been in town a little while. What reason could they have?"

Longarm took out a cheroot and lighted it before replying. "I guess I better catch you up on what I ran into this morning."

Longarm told Teddy of his morning invasion of the abandoned Land Office and his subsequent encounter with Magruder. "Now, you put that together with what the barkeep in that saloon across from the hotel told me last night," he concluded. "What he said about Delaney bringing in immigrants from Europe, to sell 'em land, and see what sort of answer you come up with."

"Obviously you think that Creighton Delaney's the man behind all this. But I still don't understand why. I could see at once that Delaney's a bunco artist, but he didn't impress me as being a killer."

"A man like him don't do his own dirty work. He'd hire it done."

"But why would Delaney need gunmen if all he's doing is cheating people?"

"You remember when you were admiring the badlands, Teddy, what I told you about 'em?"

"That the ground was sterile, wouldn't grow grass or grain?"

"Or anything else. Well, there's a lot of the badlands you couldn't see from where we were sitting. They stretch on south for quite a ways, and a hell of a lot of miles west. It's all public land, open to anybody who wants to buy it or file for a homestead on it."

"But nobody with any sense is going to file for a homestead on land like that, or buy it for rangeland," Teddy objected.

"That's right," Longarm agreed. "Nobody except an immigrant from Europe, who maybe don't know how to read a land title deed, and who'd think he was buying a piece of good land some slick bunco artist showed him."

"Sooner or later the buyer would be sure to find out he'd been cheated. I don't see how anybody could keep operating a swindle like that."

"Not unless he's got control of the Land Office and all its records. A local land office has to send copies of every homestead filing and every land sale to the office in Chicago. They record that stuff there and send copies to Washington. Sooner or later, somebody in one of those offices would be bound to notice that the same piece of land had been sold two or three times."

"Then there'd be an investigation, of course." Teddy nodded. "But if the local land office sends in the title documents, they could be falsified."

"Now you see what I been getting at," Longarm said. "Hell, it's an old swindle out here in this part of the country, Teddy. A lot of big ranchers ain't sure where their land stops and somebody else's starts."

"Yes, I've heard that. It's hard for someone from the East to realize how much land there is here in the West. It'd be still harder for an immigrant from Europe to understand it, because Europe's even more crowded."

"And it'd be real easy for a swindler to sell an immigrant a good piece of land and make up a false title to it. Maybe it'd be railroad subsidy land or rangeland some big rancher's got title to but don't use."

When Longarm paused for breath, Teddy picked up where he'd left off. "But the title that was sent east, the real title, would show the land the immigrant bought was in the badlands."

"Now you've got the whole picture."

"Sooner or later, that kind of swindle is going to blow up

in the face of the swindler, though," Teddy said. "Someone he's given a false title to will find out he's been cheated, and go to the authorities."

"Which is why I got a hunch I'd better keep a real close watch on Delaney and Magruder both," Longarm said. "Magruder always did strike me as a man who wouldn't look to see whether or not a dollar was honest before he snapped it up."

"You'll still want me to help you, then," Teddy said at once. "At least, I hope you will. I've got a personal reason now in seeing that Delaney's swindle is stopped."

"Maybe we both better think about that a while," Longarm suggested. "This case has become rougher than I had any idea it would. And while you're doing your thinking, don't forget that sweet, pretty girl who's waiting to marry you."

"Alice would want me to do what I think best," Teddy said stiffly. "We've already agreed that it's the man's place to make the decisions. As far as I'm concerned, I want to go on helping you, Longarm."

When Longarm did not reply at once, Teddy added, "Delaney and everybody else connected with the swindle will know we were together fighting off those men who ambushed us. I'd probably be in as much danger now if I stopped helping as I will if I keep on."

"I told you before, you're going to make a real good lawyer one of these days," Longarm replied. "I'd have a hard time arguing against what you just said."

"Then I'm going to keep on?"

"If you still want to, at least for now. And you're right about it not being a secret any longer that we're in this mess together. So you might as well come along when we get back to town and I go tell Magruder what happened."

"If he's just a town marshal, he won't have any jurisdiction over what happened back there."

"I know that, Teddy. But seeing what happens after I tell him might give me an idea whether or not I'm wrong about him being Delaney's man. And that might make a lot of difference before this case is closed."

"Why in hell are you coming to me with this yarn about you and your friend being bushwacked, Long?" Magruder demanded.

"Mainly because you're about the only lawman anywhere

"close at hand," Longarm told the Interior town marshal.

"If it happened where you say it did, you know I don't have any jurisdiction out there," Magruder went on.

"Call it professional courtesy, then," Longarm said. "I figured you'd like to know there's a couple of desperadoes in the neighborhood, in case anybody else gets shot at or held up."

Magruder stared angrily at Longarm for a moment, seemed about to explode into an angry tirade, then controlled his anger and said, "You'd do better to ride up to Fort Buford and report it to the army. Chances are it was a couple of renegade Sioux. You know them damn redskins," Magruder said.

Longarm turned to Teddy. "You had as good a look at those two fellows as I did. Would you say they looked like Indians?"

Young Roosevelt followed Longarm's lead. He said soberly, "Not to me, they didn't."

Longarm said seriously, "The real reason we dropped in to tell you about that bushwhacking, Magruder, is so you can pass the word there's outlaws in the neighborhood. I heard that your friend Delaney's bringing in some more immigrant land buyers real soon, and I know you wouldn't want 'em scared off."

"Where'd you get the idea Delaney's a special friend of mine?" Magruder exploded. "Just becuase he's a big man in this little town don't mean I go running to him every time I want to blow my nose or wipe my ass."

"You sure changed your tune since this morning, Magruder. Or maybe I just didn't understand you."

"Maybe you didn't," Magruder said curtly. "Delaney'll hear about them bushwackers soon enough without me telling him. So will everybody else in town. But I guess you was just trying to do the right thing, Long."

"Sure. That's all I had in mind." Longarm nodded. "Even if me and Teddy here did miss eating our dinners because them bushwackers had us pinned down, we come right here to tell you about it." He turned to Roosevelt and said, "Let's go, Teddy. We'll go on over to the hotel and make up for the meal we missed at noon."

As they walked across the street, Teddy told Longarm, "Several times since I've been with you on this case I haven't quite understood your objective in doing something, and this is one of them. Just what are you trying to do?"

"Stir things up. Did you ever toll antelope, Teddy?"

"No. I've never hunted them, and don't know exactly what you mean by tolling them."

88

"Well, antelope have more curiosity than any animal I know. When you want a sure shot at one, you tie a piece of white cloth to a stick and poke it into the ground and then move away from it a bit. Pretty soon, the antelope will see that piece of cloth fluttering around, and he'll come up to see what it is. And then you got your sure shot and your supper."

"Antelope don't shoot back, though, Longarm."

"Well, that's the risk you take, I guess. Before I can break this case, I've got to have some evidence. Right now, I don't even know where to look for it, so all I can do is stir things up and make 'em lead me to it."

They went into the hotel and crossed the lobby to the open doors of the dining room. Longarm said, "I don't know about you, Teddy, but my belly thinks my throat's been cut. I can't get my feet under a table any too soon."

Longarm and Teddy found the big square room buzzing with activity. Waiters were scurrying in all directions under the supervision of the hotel manager, rearranging tables to form an open area in one corner of the room where a single large table had been set. A waiter saw them and came over.

"I hope you gentlemen won't mind a slight delay," he said. "We have a special guest who has asked us to make some changes to accommodate her."

"Her?" Roosevelt asked, raising an eyebrow.

"Baroness Sylvie deJough from Vienna, Austria," the waiter said proudly. "She will be staying here for several weeks, I understand."

"Well, that's right nice," Longarm said, "but she ain't the only one staying here. So as soon as you get the time, me and Mr. Roosevelt would like to eat our supper."

"Yes, yes, of course. I will serve you as quickly as possible."

Longarm and Teddy sat down at a table across the room from the corner that was being prepared for the baroness. While they waited to be served, a handful of other hotel guests straggled in, only to be shooed away from the special corner. Waiters appeared with reasonable promptness, and the dining room returned to normal. Teddy and Longarm were just just finishing their soup when a buzz of voices sounded in the lobby.

"I wonder what all the noise is about," Longarm said to his companion.

"My guess is that the Baroness What's-her-name is coming in for dinner," Roosevelt replied.

They turned toward the door. The hotel manager entered first, his eyes darting around the room to make sure everything was in order. Behind him came a tall stone-faced man wearing a livery of light blue velvet with gold facings. He, too, inspected the room carefully before moving toward the corner set aside for the noble guest.

Finally, the baroness entered, on the arm of a dark-haired, saturnine man whose eyebrows were almost as wide and thick as his full mustache.

Longarm paid little attention to the man. His eyes were caught at once by the baroness. She was a striking blonde with a fair complexion. She looked neither young nor old; she could have been any age from twenty-five to forty-five. Her mouth was a vivid scarlet, full lips opened now in a smile as she responded to a remark made by her escort. Her large eyes were a surprising deep violet.

She wore a low-cut gown of creamy watered silk, cut to leave her shoulders free and to emphasize the fullness of her breasts which the tight bodice had pushed up into high white globes. A triple strand of pearls glistened against the expanse of soft flesh the daring gown revealed. Her golden hair was piled high on her head, and in it tiny gemmed clasps threw sparkling reflections.

"Now, that is one hell of a woman," Longarm remarked to Teddy as they watched the couple.

"Yes, indeed. But I've noticed that European noblewomen know how to make the most of their attributes. But, pretty as she is, she doesn't hold a candle to my Alice."

"I guess that'd be her husband with her."

Roosevelt looked at Longarm with surprise. "I thought you knew. That's Creighton Delaney."

"Delaney!" Longarm exclaimed. "How would I know, Teddy? I never set eyes on the man until right now."

"Of course. I'd forgotten."

"How'd he get so chummy with the lady so quick?"

"Since he's in the business of selling land," Teddy replied, "I'd venture a guess that the baroness is doing what many of the European nobility are doing these days: investing some of her surplus wealth in land here in this country."

"Now, that's a right shrewd guess, Teddy," Longarm said. "And if you're right, I imagine it'd be a good-sized deal. Big enough to make him so anxious to wind it up that he'd get careless. And any slip he makes will give us the opening we need."

Chapter 10

Teddy Roosevelt frowned across the table and said, "Perhaps I wasn't listening carefully, Longarm, but I don't follow your reasoning."

"There ain't much reasoning to follow yet, Teddy. All I have right this minute is a nubbin of an idea. So far, the folks that's got caught up in Delaney's land swindle has been little farmers, most of 'em from Europe. Am I right?"

"Yes, I'd say that's quite true."

"Now, they ain't the kind of people that'd know how to fight back. How many of 'em you figure would take Delaney to court? They don't know the language, for one thing, and they wouldn't really know how to go about proving he'd cheated them."

All the while he talked, Longarm had been watching Delaney and the baroness. They had been served soup, and a waiter was filling their wineglasses. Delaney was explaining something to the baroness, who listened intently.

Teddy cleared his throat to get Longarm's attention. "So far your logic is quite correct, and I think I see where it's leading you."

"Now, that lady sitting over in the corner listening to Delaney is rich and educated," Longarm continued. "I imagine she talks English, too, maybe as good as you and me."

"Most members of the European aristocracy speak English almost as well as their native language."

"And she'd know how to hire lawyers and surveyors and so on to prove a case against him."

"So you propose to let Delaney carry out his sale and, if it proves to be fraudulent, persuade the baroness to take him to court?"

"Something like that."

"I can see only one flaw in your plan, Longarm. What makes you think Delaney will try to cheat the baroness?"

"Because I've seen men like him many times. Delaney's the kind that's going to find a crooked way to do something even when it's easier to do it the honest way."

"Well, you might be right. But how can you be sure the baroness will cooperate with you?"

"Why, I'll make sure of that beforehand. If I tip her off in advance that Delaney's out to cheat her, she ought to be willing to work with us and pretend to go along with Delaney's deal while we get the goods on him."

Longarm's attention had wandered to the corner table again. Delaney was moving his finger over the tablecloth as though he was sketching a plan of some sort. The baroness was engrossed in watching him.

"Look there," Longarm said. "He's showing her some kind of land layout. He's got something up his sleeve, all right."

Teddy's study of the law surfaced. He asked Longarm, "How do you intend to prove to her that Delaney's a crook?"

"Right now, I can't prove it," Longarm admitted.

"Are you even sure you can get proof?"

"That's what I've got to start working on right away. The more I study this case the surer I am that all the old Land Office records have got to be close around here someplace."

"They might even be in Delaney's office," Teddy suggested.

"No. He couldn't run the risk of keeping 'em there, any more than he could afford to burn 'em. He needs the old records for his business, and I'm dead sure he's got 'em hidden away someplace. All I got to do is find 'em."

"That's certainly logical, Longarm, but it's not going to be an easy job to find something without having a clue as to where you should start looking."

"Oh, I don't imagine it'll be easy, but it ought not to be too hard, either. I got a pretty good idea of the kind of hiding place I'll be looking for." First of all, it'd have to be private. It wouldn't likely be right in town, because he wouldn't want anybody to see him going in and out of it all the time. But it couldn't be too far from town, either, or it'd take him too long to get to it."

"It seems to me the best way to find that hiding place is to let Delaney himself lead you to it."

Longarm shook his head. "That'd take too long, Teddy. He might not have to go dig into the old papers for quite a while."

"Delaney lives in a suite on the top floor of the hotel," Roosevelt said thoughtfully. "He might have a separate room, possibly on a different floor, where he keeps the old Land Office records. That would be a private place easy for him to get to."

"Now, the hotel hadn't occurred to me. I'll see what I can find out about it, first thing in the morning. There's something else I've thought about, too, that might give me some kind of starting point."

"What's that?"

"Smothers."

"How can he help you if he's missing?"

"I need to know why he came to be missing, Teddy. Did he just get tired and quit, or was he stealing Land Office fees, or did somebody kill him?"

"Perhaps it's premature judgement on my part, but I'd bet on theft or death."

"Maybe both of 'em," Longarm said. "The only way I know to find out is to look up whoever knew him and ask them some questions. It just might be that something he said or did before he dropped out of sight could give me some ideas."

"Ideas about what?"

"Well, for all we know, Delaney might've been paying Smothers off. Maybe they were partners. Suppose the two of 'em had a falling out and Delaney killed Smothers and hid his body someplace? I'm just beginning to get my teeth into this, Teddy. We've got a lot of rocks to look under before we can say we're stumped."

"Do you want me to go with you in the morning?"

"Not this time. And not just because we ran into a mite of trouble today. It'd be better if you keep an eye on Delaney.

Like you said a minute ago, the easy way to find the papers is to let him lead us to 'em, and if he has to dig into 'em on account of this deal he's got going with the baroness lady, he might do just that."

Longarm started his search for evidence early the next morning with Paul Heenan, the manager of the Railroad Hotel.

"I guess you know why I came to Interior, Mr. Heenan," he began, facing the manager across the desk in Heenan's office.

"It's a small town, Marshal Long. News travels fast. By now, I don't suppose there's anybody in town who doesn't know you've come here looking for Claude Smothers."

"Well, his disappearance is what got me started. But Smothers had been gone quite a while before his boss in Chicago started to get worried about him."

"I've heard about that, too," Heenan said. "Isn't it eight months or more since he disappeared? I'm curious to know why it took the Chicago Land Office such a long time to get concerned."

"Maybe what I find out will tell us that," Longarm replied. "And I guess you've heard there's another government man missing, the fellow who was sent out from Chicago to find out what had happened to Smothers."

"I've heard something about that. But I'm afraid I can't help you there either, Marshal. As far as I know, I never did see the the second man."

"His name's Arthur Alberts. That's why I came to talk to you this morning. I thought maybe he'd stopped at the hotel when he first got into town."

"Well, we certainly don't have a lot of guests these days, but even so, I can't remember all their names," Heenan said. "But I can have the desk clerk check the register and see if Alberts did stay here."

"I'd appreciate that. But there's still a few things I'd like to ask you about Claude Smothers. I don't guess you saw much of him? From what I've been told, he stayed pretty much to himself."

"Yes, he did. He came to Interior before the hotel was built, of course. I think he lived in a cabin a few miles outside town, but I'm not really sure where. Smothers ate here once in a while, and I knew him well enough to say hello on the street. That's about all I know of him. I didn't realize he'd disappeared until a short while ago."

"He never rented any rooms from you?"

"No. I told you, he had a cabin outside town."

"I didn't mean a room to stay in, Mr. Heenan. What I was thinking about was that Smothers might've rented a room for somebody who'd come to visit him, or maybe to store Land Office records in—something like that."

"Now, why would he rent a room here in the hotel for storage, Marshal? He had his office for that."

"That's a pretty small office, and land records take up a lot of room. Why, I'd imagine somebody like Mr. Delaney'd need more room than he's got in his office to store records."

"I don't know what you're driving at, Marshal. Mr. Delaney rents a suite of rooms in the hotel, but he lives in them. He doesn't use them as an office, and certainly not for storage."

"Well, it was just an idea." Longarm stood up. "If you'll get your clerk to see if Arthur Alberts checked in here, I'd be obliged. I'll stop by and find out later on."

"I'll have him take care of it as soon as possible. We're pretty busy right now, so it may take a little while."

"That's right, you've got that baroness lady staying here, and I imagine she keeps your help jumping."

"Oh, she has her own maid and manservant with her. She and her party do require extra service, of course, but we're happy to see that they get it. Members of the nobility don't visit Interior every day, you know."

"I don't imagine they do. Her being nobility—does that mean she's a relative of some king or queen or other?"

"I don't think all members of the nobility are actually related to royalty, Marshal Long. But, for all I know, Baroness de-Joungh might be."

"You know, I never did meet anybody that was related to a king or queen," Longarm said thoughtfully.

Paul Heenan knew a hint when he heard one. After a moment's hesitation, he said, "I'll be glad to introduce you to the baroness, the first chance I get."

"Why, I'd appreciate that," Longarm replied. "Maybe I'll be in the dining room when she comes in and you can do the introducing."

"Of course. Perhaps this evening, or tomorrow."

"That'll suit me fine. Well, thank you for your help, Mr. Heenan. I'll be looking for that introduction, first time it's convenient."

Longarm left a note for Teddy Roosevelt telling him about the Smothers' cabin and that he was going to look for it. Then getting his horse from the hotel stable, Longarm rode out of town, heading north. He did not hurry. The search he was starting might be a long one, but Heenan's information that Smothers had lived in a cabin a few miles outside town had given him the first solid lead he'd had.

A few miles out of town might mean damn near anywhere of course, he told himself as he turned off the trail that led northeast to the badlands and began the first of what he planned to be a series of zigzags that would cover the area around Interior. *But the town ain't all that big, and there ain't all that many trails leading out of it. And it's mostly clear country, so all you got to do is look in the places where a cabin might be hidden by some trees around it, and there ain't too many places like that to look for.*

Because he'd spent a good part of the morning waiting to talk to Paul Heenan, Longarm had started late, but he'd eaten breakfast early. The going was not especially rough, but zig-zagging back and forth to investigate each small clump of trees was time-consuming and tiring. The sun climbed up to noon and passed over to the west, and his stomach began reminding him it was empty.

In a thin stand of pines, he came across the few timbers that remained of a long-abandoned cabin. The ruins were far too old to have been the place he was looking for. Beside the caved-in walls, a tiny spring-fed creek trickled in a thin line for a few hundred yards before disappearing in a sandy sink. Reining in, he ate some pieces of jerky and a handful of parched corn from his saddlebags, washing them down with a few swallows of water. Then he lighted a cheroot and sat for a while on a cleared log that had fallen from a wall while he smoked the cigar to a stub before resuming his search.

By midafternoon he'd reached the halfway point in his search, crossing the abandoned railroad right-of-way. The wide cleared swath, almost void of wheel-ruts on this side of the town, invited him to call it a day and follow it back to town. Longarm looked at the upsloping south arc of the saucer in which the town lay; it bore more growth than the portion he'd just covered, and he decided to keep on searching for another hour or so. He toed his horse ahead and started for the nearest clump of trees.

That stand of growth and the next one on the upslope were both empty, but as he rode slowly down the slope toward a third copse, he thought he could see the vestiges of a trail leading away from it.

A hundred yards from the pines, Longarm reined in. He could see now what hadn't been plain from the distance; the trail leading into the trees was distinct, and obviously still in use. His eyes narrowing thoughtfully, Longarm walked the horse to the side of the copse opposite the trail, dismounted, and led the animal into the concealment of the trees and tethered it. Then he started out on foot to investigate.

He saw the cabin before he'd walked a dozen paces into the stand of timber. It stood in a clearing; there was a small pole corral and a roofed shelter for horses at the edge of the cleared area. Longarm angled over to look at the corral and saw fresh manure inside the enclosure. The freshest droppings were no more than three or four days old.

A wide stone chimney filled most of the end wall of the cabin that faced the corral. Longarm made his way to the rear of the little structure. There were two windows cut into the rear wall, both covered on the outside by solid wooden shutters which were bolted tightly closed from inside. The shutters fit well; when Longarm tried to slip the blade of his knife into the center gap, the opening was too small to allow him to slide the bolt by working the blade from side to side. The second window also defeated him. Reluctantly, Longarm started around to the front of the cabin.

He rounded the corner and looked at the front wall. It also had two windows in it, but they were shuttered as tightly as those in back. The door was made from heavy rough-hewn timbers, and secured by a heavy metal hasp with a stout padlock.

He was starting along the wall to take a closer look at the door when he noticed the well. A low curbing of stones had been placed to enclose a spring a few paces from the corner of the cabin. A wooden bucket stood on the curbing; Longarm stepped over to the well and picked up the bucket. Its metal hoops were rusted, but the staves were firm and tight, and the inside of the bucket was smooth and felt slightly moist.

Maybe this ain't the place you been looking for, old son, Longarm told himself as he put the bucket back on the curb. *By all the signs, this cabin's been used pretty often lately. It sure as hell belongs to somebody, the way it's locked up tight, and it ain't stood vacant for six or eight months. Dry as it is in this country, that bucket would've shrunk up and fell apart if it hadn't been dipped in the well pretty regular.*

Making his way through the trees, walking at one side of the path that led past the front door of the cabin to the corral, Longarm walked to the edge of the copse. He examined the path as he moved along beside it. There were plenty of hoofprints, and he hunkered down beside the path to study them more closely. The prints were not clean-cut, with sharp edges outlining them distinctly, as would have been the case if they were only a few days old.

From the slight crumbling around their edges, Longarm judged that the newest of the hoofprints dated back at least a week or more, and most of them much longer. The oldest were almost obliterated by later prints, and there was such a profusion of them that Longarm could not tell how many different horses had been ridden up the path to the cabin.

He stood up and continued toward the edge of the copse. He was at the very edge of the stand of trees when he glanced down the trail that led to Interior and saw the riders half a mile away and heading in his direction.

For a moment, Longarm stood watching the approaching horsemen. Then, moving very deliberately to avoid attracting their attention, he retreated deeper into the stand of trees. As soon as his movements were shielded by the thin trunks of the pines, he walked briskly back to the cabin, again avoiding the path.

He looked through the grove, trying to spot his own horse, but the trees grew close together behind the cabin, and the animal was not visible. Stepping a few paces away from the rear wall of the cabin to avoid being seen from the corral or from an opened window, he found a spot where the trunks of two closely spaced trees gave him cover, and stood waiting.

In the late afternoon stillness of the isolated copse, sounds carried very clearly. Longarm heard the muffled thudding of hoofbeats on the hard dry ground long before he could hear the voices of the riders. As they came up to the trees and rode into the grove, he could hear them discussing the poker game in which one of them had been a big loser the night before. Then they were at the cabin. The hoofbeats stopped.

"Hell, we got here too soon, Blasson, just like I told you we would," one of them said.

"We won't have long to wait. Delaney said either him or Magruder was going to be here about an hour before sundown," the man called Blasson replied.

"I don't see why we can't have a key to that damn padlock," the other growled. "You'd think there was something important in that cabin instead of just a bunch of old papers."

Behind the cabin, Longarm suppressed a grunt of satisfaction. His hunch had proved correct. Now that he knew where the papers were, he was one step closer to making a case against Delaney.

"Let up on your belly-aching, Cord," Blasson told his companion. "You're still mad because your three kings didn't stand up to Pearson's full house last night."

"That damned game cleaned me out," Cord complained. "I'm flat busted right now. Ain't even got the price of a bowl of beans. Delaney's going to have to pay me something for that job even though we messed up and let that Federal man get away."

"I don't think he'll argue too much. It ain't our fault we didn't get to him. Nobody told us there'd be somebody with him."

Listening, Longarm pressed his lips together angrily when he heard these remarks, and stored in his memory the names of Cord and Blasson as a pair who required attention in the near future.

"Delaney ain't stingy with his money, give him that," Blasson said. "What's he got for us this time? Another try at that Federal man, or some bohunk homesteader that needs to be scared off his land?"

"It don't make much difference, does it? As long as I get steady work, I don't give a damn what it is."

Longarm heard the hoofbeats at about the same time the pair of plug-uglies in front of the cabin did.

Cord said, "That's Magruder."

"Well, we can get inside the cabin now, and have us a drink. Magruder's got a key."

"Who in hell's with him?" Cord asked. "It sure ain't Delaney."

"It's that new man Delaney's got, the one that used to work for the Land Office. I guess we better lead our horses back to the corral."

Longarm had been making a plan while Delaney's men talked. He'd examined the cabin's surroundings carefully and concluded that there was only one place where he could hide and be sure of hearing what the gang that was assembling had to say. When he heard Blasson and Cord moving toward their horses, Longarm went up to the wall of the cabin and pressed himself close to its rough log surface.

As soon as the two plug-uglies started toward the corral, he leaped up and got a handhold on the eaves of the cabin's roof. Muscling himself up, he threw a leg onto the low-pitched roof and rolled over until he lay stretched out on its shingled surface. He listened until the hoofbeats of the horses ridden by Magruder and his companion passed the cabin on the way to the corral.

Raising his head carefully, he looked down at the riders as they passed. He waited until they'd reached the corral and were exchanging greetings with Blasson and Cord. Then he rolled up the gentle slope of the roof to the chimney, stretched out flat, and settled down to wait.

Chapter 11

From his hiding place on the roof, Longarm heard the four men talking as they came back to the cabin from the corral.

"When's Delaney going to get here?" Cord asked.

"Pretty soon," Magruder replied. "He didn't want all three of us to start out from town together." Then the town marshal added, "Was I you, I wouldn't be so damn anxious for Delaney to get here, Cord. He ain't real happy about the way you and Blasson let that son of a bitch Longarm get away from you."

"Well, nobody told us there'd be somebody along with him!" Cord protested. "Whoever the other bastard was, he was a pretty good shot, too."

"Aw, that was some dude from back East that Longarm picked up on the way here. Name's Roosevelt," Magruder said.

"Delaney don't need to lose no sleep over the Federal man," Blasson said. "We'll get him the next time we see him."

"Don't be so sure," Magruder told the outlaw. "That Long is a hard man to kill. Plenty have tried it, but he's come out on top every time."

Cord broke in. "Cut it short and open the door, Magruder. I want a drink of that special whiskey Delaney keeps out here."

"Yeah," Magruder agreed. "It sure beats saloon whiskey."

Longarm heard the metallic grating of the padlock and hasp

as the door was opened. Counting on the noise of the men entering the cabin to cover his movements on the roof, Longarm moved quickly. He hoisted himself into a sitting position, leaning against the chimney, his head just above its top. With the flue serving as a speaking tube, he could hear the men inside the cabin even more clearly than when they'd been outdoors.

A voice new to Longarm spoke for the first time. He remembered the earlier conversation between Blasson and Cord, and tagged the speaker as being the mysteriously missing Arthur Alberts. The voice was light, high-pitched, and nasal, and Longarm knew he'd have no trouble identifying its owner later.

"I'd like one of you men to give me a hand," Alberts was saying. "Mr. Delaney wants me to make up a new plat of the land he's planning to sell the baroness, and the old one's in that big book down at the botton of this third stack." Then, after a moment of silence, Alberts said almost plaintively, "Well? Can't one of you help me?"

"Go on, Blasson," Magruder said. "Help him juggle them books around."

A sharp thunking of boot heels and the duller, sound of heavy objects being shifted around reached Longarm's ears. He formed a mental picture of the cabin's interior, lined with stacks of oversized, cumbersome books of maps and boundary descriptions, the kind he'd seen in Land Offices.

His absorption in the noises coming from the cabin almost caused Longarm to be caught, for the sounds masked the approach of a fifth rider. Not until the newcomer was well into the copse did Longarm hear the hoofbeats and duck behind the chimney. The sun had gone down by now and dusk was settling, so he did not see the newest arrival, but he knew it could be no one but Creighton Delaney.

Delaney wasted no time. "All right, Blasson, let Alberts handle his own work. I want to know why you and Cord didn't get rid of that damned Federal marshal."

It was Cord instead of Blasson who answered. "You know why, Delaney. You sent word there'd only be one man out there, but we run into two. They found a place to hole up, and there wasn't no way me and Blasson could get at 'em without getting ourselves killed."

"That's the risk you're paid to take," Delaney retorted. "I don't expect you men to back off from a job I give you just because you don't like the odds!"

"Now, that's fine for you to say," Cord said. "You sit in that office of yours and pay somebody else to take the risks for you!"

"Any time you don't want my money, Cord, there are plenty of gunhands ready to take it," Delaney said coldly. "Now, I want Long put away in a hurry, and if you and Blasson don't think you can handle the job, I'll bring in somebody who can."

"Wait a minute, Mr. Delaney," Blasson broke in. "You gave us a bum steer. You come right down to it, you're the one that's mainly to blame for us missing out."

There was silence in the cabin for a moment, then Delaney said in a more even tone, "I guess you've got a point there, Blasson. Magruder, it was your information I passed on to Cord and Blasson. I'll charge the mistake up to you instead of them. Now, let's forget the whole thing for now and get on with what I got you out here for."

"You still want Long outa the way, don't you?" Cord asked.

"Of course I do!" Delaney said. "And I'm willing to pay you double for the job. I'll leave it to you two to set up, and if anything goes wrong, you'll have nobody to blame but yourselves."

"That's fair enough, don't you think, Cord?" Blasson asked.

"I guess. All right, Delaney."

"And soon!" Delaney snapped. "You men are going to have a lot more work to do in the next few weeks."

"Sounds like you're working up something big," Magruder put in. "I'll bet it's with that fancy blonde woman from over in Europe. Everybody in town's got their tongues hanging out trying to get a sniff of her."

"Magruder, everything we've pulled before is peanut-sized compared to this." Delaney's voice managed to sound serious and avaricious at the same time. "It's so big I'm not even bothering with anything else until it's finished. But I'll tell all of you right now: We've got to work fast, and the job's got to look cleaner than we've had to worry about in the past."

"What d'you mean, clean?" Magruder asked.

"What Mr. Delaney means is that the deal with the baroness can't be handled the way we've been doing things," Arthur Alberts volunteered. "We can't show her good rangeland and then give her a deed to a piece of property in the badlands."

"Shit!" Magruder snorted. "We've always been able to switch deeds before. Why do we have to be so careful now?"

104

"Magruder," Delaney said, "until now we've been dealing with a bunch of ignorant bohunks. Most of them never owned land before, most of them don't know English, and not one in a thousand could tell the difference between a deed and last week's newspaper. This deal's different."

"Just how big a deal is it?" Magruder asked.

"Very big. The baroness wants about half of Dakota Territory for a ranch, and she's got the money to buy it," Delaney replied. "And we can't afford to have that damned Federal marshal poking around while I'm closing it. He could ruin everything for us."

"Oh, come on, Delaney! Longarm's not interested in what we're doing. He's here to find out about Smothers and Alberts."

"That's why Alberts is going to stay out here in this cabin until we get rid of Long and his friend."

"I'll have to fix up the deeds and plats, you see," Alberts explained. "All the papers must be in perfect order."

"What in hell does a woman know about stuff like that?" Magruder said disgustedly. "Why can't we just handle it like we always do, instead of wasting all this time?"

"Because the baroness has already sent her manservant to Bismark to telegraph her embassy in Washington to send a lawyer out here to make sure everything is all right," Alberts said triumphantly. *"Now* do you understand why it's so important?"

"It goes a long way past papers, too, Magruder." Delaney's voice was impatient. "Cord and Blasson are going to have to get rid of ten or fifteen of the bohunks we've already got settled on land they think they own. And you've got to see that there's no fuss made when they drop out of sight."

Cord whistled. "That's a pretty good-sized order for me and Blasson to take on by ourselves. How about we get some help? Me and Blasson stopped in at the Gold Front Saloon on the way here and run into old One-Eye Blake. He's a good—"

"No," Delaney interrupted. "The more that are in on this deal, the more chance there'll be of it leaking out. Damn it, this job's going to take a month or so! It's not like we were dealing with one ignorant bohunk for a little piece of land!"

"Well, that's the truth," Magruder agreed. "But I sure don't like the idea of sitting on it for a month or more."

"Why do you think I'm in such a hurry right now?" Delaney asked, his voice sharply impatient.

Blasson had said nothing for some time. Now Longarm heard his voice raised. "Listen, Mr. Delaney, ten or fifteen bodies is a lot to get rid of. What're we going to do, bring 'em here and bury 'em out with Smothers, in the corral?"

"No. A peddler died in Interior a month or so back, and his cart's been sitting out behind Magruder's office because nobody knew what to do with it. You men can take the cart and go around pretending to be peddlers. That cart will haul four or five bodies at a time. Take them out and dump them in the badlands. Anybody who runs into a corpse out there will blame the killing on the Indians."

"What about Long?" Cord asked.

"I don't give a damn," Delaney started, then stopped for a moment before saying, "Get rid of his body, too. And take care of that fellow with him—the dude. Just do it fast."

"We'll take care of him. Don't worry," Cord said.

Delaney said impatiently, "Alberts, have you made up the list of bohunks that Cord and Blasson will have to get rid of?"

"It's not finished yet, Mr. Delaney," Alberts replied in his strange, high-pitched voice. "I still have to check in these old record books to be sure all the names are on it."

"You stay right here until you finish, then," Delaney ordered. "Work all night if you have to. I want them to start killing off the bohunks as soon as they get rid of Long."

"Is there anything special you want me to do?" Magruder asked.

"Yes, there is," Delaney answered. "I want you and that fat idiot who works for you to spread the word that a bunch of renegade Sioux is roaming around. That ought to keep people from asking questions when Blasson and Cord start to work."

"By God, Delaney!" Magruder exclaimed. "I got to hand it to you! You cover just about everything!"

"Be glad I do," Delaney said.

Longarm heard a chair scrape on the cabin floor and decided that the meeting was about to break up. It was full dark, however, and he quickly concluded that he'd be better off holding his position than trying to change it. The risk of one of them looking up and seeing him as they departed was less than that of having them hear him if he tried to move. He ignored the cramps in his leg muscles and held himself still.

Delaney was the first to leave. He strode out of the cabin

106

and swung into his saddle. Soon the hoofbeats of his horse had faded away in the darkness.

"Well, I guess we all know what to do, now," Magruder observed. "No use hanging around out here any longer. Come on, Blasson, leave what little bit's left in Delaney's bottle, and you and Cord can ride back to town with me. This'd be a good time for you to haul that old peddler's cart out to where you're camped. Nobody's likely to notice in the dark."

"You're not going to leave me out here by myself, are you?" Arthur Alberts objected.

"What's the matter, Alberts?" Cord asked. "Afraid old Smother's ghost might walk?"

"Of course not, but Magruder and I came out together. I just thought we'd go back together, too."

"I don't see why you expect me to stay," Magruder said. "I don't know what you're doing with them books. I wouldn't be no help for you. Anyhow, I oughta be on the job back in town."

"Yes, but—" Alberts began.

Magruder cut him short. "Just blow out the lantern and snap the padlock on the door when you leave. Come on, Blasson, let's you and Cord and me get moving."

Old son, you really lucked out, finding this cabin when you did, Longarm told himself after Magruder and the two gunslicks were gone. *You know as much about Delaney's scheme now as he does himself. Except, like Teddy Roosevelt said, you still got to get proof that will stand up in court. The old Land Office books and papers that Alberts is working on will help, but they ain't going to do much good without Alberts to testify what he was up to.*

Longarm took out the cheroot he'd been too cautious to light earlier and touched a match to its tip. *Now the thing for you to do,* he went on to himself, *is to let Alberts finish up with the fake deeds. Then you can nab him when he comes out and hide him away, which ain't going to be much of a job, because Alberts is the weak sister in that outfit. If you got papers to show in court and Alberts to testify, there ain't a shyster lawyer alive that can talk a judge and jury out of putting a noose around Blasson's and Cord's necks, and maybe Delaney's and Magruder's too.*

Slowly the night wore on. Longarm's stomach growled, but

he stopped it with another cigar and later on a third. His muscles became one big cramp, for he did not dare risk making a noise by moving. The night was totally silent except for the occasional distant howl of a coyote or the hooting of an owl. The only other noise that broke the stillness was the rustle of papers and an occasional thud when Alberts moved one of the big record books.

Longarm did not even try to keep track of the hours as they passed. As the night moved toward day, he devoted his attention to staying awake and alert, and to quieting the protests of his empty belly and the twinges that began to seize his motionless legs. He knew that a long time had passed before he heard Alberts sigh with satisfaction. There was a rustle of papers being gathered up, followed by the grating of footsteps on the floor of the cabin.

A few moments later, the ground in front of the cabin was flooded with a yellow glow as Alberts emerged carrying a lantern and made his way to the corral. Longarm used the occasion to stand up and try to bring life back into the aching muscles of his calves and thighs.

He was crouched down beside the chimney massaging his legs when he saw the lantern bobbing back from the corral. In a few moments he saw Alberts coming toward the cabin, carrying the lantern and leading his horse. He dropped the reins, letting the horse stand, and went into the cabin.

Longarm estimated the distance between the chimney, where he was standing, and the cabin door. Three long steps, he thought, would bring him to the edge of the roof, and from there he could jump down on Alberts as he made ready to mount. He waited while the glow that had been spilling through the open door suddenly vanished and he heard Alberts's footsteps approaching the door. There was a grating of metal on metal as the clerk pushed the hasp closed and snapped the padlock.

Longarm's eyes had adjusted to the darkness enough to allow him to see Alberts's shadowy form moving toward his horse. He'd already gauged the length of the three long steps he had to take to carry him from the chimney to the eaves. Half-crouching to give himself a quick start, Longarm moved.

He made the first two steps without trouble. When the first thud of his boots sounded on the cabin roof, Longarm saw the white oval of Alberts's upturned face. Almost at the same moment, Longarm's foot hit the cabin roof in his second stride. His leg muscles, still not fully restored, gave way as his foot landed.

Throwing out his arms in an effort to regain his balance, Longarm hung poised on the slanting rooftop for a fraction of a second. Then the impetus of his leap carried him forward. He flailed his arms, trying to control the fall he knew was coming, but his efforts were futile. He tumbled sideways, his momentum carrying him to the roof's edge. As he went down his head struck the eaves with a stunning jolt. Unconscious, Longarm fell from the roof and landed in a motionless heap on the ground.

Longarm blinked as his eyes opened. A light shone with a burning intensity that forced him to squeeze his lids closed again. His next effort was more successful. This time he was able to keep his eyes open, though his vision was blurred and his head was throbbing.

Slowly his eyes returned to normal. He wanted to rub them, but his arms were pulled tightly in back of him in the chair in which he was sitting. He attempted to stand up and discovered that his legs were tied to the chair legs. He turned his head and saw Alberts watching him.

Longarm said nothing; he was scrutinizing the deserter from the Land Office. Alberts was undistinguished in his appearance. He was, Longarm judged, in his middle thirties, a tallish man with a clipped sandy mustache and long sideburns. He had pale blue eyes, a pallid indoors complexion, and the hands resting in his lap looked soft. There was nothing about him that would have drawn a second look from anyone in a crowd.

"It's taken you long enough to come to," Alberts said.

"I guess I got a pretty good rap on my head when I tumbled off that roof," Longarm replied.

He examined the interior of the cabin with quick glances while still concentrating on Alberts. It looked much as he'd pictured it. A table stood in the center of the small rectangular room; on it, beside a whiskey bottle, lay his Colt and his hat. The big buckram-bound volumes stolen from the Land Office were piled high along the walls. A low single bed stood in one corner and a monkey stove occupied a space near the fireplace, its pipe slanting over to the chimney. A few chairs completed the cabin's furnishings.

Alberts moved his chair around so that he faced Longarm. He said, "Mr. Delaney's going to be very proud of me for catching you. It'll make our job a lot easier."

"Don't count on ever carrying out that job, Alberts," Longarm cautioned. "From what I heard while I was listening to your bunch talk, you don't stand the chance of a snowball in hell of your scheme working out."

"I don't see why not. It's worked before."

"I'll tell you something you might not've thought about," Longarm said. "Any swindle is good for a little while. This deed-switching you've been doing has worked up till now because it's been a bunch of little bitty deals. But now you're getting it all blown up into a big deal, and that's what'll trip you up."

"That's your opinion, Marshal," Alberts snapped pettishly. "Now that I've got you, there's no one else around to stop us."

"Oh, you'll be stopped, all right." Longarm spoke with all the assurance he could muster. "Our outfit ain't run like the Land Office, Alberts. When one of us marshals turns up missing, all hell breaks loose."

"By the time you're missed, we'll be long gone," Alberts bragged. "We'll be where the government can't touch us."

"You just keep on believing that, and you'll be standing in court facing a hanging sentence, Alberts. Now, if I was in your place, I'd just give up and get on the right side of the fence."

"You're not going to persuade me," Alberts told Longarm. "Five minutes after I get back to Interior and tell Mr. Delaney I've got you tied up out here, he'll have Blasson and Cord on the way to finish you off."

"If it makes you feel any better, keep on thinking that. I guarantee you'll be singing a different tune before long."

"I'm willing to take my chances. Now, I've wasted enough time talking to you. I was just waiting to see if you'd wake up at all. Blasson and Cord will be coming out just as quick as Mr. Delaney can get word to them. I hope you have a pleasant wait, Marshal Long."

Chapter 12

After Alberts had blown out the lantern and snapped the padlock
on the door, Longarm sat motionless in the blackness until he
could no longer hear the hoofbeats of his captor's horse. Then
he began testing the bonds that held him in the chair.

For all that Alberts seemed like something of a fool, he'd
done a good job in securing Longarm's hands and feet. There
was no give in the ropes that held his wrists behind him, no
slack in the lashings that secured his feet to the chair legs.
Longarm did not waste energy struggling uselessly. As soon
as he was satisfied that he had no immediate chance of freeing
himself, he relaxed and began thinking.

Several ideas for freeing his arms and legs occurred to him,
and he tried the first two or three before deciding to use his
brains instead of his muscles.

For a moment he debated trying to overturn the chair to see
if the change made it possible for him to free his arms, but
decided it might just make the situation worse. As time passed,
whenever he became aware that his hands and feet were growing numb, he tightened and relaxed the muscles of his arms
and legs until the movements created enough blood circulation
to cause his toes and fingers to tingle.

Most of the time, Longarm sat quietly, forming and discarding one plan after another. At intervals he dozed off for a few moments, his head sagging down to his chest, his body relaxing as much as possible in his strained position.

He lost track of the passing of time. Bit by bit the darkness in the room began to lift as daylight arrived outside. Soon faint glows of gray took shape in the walls, grew brighter, and formed rectangles that outlined the door and windows. They became more and more distinct after they'd turned from sunrise-pink to the bluish-white of daylight. To Longarm's eyes, accustomed for so many hours to impenetrable blackness, the interior of the cabin was almost as light as if the doors and windows were opened wide.

By craning his neck, Longarm could now see the bonds that held his hands immobilized. Alberts had tied his wrists together, then looped the rope between Longarm's arms to tighten the strands around his wrists. He'd then pulled the end of the rope down and bound it to a rung of the chair. Longarm tried to flex his biceps and pull against the strand that held his wrists, but the position in which the bonds held his arms prevented him from doing so.

He turned his attention to the bindings that held his feet to the front chair legs. Here, too, Alberts had done a workmanlike job. Instead of simply looping a turn or two of rope around Longarm's ankles to hold them to the chair leg, he'd made a stirrup of the rope under the instep of each boot and after looping the rope around the ankles, had tied Longarm's ankles to the rungs as well as to the legs of the chair. Longarm's feet were a good three inches above the floor. Examining the loops and knots securing his feet, Longarm shook his head.

He experimented a bit, and discovered that in spite of the taut rope that pulled and held his arms straight and the stirrup-like loop under his instep, he could move his torso a few inches from side to side. He slid around in the chair for a moment, and found that it did tilt a bit. He thought once more of overturning the chair, but decided on reflection to delay that effort.

You get yourself ass-over-head on the floor, old son, you'll be worse off than you are right now, he cautioned himself. *Just eat the apple a bite at a time. Then if it's rotten around the core you won't have so much to spit out.*

Now he could see the table again, his hat and Colt resting beside the almost-empty whiskey bottle. When he turned his head, he could see the monkey stove beside the fireplace. For the first time he noticed that a low shelf level with the stove held a frying pan, a stew pot, a few plates and bowls and some kitchen utensils. He thought he could make out the wooden handle of a knife on the shelf.

The sight of the utensils gave Longarm new hope. He concentrated now on devising a way to reach that shelf. He had no clear idea of how he'd reach the knife, if indeed it was a knife, but by this time he was chafing after hours of inactivity, and badly needed to feel that he was at least trying to get free.

After a bit of experimenting, Longarm found that when he shifted his torso from side to side in the chair and twisted it with a sudden jerk, the chair moved a fraction of an inch, in spite of the restraint of his bonds. Suppressing his impatience in favor of caution, he worked his body carefully from side to side until the chair tilted. A longer period of small, cautious movements led to the discovery of the exact amount of twisting that was needed to turn the chair a few inches on the axis of the legs that remained on the floor when it tilted.

Rocking from side to side, almost overturning the chair two or three times when be became too anxious, Longarm worked the chair toward the shelf. The distance from the spot where he'd started to the corner where the stove stood was not more than a dozen feet, but each movement of the chair covered only a few inches. He'd covered less than half the distance when a series of rapid knocks on the door broke the dead stillness of the cabin.

"Longarm!" Teddy Roosevelt's muffled voice called from outside. "Longarm, are you in there?"

"I sure as hell am, Teddy!" Longarm called back. "I'm tied up tighter'n a steer at branding time!"

"Don't worry, I'll get you out in a minute or two!" Teddy promised.

Within a few moments, a loud hammering of wood on wood sounded at one of the windows in the back wall. The pounding went on until the shutters began to crack and then to splinter. Then a hand snaked in through a crack between two of the broken boards and began groping for the catch.

"Reach down a mite, Teddy," Longarm directed. "You just about had your hand on it the last time."

A moment later the catch was released, the shutters swung open, and young Roosevelt's head and shoulders appeared in silhouette against the bright morning sky. Longarm blinked at the unaccustomed brilliance. When his eyes no longer watered he could see Teddy's face, his gold-framed oval spectacles catching the sunlight in quick bright flashes as he turned his head to inspect the interior of the cabin.

"I'll crawl in and get you loose just as soon as I can see what I'm doing," he told Longarm. "It's dark in there!"

"It can't be too soon for me. What time of day's it getting to be, anyhow?"

"Not quite ten o'clock. Why?"

"Because a lot of things are happening that need to be stopped," Longarm replied. "And I been tied up here since the middle of the night."

Teddy crawled in through the window and cut the ropes that held Longarm to the chair. Longarm stood up, swayed on unsteady legs for a moment, and sat down again.

"There's a bottle of whiskey on the table," he said. "Hand it over to me. It'll help get me in shape to stand up faster'n anything else." After he'd taken a substantial swallow from the bottle and lighted a cheroot, Longarm asked, "What started you looking for me, Teddy? And how in hell did you find this cabin, anyhow?"

"Well, I got your note telling me you were going to check outside town to see if you could find the Smothers fellow's cabin, and I started wondering where you were when you didn't show up for dinner yesterday evening. When you hadn't returned to the hotel by midnight, I walked around town, looked into the saloons, and glanced into the town marshal's office— things of that sort. I left a note for you at the hotel desk, asking you to come up to my room when you got back, and went to bed. When my note was still in your box at the desk this morning, I began to get worried, so I started looking for you."

Teddy stopped for breath, and Longarm asked him, "What was it led you out here? I put in most of yesterday trying to find this cabin, and it looks to me like you rode right to it."

"Oh, it wasn't that simple. I knew you'd started out to look for a cabin of some sort, and since we hadn't seen any when we were out on the other side of town the other day, I decided to try in this direction first. But what really located the cabin for me was your horse. I'd still have been looking if I hadn't seen it tethered in this clump of trees."

"Well, I'm sure glad to see you. Even if I was about to get myself loose, you saved me a whole bunch of trouble." Longarm stood up, found his legs steady now, and went over to the shelf where the kitchen utensils rested. He saw that the wooden-handled object he'd been trying to reach was indeed a knife. He held it up. "Soon as it got light enough inside, I spotted this, and was on my way after it when you got here."

"How the devil did you get caught, Longarm?"

"It was pretty much my own fool fault." Longarm swallowed the small amount of whiskey left in the bottle, and explained as quickly as possible the chain of events that had led to his capture. He concluded, "Now, we got a lot of ground to cover and damn little time to cover it in. We'd best get back to town and start moving."

"What about this place?" Teddy asked. "Shouldn't I stay here to guard it?"

"There ain't much to guard except the old Land Office books, and they can wait. Right now, the front side of my belly's rubbing against my backbone, and there's business in town I need to tend to besides getting a square meal. Let's skin out that window and head for town. We can talk while we're riding."

They climbed out the window and Longarm led the way to the back of the copse, where he'd left his horse.

"Are you going to arrest Delaney, then?" Teddy asked.

Longarm shook his head thoughtfully. "Not till the last minute. You see, I got a little bit of time to work in, now. It ain't likely the killers will be going after the people Delaney swindled earlier. They'll be too busy chasing after me. So I don't have to worry about any innocent folks being killed."

"Then you intend to set yourself up as bait?"

"Well, not exactly. Oh, sooner or later, I'll have to face those two, but that don't bother me."

They reached the tethered horse, both men mounted, and they started through the grove to reach the trail to Interior. As they rode, Longarm explained, "What I plan to do, Teddy, is to make myself hard to find for a little while. I'm counting on Delaney thinking he's scared me off—that I got loose by myself and ran away."

"From the little I've seen of Delaney, that's not likely."

"Now, I don't agree with you, there. Delaney's smart, but he's crooked-smart. I'm betting he'll be so greedy that he'll try to go on with that scheme he's started to gouge a big chunk of cash out of that baroness lady. I'd like to hold off arresting him till I'm certain he's so deep into his scheme that no fast-talking lawyer can get him off. Meaning no offense to lawyers, Teedy," he added quickly, "but you got to admit that there's times when the law and justice don't seem to mean exactly the same thing."

"Yes. Unfortunately, a few members of the profession I plan to enter stoop to using legal technicalities to distort justice. It's something I've noted with a great deal of regret."

"Well, since there ain't much you or me can do to change that, I want to make a real good case. That means giving Delaney enough rope so he'll hang himself."

"How do you plan to do that?" Teddy asked.

"I'm aiming to have little talk with that baroness and tell her what Delaney's doing. I'll ask her to play along with his scheme until he's got it so far along that everybody can see what he's been up to. That's when I'll step up and put the handcuffs on him."

For a few minutes young Roosevelt rode in silence. Finally he said, "Well, I don't see any legal flaws in your idea, Longarm. Delaney's scheme was already in progress before you entered the case. But you're going to have to prove that he's directly involved in the murders that you heard him and his men discussing last night. Your testimony wouldn't be enough. Now, if one of the principals confessed and implicated Delaney—"

"Don't worry, Teddy. When things get hot enough, there'll be one of 'em that'll testify against him. My guess is it'll be that Alberts fellow. He's the weak sister of the bunch."

"What do you want me to do to help you?"

"I ain't planned that far ahead. Wait till we see what happens. My belly's so empty right now that all I can think about is putting some steak and potatoes into it. After that, I'm going into the barbershop there at the hotel and get shaved, and take a bath. Then maybe I'll feel up to doing some more planning."

They rode the rest of the way into town in silence, left their horses at the hotel's stable, and went into the hotel. They started across the lobby to the dining room. Just as the two men were passing the foot of the stairway, they almost collided with the Baroness deJoungh, escorted by Paul Heenan, the hotel manager.

When he saw Longarm, Heenan hesitated for a moment.

Then, with a heartiness that was only a little bit forced, he said, "Marshal Long! Mr. Roosevelt!" Longarm and Teddy stopped and Heenan turned to the baroness. "Baroness, may I present two gentlemen who, like yourself, are visiting Interior?" Without waiting for the baroness's nod, he continued, "Baroness deJoungh, Marshal Custis Long of Denver, and Mr. Theodore Roosevelt of New York."

Both men removed their hats. Longarm tried not to stare openly at the baroness, but he was observing her closely just the same. Seen at close range, he could tell that she was younger than he'd guessed her to be; from the softness of her skin and the smoothness of her unlined face, he guessed her to be several years short of thirty.

He managed to fumble with his hat long enough to let Teddy speak first and give him a clue as to the proper way to address a baroness.

Young Roosevelt grasped her extended hand, bowed over it, released it, and said. "I'm honored, Baroness. I hope you're enjoying your visit here as much as I enjoyed my stay in your country a few years ago."

"Ah, you have visited in Austria, Mr. Roosevelt?" The baroness had only the suggestion of an accent, an almost imperceptible shading. "We must visit together later and exchange our impressions of our so-different countries."

"It would be a pleasure, Baroness," Teddy replied with another bow. He stepped aside, looking at Longarm.

Longarm took his cue quickly. His horn-hard hand engulfed the woman's small fingers as he took Teddy's place. His nostrils widened as a wave of heavy perfume drifted to him.

"A marshal of the United States?" she asked, a little frown of puzzlement of her face. "This is an important position, not so, Mr. Long?"

"Oh, it ain't such a much, Baroness," Longarm replied. "I guess you'd say I'm nothing but a kind of policeman, only I don't wear a uniform."

"But how interesting! You must have had many exciting adventures in such a vast country, with its wild savages and animals! I would enjoy hearing of them later."

"Well, they ain't as exciting as you might think, but I'd sure like to get better acquainted with you." Longarm floundered for words as he felt the pressure of the baroness's fingers and realized that he was still holding on to her hand. He released it quickly and added as he stepped back, "It's been real nice meeting you."

"Remember, you are to tell me of your adventures the next time we meet," she said, smiling. Then she placed her hand on the hotel manager's extended forearm and the pair swept past Longarm and Teddy into the dining room.

"Now, that sure is one fine-looking woman," Longarm remarked to Teddy as they followed the baroness and Heenan in and sat down at a table near the door. "Talks real good English, too."

"I'll grant you she's attractive," Teddy agreed. "But my observation is that European women of the upper class are a bit on the artificial side. No, Longarm, give me a sweet, unspoiled, all-American girl like my Alice any time."

"Do you think she really meant what she said about wanting to visit with us some more, or was that just polite society talk?"

"About half and half, I imagine. It was the right thing for her to say, so she said it."

"It ain't that I'm interested personally," Longarm went on. "But it'd sure save me having to think up some reason for going to talk to her about Delaney."

"Act as though you assumed she meant it, then," Roosevelt advised. "But that badge you carry relieves you of having to find an excuse to talk with her."

"So it does," Longarm said thoughtfully, watching the table across the room, where Baroness deJoungh was chatting animatedly with Paul Heenan. "So it does, Teddy."

Longarm demolished a tremendous porterhouse steak with a heap of fried potatoes, and topped off his meal with a quarter of an apple pie. When he pushed aside his plate and leaned back in his chair, he lighted a cheroot, picked up his freshly filled coffee cup, and sighed contentedly.

"Now, that makes up for missing my supper last night and my breakfast this morning," he said. "After I get these whiskers off and soak away three or four layers of the dirt of that cabin, I should feel pretty good."

"While you're getting your shave and bath, I'll go up to my room and write to Alice," Teddy said. "She suggested in her last letter that it's time for us to set a date for the wedding, and I'm as anxious as she is to get it settled."

"I'll bet you are. Soon as I get cleaned up, I'll knock on

your door, and we'll figure out our next move. It won't take me more'n half an hour or so to get decent again."

In the lobby, Teddy headed for the stairs while Longarm went into the barbershop. He took off his coat first, hung it on the clothes tree, and was reaching for his hat when the barber motioned to Longarm's holstered Colt.

"I'm sorry, Marshal Long, but I'll have to ask you to hang up your gunbelt while you're in the chair," the man said. He pointed to a large broken area of plaster on the wall at the end of the shop. "I guess you haven't heard about that. It only happened yesterday afternoon."

Longarm shook his head. "I was gone all day yesterday. How'd it come about?"

"A customer was lying back in the chair having a shave and his revolver slipped out of his holster and discharged when it hit the floor. There were two or three other customers in the shop, and it's a wonder no one was hit. Mr. Heenan put a new rule into effect right then. All customers must take off their gunbelts now before getting into the chair."

Longarm indicated his Colt, butt-forward in the crossdraw holster on his left side. "That ain't going to happen to my gun, not the way I wear it."

"No, your weapon probably wouldn't fall out," the barber agreed after looking at Longarm's rig. "But a rule's a rule, and it'd mean my job if I didn't do what Mr. Heenan said."

"Well, I wouldn't want to get you in trouble," Longarm told the barber.

Longarm didn't mention the little twin-barrel derringer nestled in his vest pocket. The derringer wasn't in a belt holster, he reminded himself, so the rule didn't apply to it. There was no way the stubby little gun was going to fall out of his pocket anyhow. It was connected by a chain to his watch in the pocket on the opposite side of his vest. Taking off his gunbelt, Longarm hung it on the clothes tree, then hung his hat over the Colt and sat down in the chair.

After leaning the chair back so that Longarm was lying full length on its plush-upholstered seat, his head on the rest at the top of the back, the barber draped Longarm with a cloth that covered him from neck to knees. He took a hot towel from the steamer and covered Longarm's face with it until only his nose protruded.

Picking up a mug and a brush, the barber dripped a trickle

of hot water into the mug and began working up a lather. Turning Longarm's head sideways, he slathered the exposed cheek and chin with the warm lather, then turned Longarm's head to apply lather to the other cheek.

In his new position, Longarm was looking into the mirror that covered the rear wall of the barbershop. In it he saw the lobby reflected. Baroness deJoungh and Paul Heenan had just come out of the dining room and were crossing the broad carpeted lobby. Following their progress with his eyes, Longarm almost missed seeing the man behind them until he was within a few feet of the barbershop's double doors.

The man was carrying a newspaper draped over his right arm, which he carried horizontally across his chest. When he saw the black patch covering one eye Longarm's sixth sense suddenly clamored an alarm.

Sliding his hand up the watch-chain, Longarm eased the derringer out of his pocket. When the approaching man stopped in the doorway and began swinging his newspaper-covered arm in Longarm's direction, Longarm lifted the muzzle of the derringer and shot through the barber's cloth.

The slug tore into the stranger's chest. The man's dying reflex triggered the revolver he'd carried under the folded newspaper. The muzzle blast exposed the gun as it went off, its slug screaming as it ricocheted off the marble floor of the barbershop and thunked into the back wall, knocking another hole in the plaster.

A surprised look stealing over his face as he died, the would-be assassin crumpled to the floor.

Chapter 13

For a moment after the two shots echoed through the hotel, there was dead silence in the lobby. Then Baroness deJoungh screamed, a small throaty cry of mingled surprise and fear. The cry broke the hush and the lobby buzzed with voices. Heenan ran to the barbershop door. Longarm reared up out of the chair and went to look at the man he'd shot. The barber began talking to Heenan, and the few guests who had been in the lobby joined the desk clerk and a handful of waiters and customers who'd rushed from the dining room when they heard the shots.

Disregarding the fact that half his face was clean-shaven and the other half still covered with lather, and that he was draped from neck to knees in the white barber's cloth, Longarm took charge.

"All right, folks," he announced, raising his voice to cut in above the babble of sound. "It's all over and done with. I'm a deputy U. S. marshal, and I'll take care of things until the local lawmen get here."

"Since I happen to be the manager of the hotel, Marshal Long, perhaps you'll tell me what this is all about," Heenan said.

"Why, it's real easy to explain, Mr. Heenan," Longarm

121

replied calmly. "This man was about to shoot me, only I saw him in the mirror and shot first. That's all there is to it."

"Do you know who he is?" Heenan asked. "He's certainly not a guest here."

"I've never seen him before, but I'm right sure his name's Blake. People call him One-Eye Blake because of that patch he wears. And you can see he's still got his gun in his hand."

Baroness deJoungh had recovered from her first shock and now worked her way up to the front of the little group of onlookers around the corpse. She gazed at the dead man, then at Longarm, who still had his derringer in his hand. She asked, "Is it you who have killed this man, Marshal Long? And with the so-small pistol you are holding?"

"I sure did," Longarm answered.

"I have not a thing like this seen before, though I have heard of what you Americans call a shootout. This is a shootout, no?"

"I guess you could call it that," Longarm agreed.

Gazing wide-eyed at the corpse, she went on, "And because each of you had guns, there will be no blame placed on you?"

"Why, I don't suppose anybody in his right mind would blame me for killing him, seeing as how he was doing his best to kill me. All I did was shoot first."

"Why should he want to kill you?" She frowned. "Was he a criminal, who feared you would to prison take him?"

"He's a known killer, if that's what you're driving at," Longarm told her. "I wasn't out to arrest him, though. And I ain't got an idea in the world why he'd be gunning for me. But maybe I'll know more about it before the day's out."

"Then you must come and tell me," she said. "I have a great curiosity about what you call your shootouts."

"I'll do that, Baroness, and that's a promise."

"Come to dinner in my suite," she said, in the manner of one accustomed to giving commands. "I will expect you at seven-thirty."

Pudge Sampson, the chubby deputy who had arrested Longarm in the Land Office, pushed his way through the crowd. He was panting as though he'd been running. He looked at the derringer in Longarm's hand, then at the corpse and the .38 Smith Wesson revolver the dead man's fingers still clasped.

"Somebody come running down to the office and said there was a shooting here at the hotel," Sampson said. Frowning, he asked, "Was it you done the shooting, Long? And is this the man you shot?"

"That's the only dead body I see lying around," Longarm replied. "Where's Magruder?"

"Damned if I know." Pudge shrugged. "He ain't been around all morning." He turned from Longarm to face the little huddle of spectators. "All right, folks, there ain't nothing else going to happen, and there ain't nothing else to see. I'll thank you to go on about your business now, and leave the law to handle this."

A few at a time, the onlookers trickled away. Even Heenan left, escorting the baroness to the stairway. Longarm, Pudge, and the barber were the only ones remaining beside the corpse.

"If it's all right with you," the barber said to Pudge, "I'll get something to cover him up with, until you can have the undertaker get him out of the way."

"Go ahead," Pudge nodded. "I sent word to Leary, and he'll be along soon as he gets his team hitched up, I guess." While the barber spread cloths over the corpse, the Interior deputy marshal turned to face Longarm and said, "Suppose you tell me why you gunned this fellow down, Long."

"Because he was about to cut down on me. I saw him in the mirror, coming up with that newspaper folded over his arm in a funny way. Nobody carries a newspaper that way. I got a glimpse of his gun just as he turned to throw down on me, and got off the first shot. You can see where his slug hit, in the plaster there."

"Why'd he wanna kill you?"

"Damned if I know. But he ain't the first one to try, of course."

"You know, I seen that fellow last night while I was making my rounds," Pudge said thoughtfully. "He was having a drink in the Gold Front Saloon. Noticed him because of that eye-patch and because I'd never seen him before. But it didn't occur to me he was a hired killer."

"If you go through some of the old wanted flyers in your office, I imagine you'll find his name on a few," Longarm said. "I wasn't looking for him, if that helps you any."

"If you wasn't on his trail, why'd he shoot you?"

"His gun was for hire," Longarm told Pudge. "My guess is that somebody paid him to come after me."

"You got any idea why?"

123

Longarm evaded answering the question. "Well, now, you know how it is, being a lawman yourself. Most anybody in our line of work's made a few enemies who'd pay to see us put six feet under."

"That's true enough," Pudge nodded. "And you say you never did see this man before?"

"If I had, it ain't likely I'd forget him, is it?"

"No, I suppose not." Pudge looked around, obviously at a loss what to do next.

Longarm said, "If you want to talk to me some more, or if Magruder's got any questions after you report to him, send word to me, and I'll drop in at your office. But if you ain't got anything else to talk about, I'll go sit down in the chair again. This lather's starting to pucker up on my face."

"I guess that's all there is to ask. Magruder might want to talk to you, though."

"If he does, he'll know where to fine me."

Longarm went back to the barber chair and sat down. Pudge stood looking at him for a moment, then shrugged and left. The barber got busy with a fresh hot towel, wiping off the old caked lather and finishing the shave. He didn't seem inclined to talk, and Longarm saw no reason to make conversation. The shave finished, he went upstairs to find Teddy Roosevelt.

Young Roosevelt was in the middle of the letter he was writing to his fiancée. Several sheets of paper covered with his sprawling script lay on the table in front of him, and he was in the middle of another page when Longarm arrived. He waved to an easy chair, capped the inkwell, and pushed the partly written letter aside.

"I wasn't expecting you to be finished this soon," he said. Then he saw the serious cast of Longarm's face and asked, "Has something new come up?"

"I guess you could call it new, Teddy." Longarm sat down and put his hat on the floor beside his chair. He took out a cheroot and lighted it. When the cigar was drawing satisfactorily, he announced, "I just had to kill a man in a gunfight downstairs."

For the first time since meeting him, Longarm found young Roosevelt at a loss for words. He stared unbelievingly at Longarm and listened open-mouthed to Longarm's brief account of the affair.

For a moment after Longarm had finished telling his story,

Teddy sat silent. Then he asked, "You're sure this one-eyed gunman who tried to kill you was the man Cord mentioned while you were listening to them talk in the cabin?"

"It isn't likely there'd be two men matching that description in a little town like this," Longarm replied.

"No. It must be the same man," Teddy agreed. "But how did he know where to find you? Alberts surely must've reported to Delaney that you were tied up out at that cabin."

"Likely he did. And likely somebody seen us ride into town, too. It could've been Alberts, for all we know, or even Delaney himself. We didn't try to sneak in here at the hotel, if you'll recall."

"Maybe that was a mistake."

"No. It'd've worked out the same, either way, in a place as small as Interior."

"And you think Delaney heard we had ridden into town, deduced that you'd escaped, and arranged for that gunman to kill you?"

"That's about the size of it. Cord told Delaney last night that this One-Eye Blake was in town looking for work. Said he'd run into Blake at the Gold Front saloon. And the deputy they call Pudge remarked he'd seen Blake in the saloon last night."

Roosevelt nodded. "It all hangs together."

"I'd say it's nailed down pretty tight. Magruder must've told Delaney he couldn't get hold of Cord or Blasson soon enough, and Delaney hired this other gunhand."

"Do you think he'll try again?"

"Oh, Delaney ain't giving up, Teddy. He just sent this One-Eye Blake after me because Blake was in town here and looking for a job. Next time it'll likely be Cord or Blasson or both of 'em. What bothers me is that he might send somebody after you next time."

"That's a risk I accepted when I asked you to let me go with you on this case, Longarm. I still accept it."

"Damn it, Teddy, I can't risk letting you get shot up on a job you're not even supposed to have anything to do with!"

"How much trouble would you be in if something happened to me?" Roosevelt asked.

"Now, you know that isn't what I'm thinking about! But how do you think I'd feel if something happened to you?"

"You wouldn't be to blame. I invited myself along. You

125

didn't ask me to help you. If I remember correctly, you didn't even like the idea at first. For all I know, you may not like it now. Is that why—"

"You know better'n that, Teddy. But here you are, a young man just setting out in life, maybe going to make a big name for yourself—it'd be a shame to have you hurt or killed trying to help me nab a cheap swindler!"

"Longarm, it's what I want to do. All my life I've been handled with kid gloves, first because of my asthma, then because my family's—well, not exactly rich, but comfortably fixed. Now I'm on my own, and I'm enjoying every minute of it. I'm learning things about people that Harvard never could teach me. No, I'm not going to quit—not unless you tell me to!"

"If that's the way you feel, we'll stay together till we bag Delaney."

"Do you think there's a chance we can do that?"

"Hell, Teddy, it depends on the way the cards fall. We'll just have to play what we get dealt out."

"Now that we've settled that matter again, what's our next move?" young Roosevelt asked.

"We'll see if we can tilt the odds against Delaney by getting that baroness lady to take a hand on our side. She was down in the lobby when Blake and me tangled. She's asked me to have supper with her this evening."

"Well, I hope you're a persuasive talker, Longarm."

"Oh, I imagine she'll come around, after she hears about all the dirty work that's part of the deal Delaney's trying to put over. If she doesn't, I'll just have to come up with something else. Now I'll go have that bath I've been putting off."

Promptly at seven-thirty, Longarm knocked on the door of the Baroness Sylvie deJoungh's suite. Since his travel wardrobe was limited, he'd done the best he could by putting on fresh underwear and a clean shirt after his bath. His longhorn mustache had been freshly brushed by the barber after his shave, and his sun-bronzed cheeks still exuded a faint trace of bay rum. He'd given his coat and trousers a good brushing and rubbed his boots to the highest polish possible, considering their age and condition. He'd also cleaned his derringer before reloading it, and checked the condition of his Colt.

126

A rosy-cheeked young maid opened the door. She wore a black ruffled skirt that reached just below her knees, a white blouse, and had a tiny ruffled cap perched atop her blonde hair. She bobbed a curtsey to Longarm and said, *"Bitte, mein herr,* come in, please, yes."

Doffing his hat, Longarm went in. He felt a tugging at the brim of his hat and his fingers tightened on it instinctively before he realized that the maid was trying to take it. He opened his hand and she placed the hat on a clothes tree, then motioned for him to follow her. She led him to the next room. In its center stood a table spread and set for two. Along one wall was a divan flanked by lounge chairs. The maid indicated the chairs. With another bobbing curtsey, she disappeared through a door across the room.

Longarm sat down, looking around the room and comparing it with his own somewhat bare accommodations. Candelabra as tall as he was stood on both sides of the room, each holding a dozen candles, providing soft light. Longarm's eyes went past them and then jerked back to look at them again when he realized that they had the unmistakable sheen of solid silver.

A huge tapestry covered one wall; the woven scene depicted an armored man mounted on an armored horse, being offered a wreath by a fleshy woman, who was nude except for a thin veil across one shoulder. A large oil painting dominated the opposite wall. It showed half a dozen sparsely draped women dancing around a figure—half-man, half-goat—who played on a reed pipe. Tall pier glasses with gilt frames stood on each side of the door opposite the sofa on which he was sitting.

He was still studying the painting when the door through which the maid had left opened and the baroness entered the room. She was wearing her blonde hair twisted high on the nape of her neck. Her gown was soft gray, with a full skirt that swirled around her legs and thighs as she moved and accentuated their curves. It was cut extremely low, plunging at the neck below the cleft of her full breasts. Her only jewelry was a triple strand of pearls which complemented the gown's color with their shimmering iridescence.

She came up to Longarm and extended her hand. Remembering his earlier mistake, Longarm held her hand for a moment while he bowed over it as he'd seen Teddy Roosevelt do, and released it.

"Marshal Long," the baroness said, "it is kind of you to join me. I have been waiting anxiously to hear from your own lips what occurred this afternoon."

"Well, it really wasn't much, Baroness," Longarm began.

She silenced him with a gesture. "Later, Marshal. Ilse has gone to tell the kitchen staff that we are ready to be served. But while we wait, we must have a small drink to sharpen our appetites, no?"

"Well, I never refuse a little swallow of Maryland rye before I sit down to supper."

"Maryland rye?" She frowned. "This is a liquor of one of your American provinces—no, no, you call them states here. A special liquor, yes?"

"I guess you'd call it that," Longarm replied. "But whatever you got handy is fine with me."

"*Schnapps*, perhaps, Marshal? Or vodka? Or some of your American bourbon whiskey, which I have just learned about?"

"I'll take whatever you're having, Baroness," Longarm said, realizing that there'd be no Maryland rye.

"Vodka, then," she decided, opening a cabinet beside the sofa and revealing an array of bottles and glasses. "And if we are to be friends, you must call me Sylvie."

"Why, I'll be proud to."

Sylvie was removing a bottle and tall, fragile fluted glasses from the cabinet. "Tony warned me I would not be able to buy vodka here, so I have brought good Russian vodka from home."

She bent to pour the drinks and the low-cut neck of her gown billowed out. Longarm got a glimpse of creamy breasts swaying gently as she moved. Stepping to the divan, she handed Longarm one of the glasses.

"Is it not your custom in America for friends to call one another by first names, without using titles?" she asked.

"Well, that's generally the way we do," he replied.

"Then I should not call you 'Marshal,' no? Tell me, what is your given name, Marshal?"

"It's Custis, but my friends don't call me by it much. They call me by a sort of nickname I picked up quite a while back. It's Longarm. And I'd be real pleased if you'd call me by it."

"So I shall, then." Sylvie raised her glass and held it out to him.

Longarm touched the rim of his glass to hers, watching to follow her example in drinking the clear liquor. He saw her drain her glass and courtesy demanded that Longarm empty his, too. The tall flute held three times as much as the liquor glasses to which he was accustomed, and the fiery vodka seared Longarm's gullet as he swallowed. He gulped as the draught went down his throat, and shook his head.

"Now, that's a real strong liquor," he told her, and added quickly, "but right good, Sylvie."

"Another, then," she said, taking his glass and refilling it as well as her own. "And we shall sit down and chat while we are waiting for our dinner to be served."

They settled on the sofa, a discreet distance between them. The baroness noticed the butt of Longarm's Colt in its cross-draw holster. "Do you wear a weapon wherever you go, Longarm?"

"Why, sure. There's still a lot of renegade Indians, and I guess about as many renegade white men, in this part of the country, and they don't leave their guns at home."

"It is still here as it was many years ago in Europe, I think," Sylvie said thoughtfully. "The days when knights in armor roamed the land to protect its people in the name of their king. But in my homeland there is no longer need for armed knights. The land is all taken, all settled."

"Well, there's a whole lot of land here that ain't. And I don't know too much about the old days where you come from, but I guess maybe you're right."

"Then should I be carrying a weapon, too, while I am here?"

"Not as long as you stay pretty close to places that are settled up. But you'd better know how to use a gun, if you're going to carry one."

"I have fired revolvers often enough." Sylvie shrugged. "But always at a target only. And never have I had a gun fired at me. Tell me, Longarm, is it a frightening thing to see a pistol pointed at oneself, and know the person holding it is ready to kill?"

"Well, it ain't a real comfortable feeling. But you can't take time to be scared when that happens. All you got time to think about is shooting first."

"If I am to go through with my plans and buy an estate here on which to raise cattle, I suppose I must learn to follow the customs." She frowned.

"That's what you're aiming to do?"

"Yes."

"Whatever gave you that idea, Sylvie?"

"It is something that was—" Sylvie broke off as the maid came in, followed by a small procession of tray-bearing waiters. "We will talk of this during dinner," she told Longarm. "But let us sit at the table now, for I'm sure you are hungry."

"Now that you mention it, I am, just a bit. I missed a meal or two lately, and ain't had a chance to catch up yet."

They had little to say during the first part of the meal. It began with a clear soup, followed by poached trout, and went on to rare roast beef awash in its own pink juices, with boiled potatoes and lima beans. Longarm did little more than pick at the fish, but he attacked the beef with relish.

When the waiters removed the dinner dishes and placed a platter of small cakes and a silver coffeepot on the table, the baroness told one of them, "You may bring a bottle of Maryland rye whiskey, now, and when you have cleared the table, you are dismissed. My maid will attend to any other service we might require."

After the waiters had gone, Ilse filled Longarm's coffee cup and placed some cakes on his plate. He pushed the plate aside and took one of his long slender cheroots from his pocket. He asked the baroness, "I don't guess you'll mind if I light up?"

"But, of course not," she said. "A cigar with coffee after dinner makes conversation much more enjoyable, and I must hear of your encounter with that man this afternoon."

She nodded to Ilse, who brought a silver humidor to the table and placed it in front of her mistress. Taking out a cigar even longer and thinner than Longarm's, Sylvie went on, "And while we sip our coffee and enjoy our cigars, Longarm, you shall teach me how to drink your Maryland rye whiskey. Who knows? Perhaps we shall find that we have even more tastes in common."

Chapter 14

Longarm flicked a match across his thumbnail and leaned forward to light Sylvie's cigar. He puffed his own into life and leaned back in his chair, cheroot in one hand, coffee cup in the other.

"You know, that wouldn't surprise me one bit," he said. "But there's one thing I been wondering about ever since you showed up here. What was it brought you all the way from Europe clear into Dakota Territory?"

"Curiosity," she replied, "and money."

"Both of them make folks do unlikely things. But those two words don't answer my question, Sylvie."

"Of course not. Very well, curiosity, first. I have read some books about your American West, and my reading excited me to learn of it first-hand."

"You said money came into it too, in some way."

"Oh, there is more." Sylvie beckoned to Ilse to open the bottle of whiskey, and went on, "I have a cousin, Longarm."

Ilse poured drinks for Longarm and Sylvie into brandy snifters. Sylvie brought the glass to her nose and inhaled the aroma of the liquor. She took a sip of the rye and nodded. "It is very good indeed, Longarm. Much more pungent than vodka."

"I'll settle for it any time," Longarm said. "But you started

131

to tell me how your cousin got you interested in coming up here to Dakota Territory."

"Yes, so I did. But let us sit on the divan."

Longarm followed her to the sofa and sat down beside her. Ilse placed a small table in front of them and put the bottle of rye and their glasses on it. Sylvie took another sip of the rye and puffed once more at her cigar.

"My cousin," she said, "Tony—Antoine de Valambrosa, Marquis de Mores—has a mind of great ingenuity, Longarm. He visited your country a year or so ago, and while he was travelling through the West he conceived an idea. It seemed to him wasteful that the raisers of cattle should ship large herds to distant slaughterhouses. Of this I really know very little, except from listening to Tony, but you will be familiar with what I am speaking of, I'm sure."

"Pretty much. Ranchers have what we call a roundup. They gather up bunches of steers and load 'em in cattle cars to go East to be slaughtered and butchered. That's how they've been doing it as long as I can recall."

"Yes. Tony's scheme is to build slaughterhouses here in the West, where the cattle are raised, and cut their meat up at once. He will then ship only the edible portions to be sold in the East. Does that seem a sensible plan?"

Longarm took a sip from his glass and puffed his cheroot thoughtfully before replying. "I don't see why not. He'd have to build ice-houses, and hire men to cut the ice when the rivers freeze in the winter, to keep the meat from spoiling in hot weather, but that wouldn't be so much of a job."

"Yes, he mentioned that ice would be needed." Sylvie sat in silence for a moment, then said, "I know little of such things, Longarm, but I have talked with several people about Tony's scheme, and they think it is practical. And Tony is sure that a great deal of money can be made by the raisers of cattle this way. Do you think so, too?"

"I'd be inclined to agree with your cousin, Sylvie. Any rancher you talk to will tell you that shipping cattle to market costs a lot of money."

Sylvie nodded with satisfaction and motioned for Ilse to refill their glasses. "Then I shall go ahead with my plan. I will sell some of the family land in Europe, where it earns nothing, and buy land here. On it, I will raise cattle, and Tony will buy them from me, and I will become very rich."

132

"If you don't mind my saying so, Sylvie, it appears to me like you ain't hurting none for money, the kind of style you travel in." Longarm waved his hand to indicate the silver candelabra, the tapestry, and the painting.

Sylvie shrugged and took another sip from her glass. "No matter how much money one has, Longarm, there is always need for more. And at home, land earns very, very little for a family such as ours."

"That's why this cousin of yours—Tony—is going to set up this cattle-slaughtering business over here, then?"

"Of course! Since he returned from a visit here two years ago, he has talked of nothing else." Sylvie drained her glass and motioned for Ilse to pour again for both her and Longarm, and while the maid was refilling the snifters said, "But I did not ask you here to talk of my affairs, Longarm. You were going to tell me why you fought the duel with the man in the lobby today."

Longarm decided that he'd be using bad tactics if he tried to persuade his hostess to continue discussing her dealings with Delaney. At this point, any effort he might make to show her Delaney's real nature could very easily backfire.

Accepting the change of subjects, he said, "You couldn't call that shooting downstairs a duel, Sylvie. Duelling's against the law in this country."

"Oh, it's against the law in most countries in Europe, but men still fight duels over there. Usually over a woman," she added.

"I guess you've had some fought over you. As pretty a lady as you are oughta have a lot of men running after her."

"Oh, some of my admirers have crossed swords because they were jealous, but none of them have been killed. You killed that man down in the hotel lobby."

"If I hadn't, he'd have killed me. But there really ain't a lot to tell you about it, Sylvie. I was getting shaved and saw him in the mirror sneaking up on me with a gun hidden under a newspaper. I pulled the trigger on my derringer before he could get his gun aimed, and that's about all."

"And you did not feel anything when you saw him fall? No *frisson* of pleasure at having rid yourself of an enemy?"

"I've killed enough men in my line of business so it don't have that much effect on me any more. I was glad it was me standing there looking down at him, instead of the other way around, but that's about the size of it."

Sylvie sipped from her glass, looking at Longarm over its rim, her blue eyes speculative. It was a look Longarm had seen in women's eyes before. He took a swallow from his own drink and waited, saying nothing.

"You must be a very strong man," Sylvie said at last, "to be so calm when you are in great danger." She leaned forward, her gown billowing out as she moved and giving Longarm another glimpse of her full white breasts. "I must find out for myself how strong you truly are. May I?"

Without waiting for Longarm's reply, she grasped his biceps in both hands and squeezed hard. Longarm could see the nipples budding pink from the creamy globes her low-cut gown now revealed. He accepted the invitation and began rubbing the tips with his finger.

Sylvie gasped and turned her body so that he could reach both breasts. She lifted her head, her bright lips parting. Longarm bent to kiss her and felt her tongue slide into his mouth. He felt the pressure of her hands on his biceps relax and in a moment he felt her hands on his thigh, moving toward his crotch. They held the kiss while her fingers roamed and pressed and while Longarm felt his erection beginning.

After long moments, Sylvie broke the kiss. Shrugging her shoulders, she let her low-cut gown fall away and arched her back, offering to Longarm's lips the pink nipples that jutted from her ivory skin.

Longarm passed his tongue over a nipple and felt her shuddering in his arms. Distantly and without understanding he heard her murmur something to Ilse.

Absorbed in caressing Sylvie's breasts, Longarm did not at first realize what was happening when he felt a tugging at his leg. When he felt one of his boots come off, he lifted his head and looked around. Ilse was kneeling in front of him, her hands on his other boot. She tugged it from his foot and dropped it beside the first one. Longarm tried to raise his head, but Sylvie locked her arms around his neck.

"It is quite all right," she said. "Let Ilse work while we enjoy."

Longarm was in no mood to argue. He felt hands—he did not look to see whose they were—unbuttoning his trousers and pulling them off, while other fingers worked at trying to unbuckle his gunbelt. He lifted his mouth from Sylvie's breasts.

"I'd better do that myself," he said, and got reluctantly to his feet.

He discovered that his vest, shirt, and balbriggans had been unbuttoned. He dropped his coat on the nearest chair and turned to place his vest and shirt on top of it. Soft hands touched his shoulders, and his balbriggans were pulled down to the floor in one swift tug. Longarm stepped out of the heaped-up undersuit and turned around.

Sylvie had not risen from the sofa. She was still sitting with her dress bunched around her waist. Ilse was standing in front of Longarm. Both were staring at his jutting erection.

Ilse reluctantly took her eyes away from Longarm and went to the baroness. Sylvie stood up and Ilse worked at the waist of her dress until she'd unfastened it. She lowered the garment and Sylvie stepped out of it. Longarm stared at her with admiration. In the soft candlelight Sylvie's flawless skin glowed with the richness of fresh cream. Her full breasts stood out proudly above a small waist and flat abdomen.

"Well?" Sylvie asked imperiously. "Are you going to stand there looking at me forever, Longarm?"

"I sure ain't! But you're about the prettiest woman I ever did see, and I had to make sure you're real."

"I have been asking myself the same question about you." Sylvie smiled, stepped up to him, and grasped his shaft. "We will go into the bedroom, no?"

Without releasing her grip on him, Sylvie led Longarm to the adjoining room. An oversized bed stood in the center, with tall pier glasses at each corner. Oil lamps burning in shaded wall sconces lighted the room brightly but not harshly. Sylvie released her grip on Longarm's shaft and rolled into the center of the bed, her body glowing against the white sheet. The maid had followed them into the bedroom and was positioning the mirrors according to Sylvie's signals. Longarm lay down beside Sylvie, bent over her, and began to caress her body. He started at the pink tip of one perfect breast and moved to the other after a few moments, then trailed his mouth down to her taut abdomen in a series of soft nibbles with his lips and slow, prolonged sweeps of his tongue. He had almost reacher her hips when Sylvie took his head between her hands and lifted it from her body.

"Later," she promised. "The time has not yet come for you to think of pleasing me. Later we will both enjoy the greatest

135

excitement and the greatest pleasure. Come, Longarm, lie here beside me again."

Longarm lay down beside Sylvie, wondering what her idea of pleasure might involve, and got his answer almost at once. Glancing up at the mirror across the bed he was startled to see the gleaming body of a second naked woman. For a moment he did not recognize Ilse without her uniform.

Ilse was shorter than Sylvie, and tended to plumpness. Her breasts were larger and fuller, but not as firm, and the rosettes in their centers were large and dark. She was moving unhurriedly to the bed, and Longarm's forehead puckered into a slight frown as he looked at Sylvie. She read the question in his eyes before it reached his lips.

"In Europe, we women have learned to prolong pleasure," she said. "When we are with a lover, we do not hurry. We wait until we have excited him properly, and are ourselves greatly excited. Lie quietly, and you will soon find out what I mean."

Ilse slid expertly between Longarm's legs and cradled his shaft between her fingers for a moment. Then she moved her hips down, tucked his tip into her cleft, and began to rock her hips gently. She did not allow him to penetrate her, but he could feel her warmth and wetness.

Sylvie took Longarm's chin and pressed her lips to his. Her tongue became a live thing within his mouth. His eyes caught a glimpse of motion in the mirror at the head of the bed, and he saw that, while Ilse continued to caress herself with his tip, her head had now moved between Sylvie's thighs.

Ilse's exquisitely gentle caresses combined with the thrusts of Sylvie's active tongue were bringing Longarm to the point of climax. He was so engrossed in the experience that he'd given no thought to holding back. Beside him, Sylvie was trembling gently, her darting tongue working furiously in his mouth. Now Ilse began tossing her hips in quick, jerking spasms, and allowed him to enter her shallowly. Sylvie began writhing furiously and moans formed in her throat as she climaxed. Longarm let go, jetting again and again.

Gradually, the spasms that shook the trio subsided. Ilse was the first to move. She left the bed swiftly and in a moment Longarm felt her soft hands on his shrinking shaft, then the warmth of a soft towel gently washing him. He lay still until she had finished and moved to minister to Sylvie. Then he

136

turned his eyes to the mirror at the foot of the bed.

When Ilse moved the towel away from her mistress's out-spread thighs, the sight of Sylvie sprawled and opened was an invitation Longarm could not resist.

He positioned himself quickly between her opened thighs and she guided him to her. She was very wet and with his first thrust Longarm slid into her full length. Sylvie cried out, a little scream of pleasure, and when Longarm drove in hard again she began shaking in a quick, small orgasm.

Longarm did not stop. He pounded into her again and again, thrusting deeply for a few moments, then raising his hips until he almost left her, forcing Sylvie to clasp her legs around him and pull herself up to keep him inside her.

He lost track of time, and forgot that Ilse still lay at the foot of the bed until he glanced away from Sylvie's pleasure-contorted face and saw the maid. Ilse lay on her side watching them while she caressed herself.

Longarm stroked on without interruption. He held himself back while he drove into Sylvie with long firm strokes, until she began whimpering with small throaty cries, and clasped her legs high around Longarm's waist, her hips rotating wildly.

He speeded up, going quickly into an orgasm, jetting in great spurts until he was totally drained and Sylvie gave a soft flow of contented whimpers as her body sagged in Longarm's embrace.

Longarm's legs were trembling. He pulled away from Sylvie and dropped beside her on the bed. Sylvie's hand reached out to fondle him, and Longarm's last sensation as he dropped off to sleep was of her warm soft fingers curling around his shaft.

Chapter 15

Teddy Roosevelt opened the door of his hotel room when Long-arm knocked and motioned for him to come in. Longarm crossed the room to the easy chair and sat down.

"I looked for you to stop by last night, after your dinner with the Baroness deJough, and tell me what you'd found out from her about Delaney's scheme," young Roosevelt said, taking a chair. "Did you manage to persuade the baroness that Delaney's a crook? Or make any progress in getting her to work with us?"

"Not last night, Teddy. But I did find out why she picked out Dakota Territory. Seems that a cousin of hers, some kind of nobleman, has come up with a scheme to build a slaughterhouse out here and buy cattle on the hoof, instead of shipping 'em East live for slaughter. He figures if all you ship is the cut-up meat it'll save ranchers a pot of money."

Roosevelt thought this over for a moment, then said, "It sounds like a good idea. I might want to buy some rangeland and try my hand at cattle ranching if that fellow goes through with his plan. But we were talking about the baroness and Delaney. When are you going to see her again?"

"Later on today." Longarm took a cheroot out and lighted it. "I got acquainted with her good enough last night so I know how to put our proposition to her, now."

"Do you think you can talk her into helping?"

"It ought not to be too big a job. From the way I got her figured out after talking to her last night, she's got pretty good sense when it comes to business. But right now, Teddy, if you're ready for breakfast, I've got a real big case of the hungries. There ain't a thing either one of us can do about Delaney unless Sylvie—the baroness, I mean—goes along with us on the scheme we worked out. I won't know which way she'll jump until I talk to her later on today. I'll knock on your door about suppertime and let you know what she's decided."

After having slept from the time he and Teddy finished breakfast until just before lunch, Longarm sat in his room and sipped from his bottle of Tom Moore until he judged the time was right for him to make an afternoon call on the baroness. Ilse opened the door when he knocked. She greeted him and ushered him into the suite with such casual, impersonal courtesy that Longarm wondered for a moment whether he'd only imagined the role she'd played in bed with himself and Sylvie the night before.

Sylvie was more cordial, though she gave no more evidence of having any recollection of the night than the maid had. "This is a pleasant surprise, Longarm," she said. "I did not expect you at this hour, but that's not important. Come, sit down."

"I guess I ought to've let you know before I came calling, but the fact is, I got some business to talk about with you," Longarm told her as he dropped his hat on the table and sat down beside Sylvie on the divan.

"Business?" she asked, her eyebrows arching in surprise.

"Official business."

"Goodness! Don't tell me I've broken some law of your country, and you've come to arrest me!" she said jokingly.

"You know better'n that, Sylvie. You ain't broken any laws, but the man you're into that land deal with has."

"Mr. Delaney?" Sylvie's eyebrows shot up again. "Are you sure, Longarm? He seems such a pleasant gentleman."

"That's the front he puts up. He's taken in a lot of people with that nice, helpful way he has. And right now he's working to take you in, too."

Sylvie was frowning now, impressed by Longarm's seriousness. She said, "Perhaps you'd better explain."

"That's what I came up here to do. To explain things and to ask you if you'll be willing to help me get the goods on him."

Choosing his words carefully, Longarm explained Delaney's method of operating his land swindle. Sylvie listened closely as Longarm told of forged and false deeds, murders, and the other crimes of which Delaney was guilty.

"But this is incredible!" she exclaimed when he'd finished. "How could Mr. Delaney have deceived so many people for such a long while?"

"He covered his tracks very well," Longarm replied. "Which is why I came calling on you today, Sylvie. You see, I know what Delaney's done, but right now I ain't got evidence that'll hold water if I was to arrest him and haul him up in front of a judge and jury. That's what I'm asking you to help me with."

"How can I help?"

"I'm hoping you'll see your way clear to tell Delaney you're ready to close a deal with him before he starts his gunmen out on a killing spree. If I got him pegged right, Delaney won't put off closing his deal with you just because he ain't had time to fix up all the deeds. He'll go ahead and take your money, figuring he can stall you for a while until he can deliver the papers. That'll give me grounds to arrest him, and once he's put away, I can bring in the rest of his gang without anybody else getting murdered."

"But what will happen to my plans if I do this, Longarm?"

"There's plenty of land you can buy from honest men, Sylvie. You'll still be able to go ahead after Delaney's put away."

For several minutes, Sylvie sat silent, her full lips pursed thoughtfully. At last she said, "Very well. I will do as you ask, Longarm. What do you wish me to do first?"

"Send word to Delaney right away that you've made up your mind to buy that land he's been trying to sell you. I guess you can handle the money part of the deal, can't you?"

"Of course. I have put downstairs in the hotel's safe a bank draft for a great number of your American dollars. But I would not want to risk losing it by—"

"Rest easy about that," Longarm broke in. "I'll see that you don't lose a penny. All you got to do, then, is send Delaney a note and tell him you want to close your deal right now."

"Today?"

"Sure. By tomorrow, Delaney might send his gunmen out to kill those people. I've got to move fast and stop him before he turns his gunhands loose."

Sylvie nodded. "Very well, I will send the note. Then what will you do?"

"I'll be waiting in the next room while you and Delaney close your deal. The minute he takes your money, I'll step out and arrest him, and keep him handcuffed down in my room until I can haul him off to jail in Bismark. Your part in the job ends the minute I put the handcuffs on Delaney."

"Will you be ready by four o'clock? Will that give you time to prepare your trap?"

"Four o'clock's fine, Sylvie. I'll be here half an hour or so before then, and get all set. I don't know how I can thank you enough for helping me."

Sylvie smiled. "I think you do know, Longarm. Tonight, we will see if I am correct."

Longarm inched closer to the bedroom door, which had been left a few inches ajar, when he heard Delaney's voice in the next room.

"You made up your mind a bit sooner than I'd expected you to, Baroness," he said. "Luckily, I'd already started my clerk to making up the deed to the land we discussed, so I didn't have to keep you waiting."

"That is good," Sylvie replied. "I'm sure I can trust you to have everything in order?"

"Of course! There are a few minor details that must be attended to before you can take possession, but those are merely formalities."

"Ah, so? You did not mention this before. What these details, Mr. Delaney?"

"Nothing of importance. A few squatters who are on some parts of the land. I will have them removed within a week."

"Squatters?" Longarm could almost see Sylvie's frown. "I am afraid that is a word I do not understand."

"Squatters are people who move onto land they do not own legally. Unfortunately, there are a lot of them here in Dakota Territory. But they will all be gone before you take possession, I promise you."

"You will guarantee this to me in writing, yes? I wish to

have everything in order when the attorney from our embassy arrives in a few days."

"Well," Delaney said hesitatingly, "if you want something in writing—"

"It does not need to be formal. Just a note written on the deed you will give me," Sylvie said. "Then I will give you this draft and you will give me your receipt, is it not so?"

"The balance of the payment—" Delaney began.

Sylvie interrupted him. "A draft from my bank in Vienna for the remaining amount will be here by the time the attorney from our embassy has completed his examination of the deeds and other papers."

"That will be perfectly satisfactory," Delaney said.

From his hiding place, Longarm could not see Delaney, but he could read the swindler's facial expression from the barely repressed eagerness that was in his voice. He could also imagine what was going through Delaney's mind: that if a hitch developed in his scheme, he could afford to sacrifice the balance due and make a getaway with the money he was about to receive.

Sylvie said, "If you will show me where I am to sign—"

"Here, and here, and here," Delaney told her.

There was a moment of silence, then Sylvie said, "Now, you must write your promise to remove from my land the— squatters, I think you called them?"

"Yes." Again there was silence and Longarm got ready to move. Then Delaney said to Sylvie, "There you are, Baroness. I think what I have written will be adequate."

"If you say so," Sylvie replied. "Here is your money, then, Mr. Delaney."

"Ah, yes. Very good. Now we—"

Delaney stopped short as Longarm swung open the bedroom door and entered the room.

"You're under arrest, Delaney!" Longarm snapped.

"Now, look here, you can't do this!" Delaney protested. "I an engaged in a perfectly legitimate transaction with Baroness deJoungh, and you have no grounds—"

"I got plenty of grounds," Longarm retorted. "Swindling with forged U. S. government deeds, for openers. Then there's a charge of bribing Federal Land Office people, but I don't guess that's so important, because the other charge is murder."

"Mur—" Delaney began, then quickly recovered at least

142

part of his composure and said angrily, "Oh, no, Marshal! You can't make a case on any of those charges, and you know it!"

"I wouldn't want to bet on it, was I in your shoes, Delaney," Longarm said calmly. "Now, I'll relieve you of the papers you've got there, especially that bank draft the baroness just gave you, so your hands will be free when I put the cuffs on you."

"Long, you know damned well you can't make this stick!" Delaney almost shouted as Longarm snapped the cuffs on him. "I'll be out of jail before you know it!"

"Well, it'll be interesting to see what happens, won't it?" Longarm remarked. "Now, Baroness, thank you for your help."

"All the thanks should come from me, Longarm," Sylvie said. "I am glad you told me in time what Mr. Delaney planned."

"I'll get your papers back to you in just a little while," Longarm promised. "Right now, I got to put this crook in a safe place until I can take him to a jail he can't buy his way out of."

Leading Delaney by the links that connected the handcuffs on his wrists, Longarm started for the door. He opened it with his free hand and sidled out, pulling Delaney with him.

Before he'd taken the second step that would put him into the hallway, Longarm felt the cold steel of a gun muzzle at the base of his skull.

Magruder's rough voice spoke inches from Longarm's ear. "Hold it right where you are, Long! This gun's cocked and it's got a hair trigger, so don't try making no moves. Now just go right back in where you come from, and we'll settle things up our way!"

Chapter 16

Sylvie was still sitting on the divan when Longarm and Delaney stepped back into the room. When she saw Magruder behind them, his revolver muzzle pressed to Longarm's head, she rose with a startled cry.

"Shut up, damn you!" Delaney commanded, his usually smooth voice rough-edged. "Long, let go of me! Magruder, if he tries to go for his gun, kill him!"

"That'd be a pleasure," Magruder said.

"Don't worry about me moving," Longarm told them, his voice calm. "I know when the odds are all the wrong way."

Longarm stood motionless while Delaney slid the Colt from its holster. The swindler held the gun in both hands, its muzzle inches from Longarm's chest. He said, "Take the key to these handcuffs out of whatever pocket you carry it in and unlock the cuffs, Long."

Moving with slow deliberation, Longarm reached into the side pocket of his coat and took out the key to the handcuffs.

"Unlock them!" Delaney commanded. Longarm obeyed. Delaney tucked Longarm's Colt into the waistband of his trousers and transferred the handcuffs to Longarm's wrists. He snapped them closed with vicious satisfaction, and said, "You can put your gun away now, Magruder."

"What about the woman?" Magruder asked.

"You've got handcuffs, too, haven't you? Put them on her."

While Magruder went over to the sofa and handcuffed Sylvie, Delaney grabbed the chain connecting the cuffs on Longarm's wrists and swung him roughly around. Then he forced him to step backward to one of the easy chairs beside the sofa. "Sit down, Long!" he commanded.

Longarm lowered himself into the chair. He looked at Sylvie and said, "I'm sorry about this. Just don't get all upset and do something foolish."

"That's good advice," Delaney said to Sylvie. "Take it!"

"I have no plans to do anything," Sylvie said calmly.

Still looking at Sylvie, Longarm went on, "It's my fault this happened. It didn't occur to me that Delaney might've put somebody on guard in the hall."

"That was my idea," Magruder said, turning to face Longarm after making sure the handcuffs on Sylvie's wrists were tight. "I remembered you was staying in the hotel, too, and I told Delaney he better have somebody on watch in the hall just in case you happened to pass by. How does it feel to be outsmarted, Long?"

"I ain't whipped yet, Magruder," Longarm replied confidently. "I don't give up till I die, and I sure ain't ready to do that yet."

"Magruder, will you shut up so we can get down to business?" Delaney broke in impatiently. "We've got to decide what to do with these two."

"Get rid of 'em," Magruder said curtly.

"Damn it, I know we can't afford to let them go. But what will we do with them until we can work out a way to get rid of them permanently?"

"Why, that ain't no problem at all," Magruder told Delaney. "Just turn 'em over to Cord and Blasson. They'll haul 'em up to the badlands and give 'em a dose of lead poison and hide their bodies. Nobody'll ever find out what happened to 'em."

"How will you get hold of Cord and Blasson?" Delaney asked. "I thought they were holed up out at their camp."

"Well, they ain't. They was going to take that old peddler's wagon, remember. Trouble was, it'd been setting so long that the big hind wheels dried out and the tires come loose. I took it to the smithy, and they're waiting till it's ready before they start back."

"Why didn't you tell me that sooner and save me hiring that one-eyed fool to try to get rid of Long yesterday?" Delaney demanded.

"Because you went ahead on your own without telling me what you was going to do! If you'd given the job to Cord and Blasson, Longarm'd be outa the way by now, and you wouldn't be in this mess!"

"I sent Alberts out to find you, and he couldn't!"

"I was catching up on my sleep over at Liz's parlor house!"

"All right, Magruder," Delaney said more calmly. "Never mind what's already been done. I've told you I didn't want those two hanging around town. It's too dangerous."

"Now, cool down, Delaney," Magruder said placatingly. "I got them two hid out in one of them shanties that some immigrant family walked off from a while back. They won't show their faces in town. As soon as the wagon's ready to roll, which'll be this evening, they'll head back to their hideout. Then they'll start out on that job you give 'em to do."

"That job might not be necessary," Delaney said thoughtfully. "If they get rid of Long and the woman, I'll just settle for the money she gave me when she signed the papers."

Delaney stepped over and pulled the lapel of Longarm's coat open and took out the deed and purchase agreement and bank draft that Longarm had taken from him earlier. He stuffed the papers into his own pocket and was turning away from the chair when the door to hall opened and Ilse came in.

She stood frozen in the doorway for a moment, her eyes growing wide at the sight of Sylvie and Longarm handcuffed and the two men standing over them.

Magruder had started for the door the instant Ilse opened it. He crossed the room in three big strides and before Ilse could say anything brought his pistol down on her head. Ilse sagged to the floor without a sound.

Sylvie started to scream, but choked it off in a smothered gasp when Magruder whirled, his revolver swinging up.

Moving faster than Longarm thought he could, Delaney was at Magruder's side in a flash, grabbing the town marshal's gun and forcing its muzzle to the floor.

"Damn it, no shooting!" Delaney rasped. "A shot from up here will bring everybody in this hotel running to see what's going on!"

"Get hold of your nerves, Delaney," Magruder advised.

"I wasn't going to shoot the bitch, I just wanted to shut her up!"

Delaney stepped to the doorway, dragged Ilse's form out of the way, and closed the door. He bent over Ilse, held her wrist for a moment, and straightened up. He faced Magruder, his face dark with anger. "You sure as hell shut this one up! I think she's dead."

"One body more or less ain't going to matter. She wasn't nothing but a servant. Nobody but that woman's going to miss her," Magruder rasped.

"I'm not thinking about that! We've got a body to get rid of! How'll we get it out of the hotel?"

"Leave that to me," Magruder replied. He holstered his revolver and taking hold of Ilse's wrists, dragged her into the bedroom and closed the door. He told Delaney, "Now it's all tidied up in here if anybody comes in after we've got Longarm and the woman out of the way."

"And how do we do that?" Delaney asked sarcastically.

"We wait till dark. That'll give me time to get Cord and Blasson and the wagon ready. Then they'll just drive up to the service stairs and we'll all go down to the wagon and Cord and Blasson will drive right out of town without nobody being the wiser. How does that strike you?"

"Not very favorably. There's too many holes in your plan, Magruder."

"Name a few!"

"That dead woman in the other room, for one. How're you going to get rid of the body?"

"I ain't," Magruder said promptly. "These two can walk down the back stairs, and if anybody sees 'em, which ain't likely late at night, nobody's going to notice in the dark that they got handcuffs and gags on 'em. Anybody's going to ask questions if they see a body being carried out, though."

"You can't just leave her here!"

"Why not? I'll stuff her under the bed. Nobody'll find her till it's too late to raise a fuss."

Delaney mulled this over for a moment and finally nodded. "I guess that's the best idea, after all. Go ahead and handle it that way."

"Any more holes?" Magruder asked sarcastically.

"Yes. That young fellow that's been hanging around with Long. He's going to ask questions when Long disappears."

"That little four-eyed dude couldn't give us no trouble. There ain't nobody but me he can ask any questions of, and if he starts getting nosy, I'll take care of him."

"I'm still not sure about using that wagon, but I guess it's the only way," Delaney said.

"Ah, shit, Delaney! Nobody's going to notice an old beat-up wagon standing down back of the hotel. And nobody'll stop Cord and Blasson when they leave, either. I'll be around to see to that."

Delaney shook his head. "Cord and Blasson are too damned careless to suit me. I want somebody I can depend on to go with those two."

"Like who?" Magruder asked suspiciously.

"Like you, damn it!"

Magruder stood scratching his chin for a moment, then said, "I guess I can work it out, Delaney."

"That's not the only job I want you to do, but I'll tell you the rest later. Now, let's get these two into that other room and tie them up. I've got business to take care of before it gets too late."

Under the threat of Magruder's gun, Longarm and Sylvie were forced into the bedroom. There Delaney held Longarm's Colt on them while the renegade town marshal ripped a pillowcase into strips and tied their feet, then made them stand quietly while he unlocked the handcuffs and replaced them after pulling their hands behind their backs. As a final precaution, he used the remaining strips of cloth from the pillowcase to gag them.

Longarm chafed inwardly at the indignity, and swore at himself silently for allowing Magruder to capture him, but he was too experienced in such situations to try anything with the odds hopelessly against him, and refused to give his captors the satisfaction of hearing him protest. He watched Magruder gag Sylvie, bind her legs, and then push her across the bed. When Magruder gave him the same treatment, he submitted without speaking. Lying face down on the mattress, he listened to the pair making their final plans.

"That oughta hold 'em," Magruder told Delaney as he stood back and inspected his work.

"You're sure it's safe to leave them here?" Delaney asked.

"Sure, I'm sure. They won't make no noise, and they won't have time to bust free before me and Blasson and Cord comes with the wagon to pick 'em up."

"When will that be?"

"I figure about ten o'clock tonight, after the dining room's closed down and the kitchen help's gone home. Nobody uses the back stairs after that."

"It's not quite six now," Delaney said. "Four hours is a long time to risk leaving them without somebody to guard them."

"Well, if it'll make you happier, I'll send either Blasson or Cord up here to stand watch."

"Good. Do that." Delaney paused, then warned the renegade town marshal, "I'm depending on you to do a clean job, you know."

"Don't worry. I will. Oh, what's that other job you said something about a while ago?"

"Blasson and Cord. Get rid of them after they've done their work tonight. We won't need them any longer now that we don't have a lot of work to do to finish up the deal with the deJoungh woman."

"You sure you want me to do that, Delaney? They're about the best we've had since we started this deal."

"I'm sure. They know too much. I wouldn't want them to get caught and start talking."

"Sounds to me like you're getting ready to close up shop here in Interior," Magruder said suspiciously.

"Not at all. I'm just taking no risks. There might be a big stir raised when the baroness and Long disappear. If there is, I want to be ready to get out in a hurry. You'd better be thinking about that, too."

"That's one reason I like to work with you, Delaney. You're always a jump or two ahead of everybody."

"It's the best way I've found to keep from getting caught. Now, we'd better get out of here. I've got some things to look after, and you'll be busy getting ready for tonight." Delaney paused, then said, "Here. You'd better take Long's gun. I've got no use for it."

"It's a good gun. I'll hang onto it." Magruder chuckled and added, "Even if it wasn't a good Colt, I'd keep it for a souvenir."

"Keep it or get rid of it, whatever you like," Delaney said impatiently. "Now we're through. Let's get out of here."

Longarm heard the door from the adjoining room into the hall close, and a key grated in the lock. Then everything was still. Even though he was sure the chance was slim that either Magruder or Delaney would return soon, Longarm waited for

149

several minutes before trying to move. His efforts were clumsy, for when he tried to shift his position on the bed the way in which his legs were bound together forced his body off balance, and when he tried to turn over the handcuffs bit into his wrists.

Beside him, Sylvie was having the same trouble moving. They both struggled for a few minutes, then gave up. Then, almost as though they had been able to communicate, they turned their heads to face one another.

Longarm tried to speak, but the gag was drawn between his teeth, and all he could manage was an unintelligible gurgling in his throat. He heard Sylvie making a similar sound, and knew that for her, too, speech was impossible. Sylvie shook her head, her eyes showing her discouragement. Longarm could do nothing but shake his head in reply.

Abandoning the struggle, Longarm relaxed and lay still. He was racking his brain to think of a way by which he could help Sylvie, or she could help him, to loosen the strips of cloth that kept them virtually motionless, when a low moaning broke the silence of the darkened room. Longarm grew tense again, and beside him Sylvie stirred. A second groan followed the first.

This time Longarm located the source of the sound. It came from under the bed. With rising hope, he realized that Ilse had not been killed by Magruder's blow, and that in their haste to leave, Magruder and Delaney had neglected to check on the maid's condition.

A scuffling sounded from below the bed, and by bending his head, Longarm could see Ilse rising to her feet. The maid stood up, swaying unsteadily. Then she saw Longarm and Sylvie lying helplessly across the bed. A hoarse cry burst from her throat.

Ilse pawed at the handcuffs for a futile moment, but when Sylvie began shaking her head violently, the maid gave up her efforts to remove the cuffs and untied Sylvie's gag and then Longarm's.

Longarm tried to speak, but his throat froze momentarily. Then he managed to say, "Tell the girl to quit trying to get us loose, Sylvie. Remember, one of the gunmen's on his way up here now to stand guard."

"But, how will we—" Sylvie began.

Longarm cut her short. "There ain't enough to talk about it now. Just tell her to quit trying to get us loose."

Sylvie relayed Longarm's instructions to Ilse in a quick

burst of German. The maid stopped and looked at Sylvie, her face showing how puzzled she was.

Longarm said, "Now, listen carefully, Sylvie, and tell Ilse what I want her to do, because time's running short. I want her to put the gags back on us. Then, tell her to get under the bed again and play dead till everybody's out of the way in here. When the coast is clear, have her go to Room 211 and tell Teddy Roosevelt that Magruder and Blasson and Cord are taking us on the trail up to the badlands in a peddler's cart. He'll know what to do when he hears about it."

Sylvie began, "But Longarm, I don't understand why—"

Again, Longarm interrupted her. "I got my reasons, Sylvie, and there ain't time to tell you all of my plan. Now go on. Tell Ilse what she's got to do."

Sylvie did not protest any more, but relayed Longarm's orders to Ilse. The maid did not interrupt, but stood listening, a frown growing on her face. When Sylvie had finished speaking, she turned back to Longarm.

"I've told her just what you said. Now what is she to do?"

"Get the gags tied around our mouths again, then get back under the bed and lie still. One of those fellows is going to open that outside door any minute now."

Longarm's warning proved to be correct. Ilse had finished replacing his gag and was just tying the last knot in Sylvie's when a key rattled in the door of the adjoining room and heavy footsteps thudded across the carpet. Ilse pulled the knot tight and scrambled under the bed only seconds before Blasson came into the bedroom. The gunman stood in the doorway, peering through the darkness, and in a moment a match flared to light the room.

"Well, I guess you decided you'd best wait, after all," he said to Longarm and Sylvie as he took a quick look at their bonds.

Blasson held the match until it had burned down to his fingertips before going back into the other room. In a moment, Longarm heard the clinking of glass as the gunman investigated the bottles of liquor that stood on the table there. A moment of silence followed, then a long exhalation of satisfaction broke the stillness of the room. Longarm would have grinned with satisfaction if his lips had not been immobilized by the gag.

Longarm lost track of time before Magruder and Cord arrived. In spite of his discomfort, he came close to dropping off to sleep more than once. Sylvie had stopped tossing restlessly soon after Ilse scurried back under the bed, and he was sure that she was sleeping. He sighed silently behind the gag when he heard a soft knock on the door of the adjoining room, and a few moments later heard Magruder asking Blasson if he'd had any trouble.

"Not a peep outa either one of 'em," Blasson replied. "But where in hell's Cord?"

"Waiting in the wagon down at the back door. You and me can handle Long and the woman without no trouble."

"It sure took you long enough to get here."

"I told you not to look for us till a little after ten," Magruder said. "The hotel's settling down now. There ought not to be anybody using them back stairs, with the dining room closed. Come on, let's get moving."

Longarm managed to bring his bound feet up to push on Sylvie's and wake her up before the two men came into the room.

Magruder stood looking at them for a moment. The light streaming through the door threw his face into deep shadow, but the gloating satisfaction in his voice told Longarm all he needed to know.

"All right, Long," Magruder said. "It's time for you and the woman to move." He turned to call Blasson, who still had not come into the bedroom. "What in hell's holding you up? These two can't walk. We got to get 'em on their feet and let 'em loosen up a minute before we tackle them stairs."

Blasson came in then. "Just say what you want me to do, Magruder. I can't read your damn mind, you know."

"Cut their feet loose," Magruder said. "They oughta be able to walk as far as the next room, and we'll finish getting 'em ready to move in there."

Longarm felt Blasson's knife sawing through the cloth strips that had been tied around his ankles. While the gunman was freeing Sylvie's feet, Longarm stood up and started toward Magruder. His steps were careful, and he moved slowly. Magruder backed through the door as Longarm approached him. He stopped just past the center of the room. Longarm noticed that it was his own Colt Magruder held pointed at him.

"That's far enough, Long," he said. "Stand still now, till the woman gets in here."

Sylvie limped in, supported by Blasson's arm.

Magruder went on, "Now, you two listen to me. You're going to walk downstairs and get into the wagon. Nobody's gonna ask no questions if they see me taking a couple of handcuffed prisoners outa here. They'll just think I arrested you. But I ain't going to risk having somebody see you with them gags on, so we'll take 'em off before we start and put the cuffs on with your arms in front so they'll be in plain sight. But don't you get ideas, Long. I'll be right behind you with a gun in my hand, and if you yell or try any other kind of tricks, you'll be shot trying to escape. Now, have both of you got all that clear?"

Longarm nodded. Sylvie, watching him, did so, too.

"All right, Blasson," Magruder ordered. "Take them gags off while I dig out the handcuff keys."

Longarm said quietly, "You're making the same mistake I did a while back, Magruder. You're figuring the odds wrong, and it's going to finish you up."

"That's a chance we'll have to take, ain't it, Long?" the renegade marshal snapped. "Now, turn around and don't do nothing foolish while I switch them handcuffs. Then just walk quiet down the stairs and get in the wagon. You been giving us a lot of trouble, but that's over now. You're starting out on a ride that you won't come back from!"

Chapter 17

Longarm waited until Magruder had released the handcuffs and moved in front of him to replace them. As he brought his arms around and held them out for the shackles, Longarm reminded the renegade lawman, "You'd do well to keep in mind what Delaney said a while ago."

"Delaney says a lot of things. I don't recall him saying anything special."

"Maybe you wasn't listening when he told you there'd likely be a big stir when Baroness deJough turns up missing. Now, I ain't real important. When I don't report in, about all that'll happen is they'll send another Federal marshal or two up here to find out why. But if something happens to the baroness, there's going to be a regular army come swarming up here looking for her, and they'll stay on the case until they collar your whole bunch."

"I don't scare all that easy, Long," Magruder snapped. He stepped over to where Sylvie stood in front of Blasson and began to switch her handcuffs so that she could hold her arms naturally in front of her body.

Longarm saw that Magruder was in no mood to listen. He said to Blasson, "Long as you ain't doing nothing else, Blasson, you might oblige me by handing me my hat. It's on the table

154

there, next to them liquor bottles."

"Hell, you won't need a hat where you're going," the gun-hand grinned. "But I'll oblige you, just the same." He picked up the hat from the table and handed it to Longarm, who adjusted it at the angle he favored.

Magruder said, "All right, we're ready to go, Blasson. Now let's be smart when we start down them narrow stairs. Put the woman in front and Long next to her. We'll both walk in back."

"What the hell difference does it make?" Blasson growled impatiently.

"You'd look like a spavined jackass if Long shoved the woman into you and jumped me while you was tumbling down ass over appetite!" Magruder said. "Now, do things the way I tell you to! Walk in back of me! And be sure to lock the door when you leave the room."

Grumbling, Blasson stepped aside and let Magruder follow immediately behind Sylvie and Longarm. They made their way quietly down the silent hall to the back stairway.

Longarm was glad that his plan hadn't included an effort to break away from Magruder and Blasson while they were going down the stairs. He was disappointed, though, when his hope to exchange a few words with Sylvie dissolved. As Magruder had predicted, they met no one, and on the way down Magruder and Blasson carried their guns in their hands.

When they emerged from the hotel, he saw that Cord had pulled the canvas-topped wagon as close as possible to the back door, ready for Longarm and Sylvie to climb in the instant they reached the bottom of the stairs.

"You get in back and ride with 'em, Blasson," Magruder ordered after Longarm and Sylvie were inside. "I'll ride up front with Cord."

"Sure." Blasson had holstered his pistol and was tugging at the hip pockets of his trousers. "Just give me a minute."

"What in hell are you doing?" Magruder asked.

Blasson brought his hands to the front. A bottle was in each hand. Longarm was pleased. He'd judged Blasson's character right when he indirectly called the liquor to the gunman's attention by asking for his hat.

Displaying the bottles proudly, Blasson said, "I grabbed these upstairs before we left. They were just sitting there, and I figured we had more right to 'em than some clerk or maid."

"Now, that's what I call real thoughtful, Blasson," Cord

155

said, "seeing how Magruder kept us holed up all day in that damn shack without a chance to wet our whistles. It oughta be pretty fair liquor if that rich foreign woman bought it."

"There's a real good whiskey in one of these bottles, what's left of it," Blasson told his partner. "I ain't so sure about the other one. It looks like plain water, but it sure ain't gin. It's got a kick that'll damn near jar your back teeth loose."

Magruder said angrily, "Let's get this wagon moving! What if somebody was to come out of the hotel right now?"

"Hold your water, Magruder," Cord retorted. "We're ready to roll soon as Blasson gets in."

Blasson closed and latched the tailgate and jumped over it into the wagonbed. He called, "Whip 'em up, Cord! I'm in."

Moving silently on freshly greased axles, the wagon pulled out onto the short street that ran in front of the Railroad Hotel. It crossed the main street and left behind the few dark houses that faced the side street. The flat center of the saucer in which the town stood was soon traversed, and the wagon shafts creaked gently as the two-horse team started up the long slope that led to the trail which ended at the badlands.

Looking back through the oval opening of the canvas cover, Longarm could see the few lights that remained aglow in Interior. He shifted his position slightly to peer ahead, and between the bulking shoulders of Cord and Magruder, he saw the bright orange rim of the full moon rising on the horizon at the top of the long slope. The moon shed no real light as yet. It would not shine at its brightest until it rose halfway to its zenith. The landscape around them was totally veiled.

Longarm waited until the town's lights were all but invisible pinpricks in the velvet downslope blackness. Then he said quietly, "I guess you wouldn't mind if I light up a cigar, would you, Magruder? I ain't had a smoke for quite a spell."

Magruder made no reply for a moment. Then he said, "I don't expect that'd hurt us none. Blasson, you push your pistol right into Long's ear while he's lighting up. Not that I expect he could pull much on us. I got his pistol stuck in my belt, and he's got handcuffs on. But it don't hurt none to be careful when you're handling a tricky son of a bitch like him."

Longarm and Sylvie were sitting on opposite sides of the wagonbed, facing one another, and Blasson was in the back, lounging against the tailgate. He hunched forward when Magruder spoke, drew his revolver, and shoved the muzzle against

Longarm's jaw. Moving his hands slowly and carefully, Longarm took out a cheroot and puffed it alight. In the darkness of the wagon's interior the red coal of the lighted cigar glowed like a small lantern. His eyes adjusted quickly to the light, and Longarm could see Sylvie's face clearly. He glanced back at Blasson; the gunman's head was thrown back, one of the bottles he'd brought from Sylvie's suite tilted up to his lips.

"Now, that ain't polite, Blasson," Longarm said loudly. "Taking a drink by yourself without passing the bottle around."

"Damn it, Blasson!" Cord said over his shoulder. "Don't you go hogging both of them bottles! Pass one of 'em up here so me and Magruder can have a drink, too!"

"Now, wait a minute, boys!" Magruder protested. "Let's wait till we get where we're going, and do our drinking after we finish up our job!"

Cord snorted. "Quit being so damned bossy, Magruder! We ain't going to get drunk on you!"

"If it comes to that, I'd like a little swallow of that whiskey myself," Longarm put in.

"You might like one, but you ain't going to get one," Magruder said quickly. He told Blasson, "All right, I guess a drink or two won't hurt us. Pass one of them bottles up here."

Blasson started to give the bottle to Longarm, thought better of it, and handed it to Sylvie. She surprised everyone, including Longarm, by pulling the cork and taking a swallow from the bottle before anyone could stop her. Magruder had turned around in his seat and was looking at her with his jaw hanging open.

Sylvie said tartly, "This is my vodka! I have paid for it! It is right that I have one drink from it, yes?"

Magruder's open mouth folded into a grin. "I guess you got a right, at that. I like your spunk!"

Sylvie took another drink before handing Magruder the bottle. He sniffed at the neck, and said, "This don't smell like any whiskey I ever run across."

"It is not whiskey," Sylvie said. "It is vodka."

"Well, it don't smell like much of anything, but I'll take a chance on it," he said. "Here goes!"

Magruder tilted the bottle and gulped. He swallowed once and was starting a second swallow, but cut it short. He lowered the bottle, coughing and snorting.

"Godamighty!" he wheezed. "I don't know what they make

this stuff out of, but it's damn near taking the hide off the inside of my mouth!"

"Ah, you just ain't used to a real man's drink!" Cord said. "Here, hand me that stuff."

Cord managed two swallows before he lowered the bottle and began snorting and wheezing. Like Magruder, he was used to the bar whiskey served in saloons. The powerful vodka Sylvie had brought from Europe cut like a blowtorch into the mucous membranes of anyone unaccustomed to it.

His voice a hoarse, strained whisper, Cord said, "That stuff ain't got much flavor, but it sure as hell's got a bite!"

Sylvie giggled, and Blasson guffawed.

Stung by Sylvie's amusement, Cord said, "If it didn't make that female gag, it ain't going to gag me!" He put the bottle to his lips and drank again. This time he took smaller swallows, but his breath again whistled in his seared throat when he brought the bottle down.

Turning in his seat, Cord told Blasson, "Pass me that bottle of real liquor quick! I got to have me a chaser!"

Blasson handed Cord the bottle of whiskey, and Cord took a drink. He sat silently for a moment, then said to Magruder, "Now, that stuff ain't half bad, when you chase it with whiskey. Matter of fact, it tastes pretty good. Here, Magruder, see if I ain't right."

"I don't know—" Magruder began.

Sylvie giggled again, but Blasson remained silent. Magruder would not let Sylvie see him outdone by Cord. He grabbed both bottles, took a swig of the vodka followed by a gulp of the whiskey, and exhaled gustily. In a choked voice, he said, "Damned if you ain't right, Cord. It tastes pretty good that way."

"Hell, if it's all that good, maybe I better have a go at it," Blasson said. "Don't forget, it was me brought them two bottles along."

"Do not forget it was I who paid for them," Sylvie said tartly. "If drinking there is to be, I wish to share it."

Longarm spoke up. "I sure wouldn't want to be left out."

"Ah, hell," Cord said, "It won't do no harm to let 'em have a drink apiece, Magruder. Likely it'll be the last one they're ever going to get."

"I suppose," Magruder replied after a moment of thought. He handed the bottles across the back of the seat to Sylvie.

She took them, passed the whiskey to Longarm, and drank from the vodka bottle herself. Blasson grabbed for the bottles before either of them could take a second drink.

"One drink, Magruder said," he told them. "These bottles are all we're going to see for a spell, and there ain't no use wasting good liquor on you two."

Longarm glanced at his stogie and saw that he'd smoked about two-thirds of it. Without asking permission, he slipped a fresh one from his pocket and lighted it from the first. Then he swivelled his shoulders around until he could shove the short butt of the first cigar through the gap between the canvas top and the wagonbed and let it fall to the ground.

They rode along in silence for a mile or so, then Cord called to Blasson, "Damn it, I told you not to hog that liquor! Hand it up here again."

Blasson scrambled forward and handed the bottles up. Longarm snaked still another cheroot out of his pocket and, as before, lighted it from the butt of the one he then discarded by slipping it between the cover and the side of the wagon.

After a few minutes, Longarm glanced at Blasson out of the corner of his eye. The gunman was watching Cord and Magruder as they passed the liquor bottles from hand to hand. Longarm held the freshly lighted cigar up to his face, a few inches from his lips, with its glowing tip pointed upward. He pursed his lips and blew across the red coal, trying to attract Sylvie's attention. He had to blow three times before she looked his way.

Longarm held the tip of the cigar close to his face while with his lips he silently formed the words, "Play along." He watched Sylvie closely, but she gave no sign that she'd understood. He tried again. This time Sylvie's eyes widened questioningly, but she nodded. With a silent sigh of relief, Longarm lowered the cigar.

He was surprised that his plan was working so well, and working almost by accident, with only an occasional nudge from him. The scheme had burst into his mind virtually full-blown, and he'd been wishing since it took shape that he had some way of telling Sylvie about it. But since their gags had been removed there had been no chance to talk to her without Magruder and the gunmen overhearing.

Old son, you just got to go into this deal with your fingers crossed and with a lot of luck on your side, he told himself as the wagon rolled steadily ahead. *But that Sylvie's a pretty smart woman. She'll likely catch on, once you start the rest of your scheme working.*

Glancing back, Longarm could no longer see any of the pinpoints of light that had marked Interior. The moon had risen by now, turning to a bright disc of silver as it climbed the sky, and the occasional clumps of sparse growth that he remembered as having begun near the top of the saucer's slope stood out black against the bare soil around them.

"Hey," Blasson called from the back of the wagon, "it's you two that're hogging them bottles now! How about me having a little swallow?"

"There's still plenty left," Magruder told him, turning to pass the bottles back.

Blasson crawled forward the short distance necessary for him to grab them. Longarm chose that moment to change position, and just as Blasson was stretching out, brought one leg up the few inches necessary to send him toppling onto Sylvie. Her hands went out, grabbing at Blasson's waist. Then, as though the handcuffs forced their movement, she brought them downward to the sprawled gunman's crotch. She lifted her hips against Blasson as though trying to throw him off, and Blasson scrambled back to a kneeling position.

"That was my fault, Blasson, and I'm sorry," Longarm said quickly. "My foot was asleep, and I didn't see it was under you till after I'd moved."

"That's all right," Blasson said. "Man ain't to blame for a little accident."

He fell back to the tailgate and drank from each of the bottles in turn, using the whiskey as a chaser for the vodka. Neither Magruder nor Cord appeared to have noticed the incident.

Impatient to go to the next step of his plan, Longarm willed himself to wait. He knew he must bide his time until Magruder and the gunmen had dulled their caution and their reactions with the liquor.

Longarm sat quietly while he finished the third cheroot he'd smoked since the trip started. He lighted another from the butt before sliding it out of the wagon.

When Cord called for the liquor again, Longarm decided that he'd given the potent vodka plenty of time. He waited until Blasson had returned the bottles to the men in the seat and they'd had their drinks before saying, "I don't know about anybody else—and I got to apologize to the lady for saying so—but my teeth's floating. How about stopping for a minute, Magruder?"

Before Magruder could answer, Blasson spoke up. "He's got a good idea, Magruder. I could stand to find me a bush, too."

"Sure, let's stop," Cord said. "It'll do us all good."

Her voice plaintive, Sylvie said, "I would like to go off to myself a moment, too, if you will stop."

"All right," Magruder agreed. "We still got quite a ways to go, and I guess we better pull up now so we'll be comfortable. We don't need no bushes, dark as it is. Go on, Cord. Pull up whenever you feel like it."

Longarm suddenly doubted that his plan was working as he'd foreseen. None of the three men sounded as though they'd reached the stage he'd expected them to. They'd all had several drinks, but their voices showed none of the fuzziness or hesitation he'd been hoping for. The only change he'd noticed in their behavior was that they'd eased up a bit in their treatment of him and Sylvie. He had no time to waste in nursing his disappointment, though, for Cord was already reining in the team.

Magruder and Cord leaped out of the wagon, one on each side, and were on the ground while Blasson was still pulling the catches to drop the tailgate. They pair moved to the rear of the wagon and stood waiting. Blasson slid out and joined them.

In the darkness of the wagon, Longarm put a hand on Sylvie's arm as she started to crawl out. He whispered, "If you want to try saving our lives, play up to them three."

She nodded quickly.

Longarm risked another few seconds' delay to tell her, "I got a two-shot derringer. All I need's a few seconds when they ain't looking at me, and I can get two of 'em."

"What about the other one?"

"I'll think of something. Play up to 'em all you can."

Outside the wagon, standing at the tailgate, Magruder was saying to the other two men, "Here's what we better do. Cord, you and Blasson take Long off that way a piece. I want one of you to keep an eye on him every minute. I'll stay here with the woman."

Sylvie, emerging from the wagon, said angrily, "Do you intend to watch me while I pull up my skirts?"

"Listen, it's too dark for me to see anything," Magruder told her. "Anyhow, this ain't no tea party. Woman or not, if you got to go bad enough, you'll go. Now, make up your mind."

Sylvie hesitated for a moment and replied, "Very well. But you will please allow me to stay beside the wagon, where I can be in the shadow, yes?"

"I don't care where you go, as long as you get on with it." Magruder turned to Cord and Blasson and snapped, "Damn it, go on with Long! We don't wanna stay here all night!"

Cord grasped one of Longarm's biceps, Blasson the other, and they marched him a few paces away from the wagon. Longarm's earlier disappointment lessened as they walked. It seemed to him that their feet moved a little less certainly than they had when they'd boarded the wagon, and their grip on his arms was looser than it might be.

"All right, start pissing," Cord said when they stopped.

Longarm took his time. When he could force no more urine to flow, Blasson said, "I better go next, Cord, or I'll bust."

"Go ahead. I can wait."

Longarm said, in a casually innocent voice, "I bet Magruder is getting an eyeful about now."

Blasson turned his head long enough to say, "That woman is some looker. I wish it was me watching her pull up her skirts instead of Magruder."

"Ah, when you seen one woman, you seen 'em all," Cord growled.

"That ain't what I've noticed," Longarm said. "There's some of 'em I wouldn't care to look at twice. But this baroness woman, I bet she's got a pretty ass."

While he and Cord were changing positions, Blasson said, "You know, I think she's gone sweet on me. When I slipped and fell into her in the wagon a while ago, I'd swear she was trying to feel of my peter."

"Ah, hell, Blasson! You're dreaming!" Cord snorted.

"Damned if I am! She sure was feeling me. And I got a little rub in on her titties while I was sprawled all over her. They felt real nice, big and soft."

"You know," Cord said thoughtfully as they started back, "I don't see any reason why we all don't take a crack at her while we're stopped. She sure as hell ain't going to be around to tell nobody about it tomorrow."

"Now, wait a minute!" Longarm objected. "You can't do that to a real lady from Europe that's damn near a queen in her own right."

"I never heard that queens is built no different from any other kind of women," Cord said.

"Anyhow," Blasson chimed in, "you got nothing to say about it, Long. If you start acting up, we'll just take care of you first and do what we want with her."

Longarm played the ace he'd been holding back. "You're just talking, Blasson. Magruder wouldn't let you, even if you and Cord is two to his one."

"Don't be so sure!" Cord said. "By God, Blasson! I say we put it up to Magruder! Hell, he'd be getting his share too, just like us!"

"I'm game if you are," Blasson agreed. "We'll get him where the woman can't hear what we're saying and tell him what we got in mind!"

Longarm decided that in their present mood it was safe to prod the two a bit. "Like I just told you, Magruder's going to say no," he said.

"Damn it, we'll see about that!" Cord snarled. "Come on, Long! Step up! Hell, I'm already getting a hard-on just thinking about that piece of foreign tail!"

As they hurried back toward the wagon, Longarm suppressed the smile that kept trying to form on his face. His scheme was working. Now its success depended on Sylvie playing her part. And Longarm had no doubt that she would be able to do that without any trouble at all.

Chapter 18

Magruder was standing by himself a short distance from the tailgate of the wagon when Cord and Blasson led Longarm back to the rig. Sylvie was nowhere in sight.

"Where's the woman?" Cord asked.

"In the wagon," Magruder replied. "Come on, get Long in there, too, so we can start out. It ain't getting no earlier, and we got a ways to go yet."

"A few minutes more ain't going to make much difference," Cord said. "Me and Blasson wanna talk to you, Magruder." Cord turned to Longarm. "Go on and get in the wagon, Long. And keep your mouth shut, if you know what's good for you."

"What the hell's going on?" Magruder asked.

"Like Cord said, we wanna talk to you private," Blasson told him.

"Damn it, you two bastards must be drunk," Magruder said, "I ain't letting Long and the woman stay here by theirselves!"

"We ain't any drunker than you are," Cord retorted. "Anyhow, we'll be close enough to keep an eye on 'em. Come on, we'll just step a few feet away so we can talk."

"All right," Magruder said grudgingly.

Crawling into the wagon, Longarm sat down beside Sylvie and watched while Magruder, Cord and Blasson walked a few paces away.

Sylvie said, "They plan to rape me, yes?"

Without taking his eyes off the trio, Longarm replied, "That's the idea."

"You gave them the idea, Longarm? It was in my mind, too, as a way to divert them."

"I thought it might be. I don't plan to give 'em time to do no real raping, in case that's bothering you."

"How will you stop them?"

"It'll be up to you to put on a show for 'em and get their minds off me for a minute or so—long enough for me to get to my derringer."

"I have not known men like these before," Sylvie said thoughtfully. "But if they are all like Magruder, distracting them will not be hard. I have already given him a small show."

"I figured you'd be able to handle it. They're a little bit drunk, but not drunk enough so they'll get real careless."

"How careless will they have to be? And for how long?"

"Careless enough to watch you instead of me. And all the time I need is about five seconds."

She frowned. "I will think quickly of how best to do this."

"Just don't let 'em get you very far from wherever they put me. That derringer only shoots true up to about twenty feet."

"They are coming back, Longarm," Sylvie warned. "Do you think they will begin at once?"

"I figure they'll pull off the trail first."

"I will be ready whenever they start," she promised.

By now Magruder, Cord, and Blasson were close enough to the wagon for Longarm and Sylvie to hear their conversation. Magruder was saying, "Like to never got her skirt down, and after I seen that pretty white ass I begun getting the same idea. But we better pull ahead a ways and find a place off the trail."

"Just don't take too long to find it," Blasson said.

"Leave it to me," Cord volunteered. "I know just the spot, not more'n a mile ahead."

"That'll be just about long enough for us to have another drink," Blasson said. "Who's got the liquor?"

"It's up front," Magruder said. "There ain't much whiskey left, but there's plenty of that vodka stuff."

"Well, you two help yourselves, then pass the bottles back," Blasson told them.

Magruder drank and passed the bottles to Cord, who took a swig of vodka and washed it down with the whiskey, then turned to hand the bottles back to Blasson. Longarm decided he'd better stir their captors up a bit to keep them from thinking too far in advance.

"What're you talking about stopping up ahead for?" he asked.

Magruder answered, "Nothing for you to worry about, Long."

"It wouldn't have anything to do with what Cord and Blasson were talking about, would it?" Longarm asked.

Magruder looked at Cord. "Did you let Long hear what you two was saying back there?"

"What if we did? He can't do nothing about it."

"Don't be too sure of that, Cord," Longarm said. "Listen here, all three of you. The main man I'm after here is Delaney. Now, I could make things easier for you when you come up to trial if you'll agree to testify against him."

Magruder roared with laughter. "Listen to him, boys! He's talking like he's taking us in, like we was arrested!"

"Now, that's something I guess I've overlooked till now," Longarm said quietly. "As of this minute, I'm putting all three of you under arrest."

When their laughter died away, Longarm told them, "I wasn't joking. I've just put the three of you under arrest. And the baroness is a witness."

"Well, I tell you, Long," Magruder chuckled, "when you get outa them handcuffs and put 'em on me, I'll believe you."

Cord put an end to the conversation by yanking on the reins. The wagon tilted as the horses changed their direction. Cord said, "There's the place I told you about, just up ahead. That little stand of trees."

Longarm glanced ahead of the wagon. The copse was a quarter of a mile distant, black in the moonlight against the stark bare earth that surrounded it. It was a fairly large grove. Some of the cedars stood more than head-high, and there were a few pines at the center of the stand.

"Looks all right to me," Magruder nodded. "There ain't much chance anybody'd be coming along the trail at this time of night, but we might be enjoying ourselves for quite a while, and I'd sure hate to get interrupted."

Longarm nudged Sylvie with the toe of his boot. Speaking slowly and precisely, she said, "You men intend to stop behind those trees and rape me, do you not?"

"Well, now, I wouldn't call it that," Magruder replied. "We figured you might enjoy finding out how us men over here stacks up with the ones over in Europe."

"I have heard you American men are very strong."

"Hey, listen to that!" Cord broke in. "She's talking about me!"

"But I have also heard you are too impatient to satisfy a woman properly," Sylvie finished.

"Wait a minute now!" Magruder protested. "I never did have no woman complain to me!"

"But you have never had a woman of noble blood," she retorted quickly. "One who has had little else to do but learn the arts of love."

"Ah, who in hell's got time for that?" Magruder sneered. "A bunch of soft-handed loafers that ain't got nothing to do but chase after women!"

"Soft-handed, yes, but hard where a woman wants a man to be hard. And to stay hard until she becomes wild like an animal and gives him feelings he has never had before."

"Well, I been to Kansas City and St. Louis and some other big towns like that," Blasson volunteered. "They got some pretty fancy parlor houses in them places. And I never did have none of the girls complain about what I give 'em."

"I never had a woman complain to me, neither," Cord said, "and I been to a lot more places than Blasson has."

"Whores!" Sylvie said scornfully. "They think only of what you pay them. They hurry to be rid of you so they can collect what the next customer will pay them."

"You sound like you been around a hell of a lot," Magruder said, "and I get the idea you don't mind the three of us putting it to you. Matter of fact, the way you're talking, I'd say you'd like it."

"That is what I am saying," Sylvie said eagerly. Then she stopped. "But I would not be able to please any man if I knew I was soon to die." She turned her head to look squarely at Magruder. "If I give myself to you freely, and give you more pleasure than you have ever known from a woman, will you give me my life in return?"

"I figured that's what you was working up to," Magruder sneered. "We don't have to make no deals with you. If you put up a fight, we'll just take turns holding you down and fucking you till we're tired of you."

167

"Then you will never know what you have missed, will you?" Sylvie asked scornfully. She shrugged. "Do what you wish, but do not expect any pleasure, for I will give you none."

"Damn it, I'd rather have her willing, Magruder," Blasson said quickly. "She could be the hottest woman we're ever likely to run into."

"Yeah," Cord agreed. "What the hell, Magruder! I've heard a few things about them ladies in Europe, and if she's that good, we might wanna keep her around a while. Delaney wouldn't have to know about it."

Longarm could tell what was in the minds of the three renegades, and he was suddenly worried that Sylvie might have made things worse instead of better. He slid his hands up to his vest pocket where the derringer rested, but realized that with the handcuffs on his wrists he would not be able to draw and fire with his usual speed and accuracy.

He'd already made his plan of action. The first shot from the derringer would take care of the guard he was certain would be standing beside him, the second shot would account for one of the others, and with luck he'd be able to scoop up the guard's gun to get the third outlaw.

Now, with his wrists manacled, Longarm was sure only that he could fire a single shot with accuracy. The awkwardness imposed by the cuffs would slow him so much that either of the two survivors would be able to draw and cut him down before he could trigger a second shot. Even if he did make the second shot count, he'd have no way of shooting the third man in time to avoid being killed himself. The plan had started, though, and he could see no way to stop it now.

"Your friends are right, Magruder," Sylvie said. "If you free me, I will give you what you have never had from a woman before. But if I know that I am to die anyhow, you will have no more pleasure than you would get from your own hand."

"I don't know—" Magruder began.

Sylvie interrupted him. "You heard what Cord just said. If Delaney does not know, why should we not enjoy ourselves?"

"I still ain't sure whether you're just leading us on or not," Magruder said.

"There is only one way for you to find out." Sylvie was silent for a moment, then when Magruder said nothing, she went on. "Shall I tell you something? Several times I have taken two men at the same time, but never three. And this is something I have thought would excite me very much indeed."

"Three of us at the same time?" Magruder exclaimed.

His words almost duplicating Magruder's, Cord said, "Three at once? But, that'd mean—" He stopped, his mouth open.

"Exactly," Sylvie said. "And there are three of you, no?"

"By God, that's one I never thought about!" Blasson gasped.

Longarm could see that the liquor they'd drunk was now working on all three of the renegades, but he was worried that Sylvie might be overdoing her act. He flicked his eyes quickly from Cord to Magruder to Blasson. When he saw the way they looked at Sylvie, he let himself relax a bit.

Looking from one to the other of them, Sylvie went on, "Who knows? I may find that one of you is the strong man I have always been looking for."

"You sure talk good, lady," Magruder said. "We'll find out just how good you are pretty quick. Go on and pull around behind these trees, Cord, and let's get started!"

Sylvie turned to face Magruder. "I am as anxious as you are to start," she told him. "But if you really wish to enjoy me, you must let me take the time to get ready."

"What d'you mean, ready?" he asked suspiciously.

"I know many things that please men, Magruder," she replied as Cord brought the wagon to a halt and set the brake. "I enjoy getting men prepared for me. Doing this gets me ready to please them more. If I am not ready for you, I will only lie under you like a mattress, not moving, doing nothing."

"What kind of things are you talking about?" Blasson asked eagerly before Magruder could answer.

"I like to undress while men watch me. I like to show them my body and feel their hands on me. I like to feel them, and to caress them in many ways that give both of us pleasure."

"Hey, that sounds all right!" Blasson said. "Let's pile outa the wagon and get going!"

"Not so quick!" Magruder replied. "We got to fix Long so we won't have to worry about him."

"Well, shoot the son of a bitch now, instead of later!" Cord exclaimed. "Damn it, I wanna get to that woman!"

"No!" Sylvie said quickly. "I would enjoy nothing if I saw a man die now! He is handcuffed—he can do nothing."

"She's right," Cord said. "Even if she's taking on all three of us at the same time, we'd still be ready to handle Long."

"All the same, I want him out here, where we can see him,"

Magruder replied. "Blasson, bring Long outa the wagon. Here's the key to his cuffs. You cuff him to one of the back wheels, where we can watch him. Me and Cord will take care of the woman."

Blasson almost fell over himself in his eagerness to let the tailgate down and help Longarm out of the wagon. He grabbed the short chain which connected the handcuffs and pulled him around to the side of the wagon nearest the trees. His eyes kept going to the rear of the wagon, where Cord and Magruder were standing with Sylvie. Magruder was freeing Sylvie's wrists.

Holding the key in one hand, Blasson reached for Longarm's wrists. Gambling that Blasson's reactions had been slowed by the liquor he'd consumed and that his attention was diverted by Sylvie, Longarm held his right wrist higher than the left. Sylvie's hands were free now, and she was pointing to the clear area beween the wagon and the trees.

"There is the best place," she said. "Where the light is brightest, so that you can see me clearly—and I can see you."

Blasson's hands were quivering with anticipation when he grabbed Longarm's wrist. He was so engrossed in watching Sylvie as she walked ahead of Magruder and Cord into the patch of bright moonlight that he did not notice which of Longarm's hands he was freeing. He unlocked the shackle and snapped it around a spoke of the wagon wheel. Giving the metal circlet a cursory tug to be sure the snap had caught, he tucked the key in his pocket and hurried to where the others stood in the bare moonlit rectangle between the wagon and the trees. Sylvie was in front of Cord and Magruder. They did not notice that Blasson had joined them.

Sylvie moved away from them a step or two, her hands fumbling at the neck of her dress. The distance from where they stood and where Longarm was shackled to the wagon wheel was not great. Longarm could hear Sylvie clearly when she spoke.

"Do not get impatient," she told them. "I promise you, we will do things you have never done with a woman before."

"Well, don't take too long," Magruder said. "I don't feel like waiting all night."

"You will not have to wait long," Sylvie said. She drew her shoulders together and tugged the dress down over them. Her fair skin gleamed in the silvery moonlight as she worked the dress down slowly until her breasts were half exposed.

Cord involuntarily took a step toward her, but Magruder put out a hand and pulled him back. Sylvie rotated her shoulders, raised her arms above her head, and slipped the dress slowly down. Longarm watched while Sylvie lowered her arms slowly behind her, bringing her breasts up, and began shifting her torso from side to side so that her full breasts swayed back and forth, quivering in the bright moonlight.

Cord said, "Look at them titties!"

"What the hell d'you think I'm looking at?" Magruder asked, his eyes riveted on Sylvie's swaying torso.

Blasson said nothing. He was staring, his mouth open.

Sylvie stepped-up closer to the three renegades, who were staring at her as though they were mesmerized. Taking Magruder's hand, she brought it up to let him cup it around one of her breasts. Cord was standing next to Magruder, and Sylvie took his hand and placed it on her other breast. Both men tried to draw closer to her, but she held them back by dropping her hands to their crotches and stroking them as she pushed them away.

Whirling around, leaving Magruder and Cord with their hands outstretched but empty now, she moved to Blasson. He grabbed both her breasts while Sylvie's fingers worked at his fly. She opened it and worked him free. He was already erect. He stood looking down at himself for a moment, then made a grab for Sylvie.

Cord stopped Blasson's efforts. "Damn it, let her alone! Wait'll she gets around to me and Magruder."

Sylvie continued shedding her dress, and Cord and Blasson forgot to argue further as they turned to watch her. Standing just beyond the reach of the hands that were grasping for her, she worked the dress down slowly over her hips. She had to stop now and then to push their hands away, darting her own hands in and out while she pushed the dress below her hips. It fell to the ground and she stepped out of it.

"Hurry up, damn it!" Magruder growled. "I'm getting tired of being teased, girl! Let's get to it!"

"Soon, now, very soon," Sylvie said.

She turned her attention to Magruder. When she opened his fly and brought out his shaft, Cord turned and began to work at the buttons of his own trousers. Sylvie pushed her buttocks against Magruder's jutting erection. He grabbed at her hips and tried to enter her from behind, but she pulled free.

"Wait a moment," she said over her shoulder to Magruder as she reached for Cord, pushing away Magruder's fumbling hands and evading his efforts to seize her.

Longarm wondered how long Sylvie would be able to fend off the three men with her delaying tactics. The effects of the liquor must be wearing off, and as they grew sober their fascination would end. One or another of them would get tired of waiting and grab her. Longarm slid his derringer from his vest pocket and held it in his palm.

Magruder finally succeeded in getting hold of Sylvie. He began trying to wrestle her to the ground, but she whirled away from him and stepped back. Magruder followed, his hands outstretched. He caught her, but could not hold her. Each time he let go of her briefly in search of a firmer hold, his hands slid off Sylvie's bare flesh and she twisted free.

Cord said loudly, "Damn you, let her go, Magruder! Nobody said you was going to get the first chance! I wanna see how she handles all three of us!"

Blasson said nothing. His eyes fixed on Sylvie, his open mouth slack, he was stroking his erection.

Magruder did not reply. He was pursuing Sylvie. Their sparring struggle had carried them several paces away from Cord and Blasson. Magruder caught up with Sylvie and, after a moment of silent struggling, almost succeeded in pushing her down, but she did not give up. Then Longarm saw her suddenly grow limp. She sagged to the ground, pulling Magruder with her.

Longarm raised the derringer to be ready for a moment when Magruder would raise himself momentarily above Sylvie and she would be out of his line of fire.

Before the muzzle of the little gun was levelled, while his finger was just tightening on the trigger, he saw Sylvie's hand groping for the butt of Magruder's revolver. Magruder was too intent on forcing Sylvie's legs apart to notice. She freed the weapon from its holster as Longarm swivelled around toward Blasson and Cord.

The flat bark of the derringer and the louder booming of Magruder's heavy pistol shattered the night. Longarm's second shot sent Blasson crumpling to the ground beside the fallen Cord.

Chapter 19

Sylvie was on her feet, staring down at Magruder's motionless body. The revolver she'd taken from Magruder dangled from her hand and her face was frozen in a puzzled frown.

"Sylvie!" Longarm called. "Stop worrying about him. He's dead."

She raised her head slowly and looked at Longarm. "I have never before killed a man," she said. "I am trying to understand how I feel."

"Don't worry about how you feel. It's over with, and there ain't a thing you can do to change it."

Longarm took out a cheroot and lighted it as Sylvie started walking slowly toward the wagon. She had not let go of the revolver, and seemed unaware that it was still in her hand.

"I hate to ask you to handle a dead man's body," Longarm said as she got closer, "but you're going to have to get the key to these handcuffs from Blasson's pocket."

"Yes, of course. It will not bother me," she replied.

Having this simple task to do seemed to shake Sylvie out of her lethargy. She went to where Blasson lay and kneeled beside the corpse. Laying the revolver down, she searched his trouser pockets until she found the key. She did not pick up the revolver when she rose and brought the key to Longarm.

Longarm freed his wrist from the handcuff. Her voice betraying her perplexity, Sylvie said, "I tell myself I should feel remorseful for having killed a man, but I am not sorry and I have no regret. Why am I not sure how I feel?"

"You ain't pulled yourself together yet, Sylvie. You had a big shock. It'll take you a while to figure out how you feel. But when you think about what you done, it'll help if you remind yourself that if you hadn't killed him, he'd've killed us."

Longarm looked down at Sylvie as she stood naked in the moonlight. Her hair had come down at some time after they'd left the wagon, and flowed over her bare shoulders and down her back. Her nipples were puckered and firm in the soft, creamy skin of her bare breasts. He went on, "Likely you're cold, too. I'll get your dress. Then we'll find that liquor they left in the wagon and have a drink. That'll perk you up."

"Let the dress wait. It does not bother me that I have on nothing. But if there is any vodka left, I would like a drink."

She followed Longarm to the front of the wagon. He struck a match and located the bottles lying under the seat on a folded piece of canvas. He held the bottles up. The whiskey remaining barely covered the bottom of the bottle, but there was still about two inches of vodka left. He handed the vodka to Sylvie and drained the remainder of the whiskey in a single swallow. Sylvie took a sip of the vodka.

"Do you have another of your cigars?" she asked when she had swallowed it.

Longarm lighted a cheroot and passed it to her. Sylvie took another swallow of the vodka and puffed on the cheroot. She drank again, then turned and looked out to where the three bodies lay sprawled. Suddenly she was shaken by a series of wracking shudders.

"Now I am afraid, Longarm," she said. "I see those men lying there, and I think how I might have been where they are now, and suddenly I have fear. Can we get into the back of the wagon?"

"Sure. I'll get your dress so you can slip into it. Then you lie there and rest while I drive us back to town."

"No, not back to town—not yet. Come with me. I do not wish to be alone."

Longarm took the tarpaulin from beneath the seat, led Sylvie to the back of the vehicle, and quickly spread the canvas tarpaulin over the splintered floorboards. He helped Sylvie in and crawled in after her. They stretched out, side by side, not touching.

After a few moments, Sylvie asked, "Do you feel nothing, then?"

"Not much, except I'm glad we're lying in here and not outside there. Both of us came real close to being where Magruder and his cronies are, Sylvie."

"But you have seen death often?"

"More times than I care to remember."

Sylvie started to say something, but changed her mind. They lay in silence, puffing at the cheroots. Longarm's cigar burned down to a stub, and he dropped it to the ground, as he had those he'd finished earlier. Sylvie handed him what remained of hers. The glowing tip of the stub shed enough light for Longarm to see Sylvie's face. The frown it had worn earlier had vanished and her eyes were no longer troubled. Longarm dropped the stub out of the wagon.

Sylvie said, "I still cannot believe that what happened was real. But if I am not in a dream, I can feel you touch me, and this you have not done since we got into the wagon."

"I didn't figure you'd want me to, for a while."

"I need to feel your hands and to touch you, to prove I am real. Prove it to me, Longarm!"

Sylvie lifted herself on one elbow, leaned over Longarm, and brought her lips down to his. Her tongue slid into his mouth and darted about for a moment before she sucked his tongue into her mouth. Her hands were stroking Longarm's cheek, unshaven now for a full day, and when she felt the rough prickling stubble she broke off the kiss and raised herself higher, to rub her breasts over his face. A trembling sigh floated from her lips as the sandpapery stubble rasped their protruding tips.

Her fingers slid into his fly, lifted him out, and her hand grasped him, squeezing and rubbing his shaft until it stiffened. She crouched above him, her thighs spread, and rubbed herself with his tip until she began to gasp and started to lower her hips. Longarm rolled over. He went into her deeply as he moved, and Sylvie gave a long sigh of delight and contentment.

"I am alive! I am not in a dream! I am feeling you in me now! Go deeper, Longarm, and bring me all awake!"

Longarm needed no urging by now. He stroked hard and

full, and Sylvie rocked her hips and thrust them up to meet his plunges. She shuddered into a quick, spasmodic orgasm, and tossed from side to side, wailing in short cries between ragged gasps for breath. Longarm felt her muscles lose their tension, but drove on without pausing to let her rest.

He was nearing his own climax before Sylvie began to grow tense again and to rock beneath him with a tempo that matched his own. He held himself back long enough to bring her up to meet him, and as Sylvie quivered and thrashed on the rough canvas tarpaulin, keening in a broken rhythm of throaty moans, he let go. He slowed his driving thrusts to a stop, pinning Sylvie beneath his hard hips, while his muscles grew slack and he rested quietly on Sylvie's soft, warm body.

"Thank you, Longarm," Sylvie whispered softly. "Not just for proving I am still myself, but for all else you have done tonight." Her words trailed off to a contented sigh and her body seemed to grow even softer as she dropped into sleep.

Longarm lifted himself slowly and stretched out beside her. He listened to the night outside the wagon, as quiet as death itself, a silence broken only by the rhythmic breathing of the sleeping woman. Longarm closed his eyes, intending to rest them for a moment. But sleep crept up and claimed him, too.

Longarm awoke sitting up, his hand clawing at his empty holster for the butt of the Colt that was not there. In the instant required for him to recognize his surroundings, he remembered where he was and all that had happened during the hours before he feel asleep.

A soft translucent grayness had driven out the almost total dark that had shrouded the wagon's interior before he went to sleep. The wagon shook gently and one of the horses whuffled. Longarm knew then what had roused him, and relaxed. The horses had not been unhitched when they'd stopped; now, with the arrival of dawn, they were restless and hungry, and were trying to pull the wagon against the brake.

He looked at Sylvie, sleeping naked and undisturbed, her bright hair spread over the soft white arm on which she'd cradled her head. Rising to a crouch, he slid his arms out of the sleeves of his coat and spread it over her. Then, moving carefully so that he would not disturb her, he crawled over the tailgate and let himself down to the ground.

In the dimness of the pre-sunrise dawn, the bodies of Cord

176

and Blasson and Magruder were shapeless, huddled blobs. Longarm went at once to Magruder's body and took his Colt out of the dead man's belt. No dew had formed during the night, but Longarm wiped the Colt thoroughly on his sleeve. He checked the cylinder, even though he knew that Magruder had not fired the gun, saw the cartridges were intact, and returned the weapon to its holster.

With an impolite growl, Longarm's stomach reminded him that he'd eaten nothing since noon of the previous day. He lighted a cheroot and went back to the wagon. The bottles that he and Sylvie had put on the seat were still standing there. There was no more whiskey, but an inch of vodka remained in the other bottle. Hoping that anything he put into his stomach would quiet its rumbling, Longarm took a long swallow and recorked the bottle, saving what remained of the liquor for Sylvie when she woke up.

With thoughts of Sylvie's wakening, Longarm remembered her dress. He walked over to where it lay and picked it up, carried it to the wagon, and spread it across the tailgate, where she could reach it easily. The sky had brightened perceptibly since Longarm had first opened his eyes. He glanced east and saw that the first small arc of the sun had poked above the rim of the saucer. Hunkering down beside the wagon, he began thinking about the day that lay ahead.

You're getting close to the end of your case, old son, he told himself. *Last night three of 'em got put away, and there's just two more to go. That Arthur Alberts won't be any trouble to corral. Delaney's another thing. He ain't going to be suspicious when Magruder don't show up, because he ain't due back at Interior until late. And Delaney sure as hell won't be worrying about you, because he ain't expecting you to show up at all.*

Except there's one thing you still got to figure out. Delaney'll be spooked if he sees that wagon pulling into Interior, and the road that goes into town is bare as a baby's butt on both sides. Was you by yourself, it wouldn't be no problem, but you sure can't leave Sylvie out here all alone for the better part of the day. She'd go crazy looking at them bodies. So you got to do a little studying and figure how you'll get into town.

Longarm debated his moves while the sun climbed and the air grew warmer. He was still debating when one of the team horses whinnied, and he looked up, frowning. The horse whinnied again, and now Longarm heard a distant reply, the shrill answer made by another horse. He rose to his feet and circled the stand of trees until they thinned enough to let him look down the slope.

In the slanting light of the early morning sun the lightly marked and seldom-used trail to Interior stood out in sharply cut lines of disturbed soil. Two miles more or less from the grove, a saddled horse stood on the trail.

Longarm dropped to one knee. With the sun behind him, he knew that even at such a distance his silhouette would be easily visible through the thin, straggly growth at the edge of the grove. He tried to see the trail as it mounted the slope, but the brush in that direction was too dense for even his keen eyes to penetrate.

He rose as much as he dared to without exposing himself, but saw no one near the horse. He could not see whether the animal had been tethered, but it was standing quietly. Wishing for his rifle, which stood in a corner of his hotel room, Longarm stooped and half-walked, half-ran around the edge of the grove back toward the wagon.

He veered away from the wagon to the nearest of the three corpses, which was Blasson's, and slid the dead man's revolver out of its holster. The gun was a S&W; while he walked back to the wagon he broke it and checked the cylinder, finding it fully loaded. At the wagon he called softly to Sylvie. She woke reluctantly and sat up, looking at him through sleepy eyes.

"Now, don't get upset," Longarm told her. "There's somebody poking around down the slope. I saw his horse, but not whoever it is. I got a hunch he might be walking up here, and I'm going to have a look right now."

"Do you want me to go with you?"

"No. But I'll leave this gun here, in case there's trouble. You better put your dress on and stay in the wagon." He frowned and asked her, "Can you handle a team?"

"At home, I drive four-in-hand. This two-horse team will be like play to a child."

"All right. If you hear shooting, pull the team around the edge of the trees. I'll be along there someplace."

Sylvie's eyes were wide open now, the sleep gone from her face. She nodded and said, "I will do what you say."

"And don't worry about what might happen," Longarm told her. "Chances are it's just somebody passing through, but I ain't of a mind to take chances after last night."

Longarm moved quickly around the edge of the copse until the trees began to thin. He slowed down then, and started through the low-growing salt cedars that bordered the taller trees, dodging from one clump to the next. He drew the Colt as he neared the edge and dropped flat. Worming ahead, he reached a place where he could see the entire stretch of the downslope.

For a moment he stared at the man a hundred yards down the slope from the copse. The newcomer carried a rifle in the crook of his arm and was examining the ground in front of him as he approached the stand of trees. Then Longarm chuckled and stood up, waving his hands. The man looked up and the sun glinted off his oval spectacles. He shaded his eyes and peered toward the grove.

Longarm called, "Teddy! Teddy Roosevelt! If it's us you're looking for, you sure as hell have found us!"

Young Roosevelt waved, and in his high voice called, "Are you all right?"

"Fine," Longarm replied. "So's Sylvie. But I'm glad to see you all the same."

"No more than I am to see you."

Teddy started hurrying up the slope. The sun was in his face as he trudged up the long incline to the grove, and each time he looked up his spectacles caught its light and flashed twin iridescent beams. He reached Longarm and stopped, puffing only slightly from his quick walk. He stuck out his hand and they shook. Then Teddy examined Longarm quickly with a head-to-toe glance that missed nothing.

"You look a little the worse for wear, but not as bad as I'd feared," he said. "Was it a bad night?"

"Well, I've spent a few worse, but I can't recall when or where right now."

Peering through his spectacles at the stand of trees, Teddy asked, "Your wagon's behind the trees, I presume?"

"Yes. We might as well walk along that way while we talk, if you got your wind back." They started walking through the edge of the grove and Longarm continued, "There's some bodies lying around the wagon. I thought I'd better mention it now so they won't set you back when you see 'em."

"Delaney's gunmen?" Roosevelt asked.

Longarm nodded. "And Magruder. He was supposed to get

rid of Delaney's hired guns after they took care of me and Sylvie. Only it didn't work out that way."

Roosevelt stopped, took off his fur cap, and mopped his sweat-beaded forehead with a handkerchief he took from his pocket. He said, "This cap is fine for the New England woods in winter, but not for Dakota Territory in the summer. I must absolutely get myself a wide-brimmed hat like yours before I leave this part of the country, Longarm. In the East, all I can find is derbies and narrow-brimmed fedoras."

"You sound like you're thinking about going home."

"We'll talk about that later," Teddy said. "You'd better tell me the rest of the story now. I don't suppose you'll care to go into details when the baroness is around."

"There ain't much to tell, Teddy. I can finish it in about half a minute." They resumed walking and Longarm went on, "Those fellows decided they'd rape Sylvie before they shot us. They got so interested in her that they was careless, and I had my chance and took it."

"They didn't hurt her, I hope?"

"No. She's shaky, but she'll get over that."

"And Delaney's men?"

"All dead."

"You've had a rough night. Sorry I wasn't around when you needed help, but I got here as soon as I could."

"You got here a lot sooner'n I expected."

"There wasn't any point in starting until daylight. It was almost eleven o'clock when the baroness's maid got to my room and told me what had happened to you. She was excited, and my use of German's limited. I had to guess at part of what she said."

"Likely she missed hearing some of what happened. It'd've been hard for her to hear good in the next room where she was hid out when Delaney told Magruder to bring us out here."

"She'd heard the badlands mentioned, and knew you'd be in a wagon. I was tracking blind until I spotted the first of those cigar butts you managed to drop. They were a big help, Longarm. After I saw the first one I knew I was on the right trail, and I didn't have any more trouble."

Teddy stopped at the wagon and the bodies came in sight. He stared at the three sprawled figures.

Longarm said, "It ain't a pretty sight, but it could be a lot worse. If we hadn't been lucky, you'd be looking at me and

Sylvie instead of those renegades."

They walked on to the wagon. Sylvie came out of the back before they reached it, and stood waiting. She'd put on her dress, and Longarm's coat lay neatly folded over the tailgate. She had dark blue half-moons under her eyes, and her full lips were paler than he'd seen them before, but she was smiling when they got to her.

Before Longarm had a chance to speak, she said, "I am recovered from being frightened, Longarm. To prove this, I will tell you that I am ravenously hungry." Then she told Teddy, "I am very glad to see you, Mr. Roosevelt, but I do not understand how you could find us so soon."

"It was luck, Baroness. But it's bully that you're all right. I was worried about you and the marshal."

Longarm broke into the conversation. "I don't guess you brought any grub with you, Teddy?"

"It didn't occur to me. All I could think of was getting on your trail."

"We'll hold out till we get back to town, I guess," Longarm said, managing to sound unconcerned in spite of the gnawing in his stomach. "Sylvie, maybe you better start walking down the trail toward town, while me and Teddy load up the wagon. It ain't something you'd care to watch."

Sylvie had kept her eyes away from the bodies. She said, "Thank you, Longarm. Gladly I would walk to town, to get away from this place."

"It won't take us but a minute," Longarm told her. "Just head for the trail. You'll see Teddy's horse as soon as you get around the trees. Start on towards it, and we'll be along to pick you up." He watched Sylvie as she walked away, circling as far from the corpses as possible. Then he said to young Roosevelt, "Soon as she gets outa sight, we'll go to work. Just try not to think of what you're handling when we do the job, and it won't bother you so much."

"I'll hold my end up," Teddy said. He'd turned his back on the copse and lighted one of his fat Corona cigars. "Don't worry about me."

"I ain't worried." Longarm was watching Sylvie, who was still in sight, nearing the end of the stand of trees. "You didn't finish what you started to tell me about going back East."

"So I didn't." Teddy seemed glad to talk of something other than the events of the night. "I told you about my letter from

181

Alice. She's anxious to set the date for our wedding. I wrote back to tell her to go ahead. So I'll have to leave here tomorrow or the day after."

"Well, I'm aiming to close my case today. All I got left to do is arrest Delaney and that Alberts fellow."

"That's just bully!" Teddy said. "I hoped I'd be here to see the end of it!"

"I got to ask a favor of you, now, though."

"Anything you want."

"Lend me your horse, and you drive the wagon back to Interior. I need to get my handcuffs on Delaney before he finds out what's happened to Magruder and the others. If he sees that wagon coming into town, he's going to know in a minute that something's gone wrong with his scheme."

Teddy nodded. "He's shrewd enough to deduce that, all right. You're planning to surprise him, then."

"You know, you're pretty shrewd at figuring things out yourself, Teddy." Longarm smiled. "That's what I'm figuring to do, all right. On your horse, I'll beat the wagon into town by a half-hour or more. With any luck, I'll have Delaney behind bars by the time you get there."

Longarm pressed the horse until he was within half a mile of Interior. Then he reined back to a slower pace and let the animal walk into town, as though he was a traveller coming in tired after a long night on the trail. The hour was still early, and the town had not yet awakened fully. He reached the intersection where the badlands trail crossed Interior's main street. The bank was not yet open, and when he looked at Delaney's office he could see that it was also closed. He rode on to the stable behind the hotel and dismounted.

At the desk, Longarm asked the clerk, "You ain't seen Delaney this morning, I guess?"

"No, Marshal Long. Generally he doesn't leave his room for another two hours, so I imagine that's where you'll find him."

"You got a deadbeat key in your drawer that I can use if I need to?" Longarm knew that a hotel this large would keep such a device on hand. "Deadbeat" keys were fitted on their business end with claws instead of wards and lands, and were designed to turn a key that had been left in the opposite side of a lock.

"Why, yes, we have one, but I'd have to ask Mr. Heenan—"

"And you know damned well he'd say yes after I told him I needed it for official business," Longarm snapped. "Now, hand me that key and quit wasting my time."

With the deadbeat key in his hand, Longarm went up the stairs and walked quietly down the hallway to Delaney's room. He stopped outside the door and pressed his ear to its panels. He heard no noise inside. As quietly as he could, he slid the deadbeat key in the lock and turned it gently. The lock was well oiled and the bolt slid back almost inaudibly.

Longarm drew his Colt as he threw open the door. His first glimpse told him that the gun would not be needed. The room was in disarray. Papers were strewn on the table and over the floor, the drawers of the desk against the wall were open. The door into the adjacent bedroom stood ajar and through it Longarm could see that the bed had not been slept in. A closet beyond the bed stood open and empty.

Delaney had fled.

Chapter 20

"I am so sorry that Ilse should be responsible for allowing the evil Delaney to escape, Longarm," Sylvie said. "Even if she did not intend to do so."

"You ain't blaming her, I hope," Longarm said. "Is that why you sent her away so early tonight?"

"No, of course not. I was only thinking of her. The poor girl is still weak from the terrible blow she suffered."

"I'm glad you ain't put out with her, because me missing Delaney wasn't her fault, Sylvie," Longarm replied, puffing on his cheroot. "She didn't know she'd run into him in the hall that way. Of course the minute Delaney saw her, he got the wind up."

"It certainly was not Ilse's fault, at all. But you must have been able to tell that she was not able to stay with us longer. Besides, I do not need anyone except you for the rest of the night."

"Oh, I didn't mean I'd miss her. You're woman enough for anybody."

Sylvie plumped up her pillow and took a sip of vodka from the tall, fluted glass on the table beside the bed. She said, "Still, I cannot but think that if Ilse had only gone back to Mr. Roosevelt and told him—"

"It wouldn't've helped none. By the time Teddy had figured out the best thing to do, Delaney would've been gone. He's smart enough to've figured that if Ilse was coming out of Teddy's room, his game was up—so he took off like a jack-rabbit."

"You will follow him and catch him, yes?"

"I'll do my best. There ain't no place that Delaney could head for but Bismark. Close as Canada is, he wouldn't risk going up there. That's wilder country than around here, and Delaney's a city man. He wouldn't want to tangle with the Mounties up there, either. They don't let fugitives get away."

"I am sorry that I cannot go with you, Longarm." Sylvie ran her fingers down Longarm's bare chest. "But the bank must attend to formalities before my money is returned to me, and—"

"Sure. That amount of money ain't to be sneezed at."

"Now, we have talked enough of Delaney and money," Sylvie said. She leaned over Longarm and her mouth began following the same course her fingers had taken earlier. She raised her head long enough to add, "We have the rest of the night before us, and since it will be our last one together, we would be great fools if we did not make the most of it."

"Damned if you don't carry more truck with you on a trip than any man I ever run into, Teddy," Longarm commented as Teddy Roosevelt turned away from the baggage car at the Bismark depot.

"Maybe I'll learn to travel as light as you do, Longarm." young Roosevelt grinned.

"Maybe, but I doubt it. Well, I'm sorry we got to say goodbye so soon. You been a real big help to me on this case, and I won't forget it."

"I'll remember it, too. But this is a long way from a final goodbye, Longarm. I'm coming back to Dakota Territory just as soon as Alice and I have settled down in the East. We'll be living there most of the time, but I want to buy a ranch up north in that badlands country."

"I'm glad all the trouble I got you into didn't change your mind about coming back." Longarm smiled.

"Nothing could ever do that. It's bully country, and the climate seems just perfect to keep my asthma away. Do you realize I haven't had a single attack since I got here? Why, I feel so healthy that I think I might even be able to take up the career my father wanted me to."

"Lawyering?"

"No. Father wanted me to run for public office. And, if I keep on feeling as good as I do now, I just might."

"Well, I'll give you this, Teddy, you're the healthiest sick man I ever run across."

"A man's only sick when he lets his mind make him sick, Longarm. But I've taken all the medicines I intend to, and none of them ever did me as much good as this fine climate here in Dakota Territory. Oh, I'll come back and buy that ranch!"

"You let me know when you do, and when I get sent up this way on a case, I'll drop in for a visit."

"I hope you won't wait until you get sent up on a case. Our door will always be open to you, Longarm. I came up here a four-eyed tenderfoot dude, and while there's not much I can do about my glasses, I feel that I'm going back home a full-fledged Westerner—and I owe a lot of that to you."

"You don't owe me one damn thing, Teddy. If anybody owes, it's me. But I'll agree with you, nobody'll be likely to call you a tenderfoot dude again."

"There's only one thing I regret. You didn't get Delaney."

"Oh, I'll run him down. One thing I'm satisfied about—he ain't got on a train here in Bismark since he made his getaway. Now, I read that to mean that he's holed up someplace between here and Interior, or else he's cut west. Whichever, I'll track him down."

"You will, if anybody can." Roosevelt pulled an oversized watch from his pocket and looked at it. "There must be something holding up this train." He frowned. "Not that I'm anxious to leave, but I'd hoped to get another look at the country we'll pass through. We're ten minutes late now, and if we don't start soon it'll be dark before we've gone ten miles."

"Well, it'll be easy for 'em to make up ten minutes between here and Fargo, so you won't miss any connections."

"Look!" Roosevelt said, indicating a little procession coming along the station platform. "That must be why the train's been held."

Longarm turned to look. A wheel-chair occupied by a veiled woman in a black dress was being pushed along the platform toward the end of the train by a tall, angular woman, similarly attired. In front of them, the conductor was waving his signal lantern to shoo away the few people who were still standing beside the depot. Behind the chair the brakeman was trailing. Longarm and Teddy stepped aside to let the wheel-chair pass.

Just as the group was going by, the conductor turned to the two women and said, "I know we can get your chair into the parlor car through the observation platform, Mrs. Cartright. The door to the coach is oversized at that end." When the passenger in the wheel-chair did not reply, the conductor asked the woman pushing the chair, "Is your aunt hard of hearing, Miss Adams?"

"No," she replied, her voice sounding strained, "but she has a throat condition which makes speaking uncomfortable for her. However, it won't matter to my aunt which end of the car we get on, as long as we're on board when the train pulls out."

As the quartet passed on, Teddy told Longarm, "It won't take long for them to get that invalid on the train, so I suppose I'd better get aboard, too. Since they're behind schedule now, they probably won't waste any time pulling out."

"I'd imagine. Well, Teddy—" Longarm put out his hand.

Young Roosevelt grabbed it in both his hands and shook it heartily as he said, "It's only goodbye for now, Longarm. Look for me back here in a couple of years at the most."

"I'll do that. And I promise that if you ever try to get elected to something, I'll support you."

With a final wave, young Roosevelt swung up the steps and entered the front coach.

Longarm glanced down to the rear of the train. Two cars down the platform, he saw that the brakeman and conductor seemed to be having trouble getting the wheel-chair up from the station platform to the parlor car. While Longarm watched, the tall woman who'd been pushing the chair hitched up her skirts and joined their efforts to get the chair aboard.

There was something about the tall woman that struck Longarm as being out of key. He frowned, musing, *That woman moves more like a man than a woman, old son. And, come to think of it, when she answered that conductor a minute ago, her voice sounded like—old son, you just missed being took for a mortified jackass! That ain't no more woman than you are! And you've damn sure heard that voice before! That's Arthur Alberts dressed up like a woman, and you can just bet it's Delaney riding in that wheel-chair!*

Longarm started walking rapidly toward the parlor car, but before he'd covered half the distance the combined efforts of the conductor, the brakeman, and the "woman" he'd identified to his own satisfaction as Arthur Alberts in disguise had finally gotten the chair into the parlor car.

Once the wheel-chair was loaded, the conductor wasted no time getting the train under way. He leaned far out from the steps of the observation platform and, waving his lantern in to the engineer, chanted, "Bo-ard! All aboard!" The engineer responded with two short whistle blasts and the train began to move slowly ahead.

Longarm swung aboard the train. He managed to get onto the steps of the vestibule between the parlor car and the last passenger coach. Looking into the parlor car through the pane of glass set into the vestibule door, he watched while the conductor and the brakeman rearranged the wicker chairs at the rear of the parlor car in order to make room for the wheel-chair. The tall individual was busying herself—or himself—in rearranging the shawl draped across the legs of the wheel-chair's occupant.

Longarm saw the conductor speak to the brakeman and then start up the aisle to the front of the car. Stepping back from the door, he waited. The conductor entered the vestibule.

Seeing Longarm, the conductor said, "Mister, unless you've got a reserved seat ticket for the parlor car, you'll have to go find yourself a seat in one of the coaches up ahead. If you're looking to buy a drink, the rules don't allow us to serve anything at the bar within ten miles of a station, so you'll have to wait a while."

"I ain't even got a ticket for this train, but I don't expect that makes much never-mind," Longarm said. He took out his wallet and showed the conductor his badge. "My name's Long. I'm a deputy U. S. marshal."

"What's this all about, Marshal? Are you expecting somebody to rob my train?"

"Nothing like that," Longarm assured the man. "But there might be a little bit of trouble down the line. I got a suspicion them two women is fugitives trying to make a getaway."

"Mrs. Cartright and Miss Adams? Why, that's ridiculous!

"That one you call Mrs. Cartright's really a man named Creighton Delaney, and the tall skinny one is a man named Arthur Alberts. At least, I'm pretty certain that's who they are. Delaney's been running a land swindle up north of here, at

Interior, and Alberts is in cahoots with him. They're mixed up in some murders, too."

"You say you're not positive that's who they are?" the conductor asked. "How do you propose to find out?"

"I'll just watch 'em for a while. If I see they're who they say they are, there won't be any trouble. If they're who I think they are, they'll likely resist arrest, and that'd mean trouble."

"Well, I'll help you all I can, Marshal Long. What do you want me to do?"

"Not a thing right now. There's a man I need to talk to up in the first coach. He's been helping me on this case, and I'm going to ask him to give me a hand. Later on I'll let you know what I plan to do."

Longarm made his way to the first coach. Teddy Roosevelt was sitting about midway in the car, looking out the window, trying to get a final glimpse of the country through the darkness that was settling in. The aisle seat beside him was unoccupied, and Longarm slipped into it. Teddy turned from the window to see who was joining him. His jaw fell and his bushy eyebrows rose above the gold rims of his small oval spectacles.

"Longarm! What're you doing here?"

"I took closer look at that woman in the wheel-chair and the one who was pushing it, and it appears to me they ain't women at all. They're two people I'm mighty anxious to get my hands on."

"Delaney and Alberts?" Teddy asked.

"Right. My luck was in. I was standing with my back to 'em when they passed us, so they didn't see me. Maybe they noticed you, because they went past so close to us, but that wouldn't spook 'em the way it would if they was to see me. Anyhow, since you're on the train, too—"

"You want me to help you arrest them?" Roosevelt exclaimed. "Well, that's just bully! I'll be in on the finish of the case! I'll go up to the baggage car and dig my revolver out of my luggage, and—"

"Whoa, Teddy!" Longarm said. "First of all, you'd better listen to what I'm aiming to do. And if everything works out right, you might not need a gun. Anyhow, there's other passengers in that parlor car, and I don't want to risk shooting in there. Somebody might get hurt or killed."

"That makes good sense. Go ahead."

"Now, those two didn't have suitcases when they passed by us, so I figure they've checked their luggage through, and

189

it'll be in the baggage car. I'll get the conductor to go back and ask Alberts to go up to the baggage car to straighten out some mixed-up luggage. We'll be waiting just inside the car door and we'll nab Alberts the minute he steps in. If he's got a gun, you hold on to it. That'll save digging out yours. When we've got Alberts safe, I'll go back and arrest Delaney, and that'll be that."

"You make it sound so simple, Longarm."

"Well, the simpler you keep things, the better they work."

"I suppose you're right. Your plan's good enough for me. When do we start?"

Longarm glanced out the window. The train was travelling through fairly flat country now, and making good speed. He told Teddy, "I don't see a thing wrong with right now."

"Lead on. I'm with you all the way."

Arresting Alberts was as simple as Longarm had foreseen it would be. The clerk gave up at once when Longarm stepped from behind the baggage-car door and pinned his wrists with an unbreakable grip. Teddy stepped up and stripped off the hat, veil, and wig.

"It looks like you've got me," Alberts said. "Delaney convinced me we could get away with this, and I was fool enough to believe him."

"You were a fool to get mixed up with Delaney in the first place," Longarm told him. "Now, what about Delaney? Is he carrying a gun?"

"I don't think so," Alberts replied. "If he is, I haven't seen it. He has a big purse under that wrap over his legs, but that just has money in it. He gave me his word there wouldn't be any more shooting or killing. If he hadn't promised me that, I never would have agreed to help him get away."

"You wasn't thinking about the money he promised you, I guess," Longarm observed. He asked the conductor, "Have you got some rope around someplace we can use to tie this fellow up with? I only got one pair of handcuffs, and I'd like to save them for his boss."

"Why, I've got handcuffs myself, Marshal," the conductor said. "There's been so many drunk passengers making trouble on this run lately that the road's furnished us with handcuffs so we can control the worst ones."

"Fine. You keep an eye on him," Longarm told Teddy. "I'll go get Delaney."

Going back through the train, Longarm stopped in the vestibule and watched Delaney for a moment through the glass in the parlor-car door. Until that moment, he hadn't realized what a disadvantage he'd be under. Even though the parlor car was better lighted than the day coaches, Delaney's veil concealed his face and the shawl over his legs hid his hands. Longarm could not see whether Delaney was watching the door or looking out a window, nor could he watch the fugitive's hands for a sign of motion.

To avoid any stir that might be caused among the passengers if he stepped into the car with a gun in his hand, Longarm did not draw. But Delaney must have been sitting with his gun ready under the shawl, for he fired through the concealing fabric.

Longarm's alertness saved him. He saw the movement of the shawl and, as Delaney lifted the muzzle of his pistol, dived for the floor. He drew as he moved. Delaney's bullet cut the air and thunked into the end of the car.

At the sound of the shot, half the passengers in the parlor car rolled out of their seats to the floor. The others jumped up and began milling around excitedly in the car's wide aisle. When Longarm got to his feet, the wheel-chair was empty, and the door to the observation car was just closing.

Pushing his way through the excited passengers, Longarm reached the back door of the coach. He went out into the night's gathering darkness, and for a moment, after leaving the brightly lighted car, he had to stand on the platform blinking his eyes to adjust them.

Delaney was not on the observation platform, but the train was moving too fast for him to have risked jumping off. There was only one place where the fugitive could have gone. Longarm set his hat more firmly on his crisp brown hair and swung out onto the ladder that led to the roof of the car.

Lifting his head carefully, Longarm could see Delaney's silhouette against the sky in the light from the locomotive's headlight. He was standing on the narrow walkway that ran the length of the car. The long skirt of Delaney's disguise had been shredded and the garment streamed out in the wind.

Delaney saw Longarm, and the flash of his revolver cut the darkness. The slug tore into the roof of the car inches from Longarm's head.

Longarm ignored Delaney's weapon and pulled himself up

on the ladder to bring his gunhand above the edge of the roof. By the time he could get himself high enough to shoot, Delaney had jumped to the next car and was running toward the front of the train, his torn skirt flapping behind him. Longarm snapshot, but the car was swaying and his shot went wide. Delaney dropped between two of the passenger cars.

Crawling up to the top of the car, Longarm ran along the walkway. He spanned the gap between the parlor car and the passenger coach ahead of it with a leap and ran the length of the car before dropping flat again when he neared the end of the narrow walkway.

Inching along the walkway on his belly, Longarm reached the end of the coach. Cautiously, he peered down. In the glow that came from the vestibule doors he could just see Delaney. The fugitive was clinging to the grab bars between the two cars, trying to uncouple the parlor car from the front of the train.

Longarm brought his Colt up and got off a shot at Delaney. Delaney saw the gun's menacing muzzle in the instant before Longarm fired and swung back. Longarm edged back too as hot lead from Delaney's return shot zipped past his face.

Rolling to the right-hand side of the swaying coach, Longarm groped with his left hand along the end of the coach until he found the first rung of the ladder between the coaches. Abandoning any idea of caution, Longarm rolled off the car and swung down. For a moment he dangled by one hand between the coaches. Then his booted foot found a rung and he managed to steady himself for the few seconds needed to let him jump to the floor of the vestibule.

Through the open door of the coach ahead of him, Longarm saw the passengers roiling like ants whose hill has been stirred up. That was all the clue he needed. He pushed his way through the car to the front. A quick look into the next coach showed that Delaney had gone back to the top of the train, for the passengers were sitting calmly in their seats. Longarm climbed up the ladder between the cars.

Lifting his head carefully above the roof of the coach, Longarm saw Delaney ahead of him, The fugitive had run the length of the passenger car and the baggage car. He was now at the front end of the baggage car, his figure outlined in the red glow from the firebox of the locomotive. Delaney had stopped, hesitating before making the long jump that would be necessary to take him to the tender.

Longarm fired as he reached the relatively stable footing of the walkway atop the coach. Delaney whirled and let off a shot in reply, but now Longarm had gotten used to the swaying motion of the speeding train, and as Delaney's bullet zipped past his ear, Longarm triggered his Colt.

Delaney pitched backward as the heavy .44 bullet caught him in the chest. His arms flew out, his gun fell from his hand, and he pitched backward to land on the coal piled in the tender below the baggage car.

Longarm moved slowly along the walkway to the front of the baggage coach. He stood for a moment at the end of the coach, looking down into the tender. What was left of the black dress Delaney had worn as a disguise blended with the black coal. All Longarm could see in the red glow from the firebox was the dead man's white face.

Holstering his Colt, Longarm took a cheroot from his pocket, flicked a match into flame, and shielded it against the rushing night wind while he puffed the cigar alight.

An onlooker could have seen no emotion on Longarm's strong rugged features. He stood there for another moment, smoke from the cheroot streaming behind him. Then he turned and walked back to the end of the coach and went down the ladder to join his friend.

Watch for

**LONGARM
IN THE BIG THICKET**

forty-eighth novel in the bold
LONGARM series from Jove

coming in October!

SPECIAL PREVIEW

Here is an excerpt from

LONE STAR
ON THE TREACHERY TRAIL

first in the hot new
LONE STAR series from Jove.

LONE STAR ON THE TREACHERY TRAIL
LONE STAR AND THE OPIUM RUSTLERS
and
LONE STAR AND THE BORDER BANDITS

are available now!

The crew hesitated, giving her hard, belligerent looks, then slowly settled back on the benches. In the tense hush that followed, Jessica sipped her coffee and thought how they all must be silently wishing she'd go away, preferably straight to hell. Well, she wasn't about to go; she was going to stay and find out how many of *them* were going to go.

Draining her cup, she returned their glares and said, "But in another sense you're through. Through for good."

One of the feistier hands protested, "Lady, it's not—"

"Miss Starbuck, if you please. And yes, it is."

"Miz Starbuck, okay, but it's not right to fire us now. We came back and worked all day, like you wanted. It's not fair."

"I don't have to fire you. You're firing yourselves, with all your hurrawing on the ranch's time and money. And the rustlers are firing you too, by raiding and looting till the Flying W is stone broke, and Ryker can take it over as a favor." She leaned forward, sternly eyeing the shaken crew. "Ryker says he's planning to form a combine out of the ranches he buys, and you know what that'll mean? It'll mean most of you'll be canned, and those who aren't will have to work twice as hard for half the wages."

Another puncher shrugged. "Nothing we can do to change it."

"That's where you're wrong, dead wrong. You're going to start tomorrow dawn, by weeding out the stock of everything four years and older, and shipping them to Starbuck. We need them like the plague, but it'll help pay your wages, help keep you *hired*. And I want a couple of you to take some Giant powder to the west end of the valley, where the stream flows down out of that long canyon. I found plenty of tracks heading up it, and the cows didn't get there by straying."

The second puncher nodded, brightening. "Not a bad idea. A little blasting up in the rocks oughta close that gap to rustlers."

"It'll also dam the stream," Jessica continued. "It'll form a reservoir to provide extra water for the herd, and for crop irrigation."

That startled a third hand. "Crops? We're not sodbusters."

Jessica favored him with a flinty smile. "It's not hard to learn. And you'd better, because that whole section by the canyon will be fenced off for native hay and maybe some sugar beets. What you don't use for the ranch will be sold as another source of income."

By now the entire Flying W crew was gaping attentively at her. Daryl as well was studying her in wonderment. She was moving fast and decisively, this Jessica Starbuck. She was ramrodding hard—which, though unsettling, was also generating fresh enthusiasm.

And then she dropped the bomb. "You're going to need a foreman, what with Nealon gone—and from what I've seen so far, good riddance—so I'm going to ask Toby Melville to stay on awhile, as a guest of Mrs. Waldemar. From now on, you'll take your orders from him."

There was outburst of voices, including Daryl's: "But Je—"

She shushed with a wave of her hand. "Listen, Toby Melville's forgotten more about ranching than most of us will ever learn. And you all get along with the Spraddled M crew, don't you?" When she wasn't contradicted, she forged on: "The two spreads will remain separate. I'm only talking about banding together till we've licked the rustling. A common herd can be defended by fewer men, freeing others for nighthawking—and fighting."

A fifth hand balked at this. "Fighting, like in shooting? Not me. I was hired to nurse cows, not toss lead."

200

Jessica nailed him with steel-cold eyes. "You're hired to side the Flying W, a fact you've managed to ignore." Surveying the others, she added, "You're bogged down and sinking fast, and if you hope to save your ranch and your jobs, you're going to have to lay your brains and guts and, by God, all your loyalty on the line."

"By damn, I've heard all the manure I plan to," a puncher way in the back sneered, "and the only reason I say 'manure' is on account of a female's present. Leastwise, she *looks* like a female."

Daryl stiffened. "Hold on, watch your tongue there."

The third Flying W hand who'd spoken now chimed in, "Yeah, Wylie, ain't no call to—"

"Shut up, Croft," the man called Wylie snarled. "Maybe your spine is made outta smoke, but as for me, I've had my fill of bein' lectured at by strange wimmen." He got up from the table, a dark, squat man with a barrel chest and black, beady eyes. "I'm doin' nothin' till Miz Waldemar tosses these troublemakin' talkers offen the ranch. If anybody else feels the same, come with me."

The two burly punchers who'd been flanking him on the bench rose and fell in, swaggering behind Wylie as he began shouldering his way toward the door. Apparently his close buddies, they laughed when he glared at Jessica and taunted, "Yeah, if I craved preacherin', lady, I'd go to Sunday school." Then, turning to Daryl and Ki, he added, growling, "Step aside, 'lessen you wish to get busted apart."

Almost to the front of the table now, he drew abreast of Croft. Foolishly, Croft shifted on the bench and reached out to place a cautioning hand lightly on Wylie's arm. "Simmer down, Wylie," he said. "Hear them out. Maybe these folks've got something to—"

"Leggo!" Wylie wrenched away from Croft's hand as though it were a snake biting his arm, then pivoted and shoved his palm flat into Croft's face. "I'll learn you to shut up!" he snarled, and mashed Croft's head down into his dinner plate with a dull, meaty crunch. Dazed and half-blinded, Croft reeled to one side and began falling off the bench, and Wylie drew back his right foot to kick his boot into Croft's unprotected belly. "I'll learn you good!"

Ki reacted before the kick could land. With an odd smile that masked his anger, he launched himself at Wylie, who immediately turned to meet him with fists. Ki ducked Wylie's first and last punch, catching the puncher's outflung arm and angling to drop to one knee, swinging him into the *seoi otoshi,* the kneeling shoulder-throw.

Wylie arched through the air, over the heads of the seated men, and came down on the table, atop the meat platter and the bowl of mashed potatoes. He sprawled there, dazed and breathless.

Even before Wylie hit, Ki was swinging around in the cramped space between the bench and the wall, to check whatever Wylie's two friends might be up to. The nearer one was charging him with arms outstretched, as if he were tackling a drunk in a barroom brawl. Ki chopped the edge of his hand down at his nose. He purposely held back a little so he would not break it, but it struck forcefully enough to hurt like hell, and tears of pain sprang into the man's eyes. Ki followed through by kicking the man in the side of his knee, collapsing him to one side. He caught his right arm, crunched down on it with his elbow, and then brought his own knee into his hip.

The man dropped to the floor, leaving the way clear for Wylie's second pal to lash out at Ki with his wide leather belt. Ki had already seen this second one slide off his belt and fold it double, which was one of the reasons he'd had to dump the first man, for now he was able to step over the first man and catch hold of the second one's right arm and left shoulder with his hands. At the same time, Ki moved his right foot slightly in back of the man so that as the fellow began tumbling sideways, Ki was able to dip to his right knee and yank viciously. His *hizi otoshi,* or elbow-drop, worked perfectly; the second man catapulted upside-down and collapsed jarringly on top of the first man, flattening them both to the floor.

And Wylie, face purpling with rage, launched himself off the table, a well-honed bowie knife clutched in his right hand. "I'm gonna carve you apart!" he bellowed, slashing at Ki.

Ki calmly stepped aside and then kicked up with his callused foot. His heel caught Wylie smack on his chin, so hard that Wylie flew backwards onto the table again. This time he sprawled cold on his back, staring sightlessly up at the rafters and cobwebbed ceiling of the cookshack.

The rest of the Flying W crew gaped at Wylie, his two moaning pals, and then at Ki with stunned disbelief. They said nothing.

Jessica broke the silence. "If these three want to quit, then they can quit. If any of you others want to quit, you can. Or you can stay. It's up to you, but make up your minds. As I said last night, I don't have the time—and the Flying W doesn't have the time—for you to sit on your butts. Either start kicking or packing."

The feisty hand who'd first spoken, now spoke up again. "Well, boys, I reckon Miz Starbuck might have something. She sure has a powerful persuader, and she's got me convinced. We gotta pitch in and stop the raidin', else we'll all be grub-lining. 'Sides, none of us is safe from a bushwhack bullet 'lessen we do rare up and fight back."

"Okay, count me in."

"We gotta do something, I see that now."

"Sure, we couldn't face Miz Waldemar if we didn't."

A consensus of agreement quickly swelled from the crew, including the one who'd refused to fight. "Might as well," he growled, moodily building a smoke. "Guess it don't make no difference how I bleed, fast or slow. I'll be dead here anyways."

Diplomatically thanking the men for their splendid cooperation, Jessica rose and left the cookshack. Ki followed, amused as ever by how much she was her father's child, equally as competent as Alex Starbuck had been in defusing and mastering tricky negotiations.

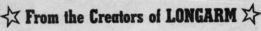